"I'll kiss you, then y

"That's not what I—"

"Not what you meant when you asked for a favor, I disagree. I think it was—you just didn't know it."

"That makes little sense."

It did, but she didn't know that either. The more Hamilton thought of it, the more he warmed up to the idea. This was perfect truly. Perhaps it was a bit untoward, but they were friends, and it didn't have to mean anything. He could simply...show Beileag what it was like. Then she wouldn't be so unattuned with the men who were no doubt making jests about tools and falling flat.

Just kiss her, something chaste of course. And he could hold her. That wouldn't be much. He'd already accidentally been doing that for days now.

She was slender, her movements graceful. She reminded him of a young tree in a gentle wind dancing to a tune he couldn't hear and bending in ways he couldn't guess.

Fitting perhaps to what she carved. Maybe there was some connection there. Another intriguing aspect to this woman...

Her hazel eyes more golden again and growing wider as she waited for him to answer.

Was there a question? All he felt was some untoward anticipation.

Author Note

Here's the upcoming story in a new series. While I promise I don't intend to make this series a long one, some of you may have already guessed that at least two more stories are rattling around. And if so, you'd be correct! (After all, I have to eventually tell you what is in Seoc's mead, don't I?)

But now, we have Hamilton who is everything I'm not. He's carefree and mischievous, a sharp contrast to the quiet Beileag, who is someone I definitely share traits with. Oh, not her whittling, but her feeling like she can't quite fit in—that is definitely me. To write about these two was very... interesting.

Hamilton and Beileag may be two unlikely people to fall in love, but Hamilton has had a few life events that changed him, enough for him to realize one pivotal fact: Beileag isn't quite whom he thought she was. And Beileag, who has had her own assumptions about Hamilton, well, she'll show him what he's been missing out on all these years...

NICOLE LOCKE

—

The Highlander's Unexpected Bride

HARLEQUIN®
HISTORICAL™

ISBN-13: 978-1-335-59575-1

Recycling programs
for this product may
not exist in your area.

The Highlander's Unexpected Bride

Copyright © 2023 by Nicole Locke

For questions and comments about the quality of this book,
please contact us at CustomerService@Harlequin.com.

Harlequin Enterprises ULC
22 Adelaide St. West, 41st Floor
Toronto, Ontario M5H 4E3, Canada
www.Harlequin.com

Printed in U.S.A.

Nicole Locke discovered her first romance novels in her grandmother's closet, where they were secretly hidden. Convinced that books that were hidden must be better than those that weren't, Nicole greedily read them. It was only natural for her to start writing them— but now not so secretly.

Books by Nicole Locke

Harlequin Historical

Lovers and Highlanders

The Highlander's Bridal Bid
The Highlander's Unexpected Bride

Lovers and Legends

The Knight's Broken Promise
Her Enemy Highlander
The Highland Laird's Bride
In Debt to the Enemy Lord
The Knight's Scarred Maiden
Her Christmas Knight
Reclaimed by the Knight
Her Dark Knight's Redemption
Captured by Her Enemy Knight
The Maiden and the Mercenary
The Knight's Runaway Maiden
Her Honorable Mercenary
Her Legendary Highlander

The Lochmore Legacy

Secrets of a Highland Warrior

Visit the Author Profile page
at Harlequin.com for more titles.

To Lori and Robert,

How unforeseen on that day, long ago, we met at the infamous Historical Romance Retreat. But how fortunate it was that we became friends. I may take forever to write a story, but that simply gave us more years to have fun before I could sneak in this dedication to you both.

Chapter One

April 1297—Clan Graham

'Get that from the top shelf,' her mother said, in that clipped precise voice that made dread descend into Beileag of Clan Graham every time.

It didn't matter if her mother was talking to someone else. All Beileag had to do was hear that particular tone and all the insecurities of her past, present and bleak future weighted her body, until everything she did for the rest of the day seemed like too much.

Her mother whirled. 'Why are you still sitting there?'

Because she knew the moment she stood her mother's derision would worsen. No hope for that though. It wasn't as though she could do anything about the length of her legs and she was far too old to be wishing otherwise.

Setting down the knife she'd been sharpening, Beileag hunched her shoulders, stood and walked to her mother's side.

She didn't have far to go. Their three-room home was barely large enough for her parents, who shared one room while she shared the other side room with her three younger siblings. This room was the heart of the house. The area where they prepared food, ate, sat by the fire and sewed their clothes for winter.

It was also the room she avoided the most when she could and the reason was exactly these moments when the only occupants were herself and her mother.

'What do you want down?' she said.

'The large linen chest.'

There were three identical chests on the top shelf which contained the carefully folded and stored linens. There was no identification of which would be housing the large linen.

Of course, her mother knew this and Beileag knew better than to ask. So she took the one on the far left and brought it to the table on the other side of the room.

'That's not the correct one,' her mother said.

Keeping her expression neutral, Beileag put the closed chest away, and stretched for another. She did it slowly to give her mother enough time to offer assistance on which one she wanted. She needn't have bothered.

'Oh,' her mother said. 'It must be nice to be your height where you can waste other people's time as you easily retrieve wrong item after wrong item. It's the last one, which you should know since you put them up there last summer.'

She tried to forget any time she was with her mother. No doubt her putting away the chests was equally unpleasant last summer.

Beileag held her tongue as she slowly pushed back the second chest and pulled out the final one to place down on the table.

After a disgruntled breath from her mother, Beileag opened it, only to see contents that weren't large linens.

'It's that one.' Her mother pointed to the first chest on the shelf.

Beileag held her tongue. If she argued now, even in the tiniest of bits, it would be worse for her.

Still her palms drew damp and her heart raced as she thought of all the retorts she wanted to say burning just under her skin. If she stayed much longer, she wouldn't be capable of holding them back.

Closing the chest with a resounding thud, she shoved the last chest back on the shelf and grabbed the first.

With a tight smile, she said, 'It *is* good we're not wasting anyone's time, isn't it?'

She flopped the lid open, grabbed the largest linen in a tight fist and turned. 'Now where do you want this?'

Her mother turned that darker shade of anger and Beileag's racing heart twisted and locked up tight.

For one flaming moment she was a child who wanted to flee again. No matter the years, her sense of worth crumpled under that familiar glare. She hated it.

Hated it more because her mother noticed.

Her mother always noticed her even when she tried to be as small as possible. But she was never as finely boned as her adventurous younger sister Oigrhirg, or her two brothers Roddy and Raibert, who wouldn't be small much longer.

Her younger brothers looked as if they'd be as big as her father. If Beileag had any fortune at all, they'd be taller than her. Maybe then her mother would leave her alone.

But since her siblings were much younger than her— Oigrhirg being sixteen, Raibert being twelve and Roddy ten—it would be years before she'd have such peace.

When she was younger, she'd sought solace with her father, who would pat her and go on his way. He never seemed to know what was happening in his own house.

Day in and out, doing his carpentry work, helping

others, dropping whatever he was doing…but never seeing how his wife, whom he adored, treated his eldest. He wasn't evil, he wasn't neglectful…he simply never noticed. And she…was long past asking for help.

Years of her father's silence and her mother bemoaning that she'd never wed. Years as her friends were courted or kissed, whereas Beileag hadn't even had a flirtatious smile sent her way. Was it truly because she was too tall? She wished someone would *see* her for who she was, or better yet, maybe not carry longing in her heart for marriage or a family of her own.

Might as well wish for herself not to be tall or her mother not to hate her.

And what care did her mother have if she married or not? They weren't wealthy, she helped out in the home—for all she knew her father wanted her there.

With her hand out, palm up, her mother smirked as if she had one. 'Hand it over.'

She didn't want to, but she also didn't want to continue this hostile argument that wouldn't resolve anything. Slowly, carefully, Beileag held out the linen over her mother's outstretched hand.

The gleam in her mother's eyes should have warned her before the linen fell to the floor, but she was expecting more words, not the claw-like grip of her mother's rough hands against her own.

Nor the yank as her mother brought her hand closer to peer at it.

Beileag knew immediately what she would see. Some callouses from chores, old scars and new cuts.

Her mother scraped her fingernail over a fresh cut, making it bleed again.

Beileag flinched and her mother gave a knowing smirk. 'Still lagging around your father's heels?'

Her father was the village artisan carpenter. He might be completely blind to the workings of his children, but Beileag hadn't been blind to him. Completely rejected by her mother simply because her legs were too long, she sought attention from her father through his craft.

No such fortune there either, but she found solace none the less. She learnt his craft, then she learnt what more she could do with her father's tools and skills. She worked hard on her craft, was proud of what she did…so she hid it.

'Merely some cuts while picking herbs in the chapel gardens.'

'Liar, too, when you're sharpening a knife right at my table?' her mother sneered. 'Your disgraced friend is the one who wanders those weeds.'

Anna was heartbroken, not disgraced. 'She is better at it than me, thus, her hands don't suffer cuts.'

'Too tall,' her mother continued as if she hadn't attempted to defend herself. 'And it's not weeds you cut. You wield tools as if you're a man. You'll never find a husband and leave the house. After everything your father and I have done, and continue to do, too!'

If only she could find a husband who'd love her! But it seemed all the men of the Graham clan agreed with her mother. She was either a friend or…not perhaps as unattractive as her mother lamented.

She wouldn't care. She wouldn't. Except, her mother could rail at her lack of beauty and her lamentable passion all she wanted and it would hurt.

But mentioning again that no one could love her pained her more than she ever wanted to say because out of everything, Beileag longed for a husband and children of her own. For a loving family, one that was utterly devoted to each other. One with a mother who was not dismissive or cruel and a father who didn't avoid all his children. Was it too much to want a joyous home and to be truly wanted?

And she'd tried and failed over the years to flirt or to smile or even to suggest her openness to being wooed, but no one seemed to notice. A few nights ago, the scouts returned after six months away. For one fleeting moment, she thought she might gain someone's notice.

But despite the absence, no man saw her any differently.

If it wasn't for her siblings, and her friends, Anna and Murdag, she'd…run away, or something drastic. Maybe someone out in another clan wouldn't care that her hands were scarred from learning to woodwork.

Wouldn't care that she spent her hours with sharp knives and hard wood, making little creatures that no one would ever see because she was too broken inside to ever have the confidence to show anyone. A brokenness which was apparent to everyone including the woman who put it there.

'If I found a husband, Mother, then who would get your baskets off the shelf?' Yanking her hand free, Beileag marched out the opened door.

Chapter Two

'So, what do you do this fine day, Murdag?' Hamilton of Clan Graham leaned against the barn wall. He wasn't one to rest in the middle of the day; he wasn't the one to be idle at all.

Unlike his twin brother, Camron, he was the most likely to be springing into some action before he even knew what the task was.

Some might call it effectiveness, others recklessness. All he knew was that, since last March, when the English King Edward had invaded Scotland to oust King John Balliol, he couldn't shake off his restlessness. It only got worse at the Battle of Dunbar, when Clan Graham had lost their laird, he almost lost his closest friend, Seoc, and all Scots had to flee to Ettrick Forest.

Afterwards, he'd had nothing but nights of sleeplessness as he and others patrolled the clan's outer borders and met with nearby allied clans. Now, he had returned to his family village, but it didn't feel like home. He had even returned to his duties as a clan huntsman, a skill he'd valued, but after Ettrick, his love of the forest was not the same.

But still he stood around and watched one of his oldest friends bend over and rhythmically move her hands about the horse's belly.

He couldn't see what she was doing, but Murdag of Clan Graham, black hair cascading down her lean build, was distracting enough.

'What does it look like I'm doing?' Murdag said.

'Something to do with the horses,' he said. 'As usual.'

'I'm cleaning this mare's udders,' she said.

Not what he expected. But then again, he didn't expect to be wooing a woman who didn't look at him long enough to realise what he was trying to do.

To be fair, he wasn't only trying to woo her. He was also trying to win a bet made with his brother: to win a marriage before summer's end.

He meant to win, but gaining the attention of this certain lass was proving somewhat difficult.

'She's arching her head and lifting her leg out now,' he said.

Straightening, Murdag looked behind her. 'She's happy.'

He been around horses all his life, but this level of care was beyond his knowledge or interest. Still, if Murdag was the woman he wanted, then he'd have to get used to it. After all, horses were her passion.

'You're a happy baby, aren't you? No more itching for you.' Murdag went back to cleaning. 'They need it more than you think.'

'Are you talking to me?' he said.

'Who else would I be talking to?' she said. 'Horses need their udders cleaned more often than you think. This one especially since she thinks she's a pig rolling around in the dirt. Is there something you need, Hamilton?'

You, he should have said. He would have if he was

flirting with some woman he had met in an inn along the way or at another clan. But his usual easy way of charming a woman didn't feel right when it came to Murdag. They'd been friends all their lives and he'd never looked at her as anything else.

Except that had changed four days ago. He and the other clan scouts had been gone for over six months and there was a feast, bonfires, plentiful ale and mead to celebrate their return.

But he and others drank more when Murdag, in her thin gown, climbed a boulder and bet the crowd around her that she could outdrink them.

Never bet a Graham on a drinking game. But she was a Graham herself and he liked her challenge. Liked the playful way about her and the fact she made jests almost as well as he did. He also liked the way the firelight lit up her form.

So, he was struck with lust and turned to his brother to tell him so.

Only to see, despite the copious amounts of ale drunk, the usual glum expression on his twin's face. For Camron, six months away didn't mean freedom, it meant being away from the woman he'd loved for years.

But Anna was older and had never looked at Camron that way; furthermore, years before she'd fallen for a liar and a cheat. Her wanting to love and marry any man wasn't likely.

And so, a terrible trick, but a wonderful scheme came to him. For though it was true that Grahams could outdrink anyone, it was equally true that he and his brother made bets.

How could they not? As twins, they were duty bound to try to outdo each other. No matter the years or adversities, if one or the other made a challenge on who could throw better, run faster, drink more, the other twin would take the bait.

So he thought of making a bet with his brother on who could marry before summer's end. Camron would then be forced to act on his feelings for Anna and, perhaps, with her sister, Murdag, he could find a woman to calm that restlessness in him.

But him making a bet wouldn't be enough. His brother could easily dismiss the suggestions as another trick. Hamilton liked his jests to play; the world was too dull otherwise.

So he knew, with absolute certainty, he needed Camron to believe he made the jest so he couldn't dismiss it. So that Camron would believe, deep in his heart, he'd done it because he was done with waiting.

It seemed to work. Before the bet, Camron, because of their age difference and then because Anna fell in love with another, waited and yearned for years. Now, the day after the bet, Camron had followed Anna to Colquhoun land so she could visit a cousin and they hadn't returned yet.

Hamilton wouldn't be surprised if they returned to announce their betrothal. Of course, in the meantime, he'd pursue his own wife-to-be, Murdag.

He liked jests; Murdag liked jests. She was full of action and adventure. Why hadn't he seen it before? The fact she was Anna's sister made it all the more perfect.

Hamilton cherished the deep connection of being a twin. He might make a world of mischief, but he loved the ties of family even more. With any hope, long before summer's end, they'd be happily wed, with families to return to after the upcoming battles. He'd keep his twin close, his friends close and have a joyous future. Then all the unease, of looking over his shoulders, would be gone.

He wanted that. Needed it.

Murdag was ideal for him. She…the situation…everything was absolutely perfect. He had no doubt Anna would fall for Camron; he merely needed Murdag to fall for him. When she looked up from her horses, that was.

'Hamilton,' Murdag said.

Shaking himself from his thoughts, Hamilton blinked. 'Yes?'

'You were deep in thought,' Murdag teased. 'Is there something you need? You're just standing there staring.'

'Making you nervous?'

Her eyes straightened and looked around her. 'What are you up to?'

Hamilton pushed himself off the wall. Now this was a Murdag he could get behind in all the ways that meant. When she was working her horses…not so much.

'When am I not up to something?' he said.

Eyes darting around, she brandished the leather cloth at him. Given what the cloth was now covered in, he'd take it as the weapon it was intended.

'Stop,' she said. 'I love a good scare like anyone else, but it won't go over well with this mare, she's too skittish.'

'What makes you think I'm here to scare you?' He intended to seduce her. Why was it so difficult? She was comely enough and they were alone. A few hints of words on his intentions to gauge her reaction should be easy.

It wasn't.

Maybe that was because of the environment—it was difficult to flirt surrounded by barn walls, tethered horses and dung. 'Are you done here? Want to go for a walk?'

Murdag threw the linen in a pile of other used linens and went to a bucket to rinse her hands.

'Where are we going?'

He didn't know and that wasn't the point, but maybe they could go do what he liked to do. 'How about down to the water for fishing?'

'Fishing? That storm just came through and everything will be wet. Are the rest of them there?'

His brother Camron was off with Anna and he had no idea where Seoc or possibly Beileag were, but he sensed it mattered to her. 'Of course.'

She waved in front. 'You go through the doorway first.'

It was his duty to go afterwards, wasn't it? As friends, he had probably never given her any courtesy that he needed to show her now. 'After you.'

With a quick grin and shake of her head, she said, 'Go through the doorway first and get a bucket of what dumped on my head?'

'What are you talking of?'

'That's one of your oldest tricks. Is that why you've been standing here this entire time? Waiting for a laugh at my expense. Hamilton, when will you stop?'

She shoved him until he stumbled through the doorway and she quickly followed. But he miscalculated the distance. When he quickly stepped to the side to give her a way to walk in front of him, she stumbled.

He immediately stepped back and clenched her arm for support. For the briefest of moments, she leaned into him.

He liked her lean body and the strength of her hand as she gripped his arm. But something bothered him. Something…shouldn't there be more? When he demanded his body become aware of their proximity to each other, he felt nothing so he forced the issue.

'Perhaps I'll stop,' he said.

'Stop?' She disentangled them.

'Maybe I'll stop the games for the right woman,' he said in his most enticing voice. It wasn't as much a hint as to his interest, but a full-out declaration. If this woman intended to refuse his lighter flirtation, and if his own body didn't react to her being against him, so be it.

Murdag pulled up hard, looked at him as if he'd grown two heads and laughed.

'Only a fool would think you'd change!' She slapped her knee as if he made the best of jests. 'Oh! There's Seoc. I thought you said he'd be by the water?'

She walked in the direction of their friend and he let her. If she could brush it off, so could he. After all, there was time enough to make good on his bet and maybe get rid of his uneasiness.

And, he reminded himself, this bet wasn't only for him, but for his brother as well. If nothing else, his brother would finally wed Anna. It was a good trick, the very best where both of them could win.

Pulling his shoulders back, he swaggered forward. Only to catch the eye of Beileag of Clan Graham. He should have expected Beileag to be near; they'd all been in each other's proximity for most of their lives.

But he didn't expect the slight tilt to her long neck, or her expression to be so perplexed. Had she been standing there the entire time since he and Murdag emerged from the barn? Had she heard him flirt with her friend and fail?

She said nothing, which wasn't surprising. Beileag was the quiet one of the group. Though there were times when he caught her in an animated conversation with Anna or Murdag, but only when he was at a distance.

'We're fishing this morning, if you care to join,' he said.

She folded her hands in front of her. 'Why?'

The reason was to court her friend, but he couldn't say that. 'I like fishing.'

'You like hunting more,' she said.

How did she know that? 'Fishing's best today.'

Murdag was talking to Seoc now—were they standing a bit close? He couldn't see anything overt in their manners towards each other. They, too, were old friends, but then he'd never paid attention to Murdag before. Of course, since that night when she'd brandished her goblet, many other men commented on the beauty Murdag had become. Did Seoc have interest now as well? He'd have to declare his intentions.

Which would be easier if Murdag paid him any attention, but she barely looked at him. Certainly not the way she was currently conversing with Seoc. She was practically beaming at his friend.

For a flash of a moment, he wanted to declare his intentions right there and then, but Hamilton could feel Beileag's assessing gaze on him and, with effort, he turned his head towards her.

'Isn't it a bit late for fishing?' She arched her brow.

It was, but it was an activity where he could spend more time with Murdag. Though how much time now that Seoc was involved he didn't know. What he didn't understand was that if he couldn't get Beileag, her closest friend, to fish with them, Murdag wouldn't stay. 'You want to come?'

She looked towards the forest and clenched her hands before turning to him. 'Why not? What else do I have to do?'

He needed her with them fishing, but he didn't want to force her. Days were going by where Camron was wooing his Anna and he was no closer to any understanding with Murdag, but still, he wouldn't be an ass about it.

'It'll probably be dull what with the late hour, so I understand if you care to do something else.' When she looked at him, her eyes wide, he pointed to the forest where she was just gazing. 'If there's some place else you'd rather be...'

Her hands flew apart before she grasped them again. If possible, her golden-hazel eyes, which unerringly matched her hair, got a bit wider. They were really pretty eyes, especially when the morning sunlight hit them like this.

But the expression inside them wasn't so pleasant. Beileag, his friend, looked wary. He pointed to the forest. 'It's okay if you want to—'

'Why would I want to go to the forest?' she said. 'What could possibly be there this time of day?'

'Nobody, but then maybe that's what you're wanting instead of our company?'

He didn't know why he was pushing the matter when he actually needed her to go with them to the water, but he felt as though it was important to give her the chance since she seemed rather preoccupied...at least more so than usual.

She looked to Seoc and Murdag who were now walking side by side towards the water, then looked to him. A shallow smile reached the corner of her lips. 'You want me gone now to gossip about me?'

Was she teasing him? How...unusual for Beileag, but then he'd been gone for months; maybe this was how she was now.

'Oh!' She frowned. 'You do want to talk without me and were only being polite.'

'When have you known me to be polite?' He waited until she gave him a small agreeing smile, then waved in front of him. 'After you.'

Beileag lifted her skirt, and gave him a hesitant nod, but any wariness or awkward talking faded as they made their way through the rest of the village.

As he was wont to do, Hamilton quickly shook off any misgivings about Beileag and her observations and hesitancy. They'd known each other since before they could walk. He was only feeling out of place a bit because of this new interest with Murdag and his long absence from the village. He obviously was reading too much into this day because Murdag didn't once notice him all the time he leaned against the barn wall.

He was only a bit wary because there was a possibility Beileag had heard him failing to charm her friend.

And simply because Beileag was watching him a bit more closely, that didn't mean anything either. He'd been gone and probably was a bit of a curiosity, the way he was finding her curious, too.

No, all was fine with his world, and his plan to marry Murdag and his brother to marry Anna was better than fine. And he was doing nothing out of the ordinary by walking with friends towards the water to go fishing.

This was simply Beileag, slender limbed with a stride as long as his. No surprise there since she was a wee bit taller than him. She'd always been taller than him; he couldn't imagine her any other way. And he liked her long, wavy, golden-brown hair that matched her eyes, and the hue of her skin when it was kissed by the sunlight like now.

No, he wouldn't change one thing about Beileag.

What was wrong with him? That sounded conceited even to him. Why was he even thinking of Beileag or her appearance? It wasn't that he was attracted to her. He couldn't imagine anything more faulty. She was a friend and she wasn't like him at all. Quiet, subdued, with no loud gestures or activities. Other than helping around the village, he didn't know what she liked or did with her days. Which was saying something since he'd known her for years.

She wasn't like Murdag, who challenged, and whom he knew adored her horses. The whole village knew Murdag enjoyed her horses. Beileag with her quiet ways and looks and Murdag with her striking colouring and grand ways. Two women could not be more opposite to each other or to him and—

Why was he now comparing them? He needed to let it go for the day and stop observing how lively Murdag was around Seoc, how far ahead they were so he couldn't even hear their conversation to guide it to more appropriate talk. Like himself. Without a doubt this very day, he needed to have a talk with his friend regarding his feelings for—

'Are you certain you want me to go?' Beileag said.

He glanced her way only to be hit with that assessing gaze of hers again. Had she always had such a studying look? For several heartbeats he felt…caught, until he blinked and inwardly shook himself.

He probably only felt this way because of the way the sun warmed her cheeks and brightened her hair and eyes to gold. It truly was quite remarkable and he wasn't much of a friend to have not noticed before.

'Of course, I—*we*, want you to go.' He coughed to clear his throat from the sudden huskiness there. 'Don't you like fishing?'

'It only seems you're a bit preoccupied.'

He was right about her observations if she was noticing his thoughts on Seoc and Murdag. That wouldn't do! 'Wondering whether there'd be any fish is all.'

Beileag hummed under her breath, but they continued on towards their friends.

A few more steps together and they were almost in sync and he found himself breathing a bit easier. There was something comfortable about Beileag and her silence and accepting ways, especially after Murdag's laughing at him and her smiles towards Seoc—

'It's difficult when they ignore you, isn't it?' she said.

He stopped walking and gaped. It was Beileag's reddening cheeks more than her words that registered with him. She hadn't meant the conversation with Murdag, had she? They had been some distance away, it wasn't possible, though he'd been concerned that she'd overheard him.

They'd been talking of fishing and forests and everything else. There was no reason to have noticed or say anything about it.

Even if she did overhear, this was Beileag who kept her own counsel. So maybe he didn't have to say anything back, they could merely continue walking. That would be fine, wouldn't it?

But she clenched her hands tight and her eyes widened even more. If possible, her blush deepened and she looked close to tears.

He desperately wanted to say something to stop the flood of emotion, but that would mean he'd have to talk about Murdag's rejections and his own flirtation, and all the reasons, and… This was so difficult; he had no idea how to respond.

'Oh, I'm sorry,' she blurted before hitching up her skirts and running the other way.

Chapter Three

Horrified, Beileag tried to escape, but a strong hand on her arm spun her around.

She tumbled into Hamilton's broad chest and his free arm went around her waist. A heartbeat, maybe two at the most, and she knew she wouldn't be the same.

It was the breadth of his hold, the flat of his hand splayed wide against her lower back, the gentle grip of his other hand on her arm that instantly went from tugging to cradling.

It was the way he smelled of crisp air and hay. It was the feel of the gust of his breath against her neck when her shoulder battered into his sternum and the nimble way he righted them again as if their collision was nothing.

As if *she* was nothing but some small little creature and not the giant she knew she was.

'Hey, there, are you all right?' Hamilton said, his brown eyes holding nothing but concern when she expected annoyance, or, worse, some sort of hatred because she'd blurted something she shouldn't have.

Why did she say anything at all?

'I didn't hurt you, did I?' he said, rubbing her shoulders before he dropped his hands.

Hurt her?

'I think I got you.' She pressed the middle of his chest. His brows drew in and he stepped back.

She was so clumsy! 'I'm sorry. I didn't mean to ram into you and then poke exactly where I hurt you.'

'You think you poked me?' If possible, his brows drew down even more before he dropped his head and looked down at himself. His expression wasn't exactly assessing, more puzzled, but by what she didn't know. Other than…other than she guessed he had an interest in Murdag.

What if what she'd observed was merely her own longing for a family, and she'd embarrassed him for no reason at all?

If possible, she was more embarrassed. That had to be it. Hamilton was friends with Murdag, his brother was gone, so he was catching up with friends! He was simply up to his usual jests and mischief, and here she was implying he had an infatuation! Her skin heated even more and she would have run again, except she needed to apologise.

'Did I hurt you?' She tried to convey with her eyes that she was sorry for her foolish tongue and her bony shoulder.

He shook his head as he snapped his gaze back up to hers. 'No, not hurt.'

'Bruised a bit?' she pressed when his expression still hadn't eased.

The corner of his mouth lifted. For the first time in her life she had been held by a man. Something she was counting no matter how brief it was. And also, despite the other truths that she'd seen Hamilton fully laugh many times over and that puzzling gaze, his almost-smile flipped her heart several times over.

He seemed to guess it because his eyes looked at her chest down to her feet and then back up to her, but he didn't move or say anything.

Which was very un-Hamilton-like, but nothing in her wanted to protest or break whatever this was.

'Not bruised,' he said it as though it was a question.

'That's good,' she replied, but her voice sounded thready.

The wind picked up, causing his brown hair to ruffle and the tips of his ears to show. Why that would be the detail she noticed she didn't know. She didn't know any of this sudden fascination with Hamilton.

Liar.

Out of all the men on Graham land, she had always noticed Hamilton. First as a child, when she thought his antics were brave and humorous, next as a young woman when his charm revealed itself. He had so much appeal, even when he wasn't calling attention to himself, people followed him.

Whether it was making or taking a bet with his twin Camron or luring Murdag or Seoc to help him with some trick against the pantler or dairymaids or whoever else was the prey for the day, Hamilton loved being the centre of mischief. He was noticeable, but that wasn't why she watched him the most.

It was his easy smiles, his ease with life; he intrigued her and it went far beyond the fact he was far too handsome for his own good.

She wished she could be a bit more like him at times. Not that she wanted the attention, she received more than enough from her mother, but maybe she wanted some…connection with someone.

But every time she tried to help out with a trick or play a game with her friends, she floundered. Not because she was overtly clumsy or her height was noticeable, she simply didn't feel as though she knew what everyone was doing around her.

They were having fun and she couldn't always see the fun. But she tried, at least until the lure of the quiet woods and what she could create became more appealing. These people were her clan, her family, her friends, but a deep part of her was broken.

She was old enough to know she wasn't like everyone else and she was almost fine with that knowledge. Except for now when she so desperately wanted to understand the odd situation she found herself in, with her staring at Hamilton and him looking right back.

This had never happened to her. No one had ever merely stood and looked at her. She felt...she felt *seen*.

'Beileag—' he said.

'Hamilton—'

He stopped, cleared his throat.

When he didn't say anything more, she continued. 'I—'

'You ran away,' he said.

That wasn't what she expected him to say. 'You stopped me.'

'Yes, I thought maybe I—'

Splashing and laughter beyond the trees and Hamilton swung around.

The softness she saw in his face disappeared as he glanced her way again. 'Maybe we should catch up to them before they scare the fish away.'

Whatever they'd shared between them was gone or perhaps she'd only imagined it. In truth, she hadn't expected anything between them so what else was new for her?

'Maybe we should,' she said.

In far too soon a time, they cleared the trees, only to see Seoc brandishing a branch over his head and Murdag shrieking, looking for her own weapon.

Hamilton stopped walking and Beileag almost ran into him again, but he quickly shook off his shock and laughed. 'Oh, I know this game. I'll protect you!'

Grabbing a similar-sized stick, Hamilton raced to the water's edge.

'Don't you dare, Hamilton,' Murdag said. 'He's mine!'

Helplessly, Beileag watched adults take up a game as they had when they were children. Their branches in the air, feet crunching on rocks, shouts when boots slid into water.

She understood somewhere inside her that it probably wasn't effortless. They were grown with all the awareness of the world that came with the burden of years. And this world with its political challenges wasn't carefree.

And Seoc, the gentle giant, carried the scar across his chest from the wound that almost took his life at the Battle of Dunbar. A scar he touched with a frequency almost like an afterthought, but that she feared was a conscious reminder of the pain he endured.

Did he still feel any and not let anyone know, or did the ghost of the agony haunt him? No, Seoc wasn't the same as when he'd last played this game.

Neither was Hamilton.

Beileag looked behind her to the beckoning woods, to where her tool chest was buried under a hollowed log and next to it, wrapped in worn linens, were bits of wood mutilated into figurines. Some pieces were more recognisable than others and those still rough-hewn needed her knife and hands or they would never be anything other than sticks.

She should go... Beileag turned back to her friends.

Hamilton was as beckoning as her treasured sticks. Were the differences she saw in him because he'd been gone for six months, or was there something more?

He was still carefree in ways she could never be, his brown hair tousling with his abrupt movements and a happy colour to his cheeks, but his body had muscle and sinew and memory from true battle. Hamilton grinned and shouted with glee, but everything from the breadth of his shoulders, the thickness of his thighs, the way he jumped and feinted, was of a man who knew loss.

It was good for them to do this familiar playful game. They needed it and it was time for her to leave.

Murdag brandished her branch, stumbled into the water and was desperately trying to get to dry land. They were making so much noise, it was a wonder no one else joined or tried to stop them.

It looked as though a mock argument was beginning, what with Hamilton getting between Murdag and Seoc. Of Seoc taking the bait, clearly thinking Hamilton was the greater threat, only to see Murdag sneak past his side and tap him on the back.

Seoc bowing gracefully as Hamilton, with a victorious smile, threw his arm around Murdag's shoulders and squeezed.

Frowning fiercely, Murdag threw off his arm, tossed her branch away and exchanged words with the men. Beileag couldn't hear what they said, but Seoc shrugged, and Hamilton's grin fell. It fell even more when Murdag strode up the hill towards her.

Beileag didn't know what to make of Hamilton's expression. He seemed bewildered, but he quickly turned away and faced Seoc, who was talking again.

Murdag stopped next to her and huffed. 'All week, he's been like this!'

She couldn't hear or see much of the men's conversation, but it appeared as if Seoc was teasing…though it was always difficult to know what Seoc was feeling.

She didn't know what was going on and she wasn't certain she wanted to. A stabbing twist had happened deep in her stomach when Hamilton threw his arm around Murdag's shoulders. She could still feel that moment when Hamilton had his arms around her.

It wasn't the same! Hamilton had purposefully held Murdag, held her tighter to him. Whereas for her, he'd only waited until he was certain she wouldn't fall at his feet. What was wrong with her today?

'Who and what?' she said.

'Has Hamilton been following you?'

Other than that strange moment by the barn, she'd hardly seen him. 'Is he supposed to be following me?'

Murdag grinned. 'Oh, Beileag. I love that you don't care.'

Hamilton and Seoc appeared to be deep in a friendly conversation, but there was a tension in Hamilton's neck and shoulders when before he had been at ease. Friendly with Murdag even. Protective, too. Touching her a bit more than she'd seen before. Had he been overly friendly? Did he more than care for Murdag? Perhaps she hadn't been wrong when she thought she saw Hamilton's interest in her friend.

Then had Murdag inadvertently hurt Hamilton with her rebuff? 'What am I to care about?'

'What do you think he's doing? I can't breathe or turn around without him suddenly popping up.'

I think he likes you, Beileag wanted to blurt.

But she couldn't say such a thing. For one, she

couldn't actually see Hamilton and Murdag together. They had been friends all their life, but they were both the same. Both liked their freedom, their space. Both liked to make jests and create mischief. Maybe to some this would make a great match, but…it felt as though something was missing.

But then…maybe she was biased. After all, Anna was always being courted by Camron—why shouldn't Murdag have Hamilton, too? This conjecture was torture! Especially, when it could be her own wishful thinking for a family of her own that she saw mere friendship as something more.

'Maybe he's lonely,' Beileag whispered, then cleared her throat. 'His brother and Anna are gone and that leaves you, me and Seoc.'

'He's been with Seoc this entire time and you're always disappearing doing what we cannot name…'

Murdag and Anna were the only ones who knew she carved and she wanted to keep it that way. 'So that leaves you.'

'Something seems off, though.' Murdag wrinkled her nose.

It did to her as well. Merely the thought of Murdag and Hamilton wasn't pleasant. Was she jealous or self-ish? That didn't sit well either. She'd always preferred Hamilton to any boy or man in Graham land, but that didn't mean he was for her! No matter how well his tunic outlined the lines of his back, or the way his breeches hugged his legs in their widened stance.

It didn't do for her to think of him, or of any Graham man. If they hadn't noticed her by now, they never would. And despite her mother's debilitating words, she knew she held some worth. She hoped at least.

But Murdag either didn't know her worth or forgot a

very important fact. 'He did see you in that sheer gown the night of the festivities.' Beileag smirked.

'Why didn't anyone pull me from that boulder?'

'We tried, but you swung that goblet at our heads and we thought it best to leave you at your little game.'

'Little? Hah!' Murdag poked her shoulder. 'I had half the clan making bets on ale.'

'And the other half getting sick in the woods. *My* woods.'

Murdag winced. 'Sorry about that.'

She truly was a good friend. Maybe Murdag would like Hamilton? 'He might like you.'

'I hope not!' Murdag put her hands on her hips. 'When would that have happened? They just got back, Anna and Camron are gone. I won't tolerate it. It has to be impossible, but just in case, I'll give him time to get over it. Will I see you later?'

'Where else will I be?' Beileag hadn't meant for it to sound forlorn, but she did.

Murdag frowned. 'Are you well?'

She tried to smile. 'Of course, now go before they really make us fish.'

Murdag patted her shoulder and took off.

Still listening to whatever Seoc was saying, Hamilton looked over his shoulder. His happy expression entirely crumpled as he watched Murdag's retreat before he turned away again.

As much as Beileag wanted to belong, for as long as she'd known her Murdag had wanted her freedom. She didn't know if it was because of what had happened to her older sister Anna, who fell in love with a man who was disloyal, or if she simply was like her horses and needed to run. Either way, if Hamilton was interested it would make for an entertaining, torturous summer.

Looking over Hamilton's shoulder, Seoc gave her a wave and she waved back as he turned and walked further away down the winding river to go and do what, she had no idea.

But Murdag was gone, as was Seoc, and Hamilton now strode her way.

Her entire body felt like that moment when she'd first held the blade to an uncut piece of wood. Some sort of anticipation mixed with trepidation.

She truly should go. She'd already talked to Hamilton today. Most likely he was simply heading her way and would walk right past her.

But he didn't. Instead, he stopped just shy of two feet's length. A respectable distance for a conversation, but it didn't feel that way to her. To her it was too soon for anything Hamilton-related.

'Beileag, do you have a moment?' Hamilton said.

She wanted to say no, but couldn't think of a reason. Why shouldn't her friend ask her a question? The feeling of dread and uncomfortableness was most likely left over from the unusual encounter they'd had earlier. Nothing more than that. Her and Murdag's talk, her observations, were most likely wrong and there was nothing to worry about.

'Of course.' She clasped her hands in front of her.

Chapter Four

'You're…' Beileag pulled in a calming breath through her suddenly tight throat. 'You're playing a game with our friend's *lives*?'

Horror flushing hot through every vein in her body, Beileag stared, but Hamilton didn't break out in laughter and tell her it was a jest. She would have expected mischief from him and, if so, she could just laugh and dismiss it all. No one took Hamilton altogether seriously because if a person did, then they could find thistles in their boots, or some such nonsense.

Instead, Hamilton looked serious. In truth, since they'd returned from Dunbar's battle, and then this last scouting mission, much of Hamilton's countenance seemed changed, but then he'd flash one of his easy smiles and she believed she was imagining that wary look in his eyes.

Except she wasn't imagining what he'd just told her.

She should have left for the woods instead of watching them play, instead of feeling uncomfortable because she didn't belong, because she'd guessed Hamilton had feelings for Murdag and he stood in front of her and said that he did.

And then…

And *then*! Oh, she was so angry she was surprised he wasn't taking steps back to protect himself.

His grin fell and his eyes became completely sober of mischief. 'It's not a game.'

Trying not to unleash on him, she crossed her arms. 'A bet between people usually involves a game.'

She'd never been full of venom in all her life. She wanted a family, children, something she'd never have because no one wanted her and he—with his brown hair that curled around his ears, lively eyes and muscles on top of muscles—just thought, why not? As if was easy to get a family and have everything. As if it was as easy as a thought and it was done.

But then look at him! Of course, someone would marry him. With his easy grin and fun ways, he was always pursued by women. Even she was attracted to him, as foolish and ill spent those wayward thoughts were.

'A bet is usually like a game,' Hamilton said. 'But this isn't a usual bet.'

'It shouldn't have been a bet at all,' she bit out. 'The fact you even thought of—'

'Wasn't me.'

She counted her whittling tools in her head. Then counted them backwards in case she missed any before she could say, 'What?'

'It wasn't me who came up with the bet.'

Hamilton was always coming up with bets. 'Are you telling me someone else in this clan challenged you to marry before the summer's end?'

Hamilton winced. 'Not someone else. Camron made the bet; I merely agreed to it.'

She believed that as much as a stranger riding in and declaring his devotion to her. 'Your brother, Camron.'

'Is there any other Camron in this clan?' He shrugged. 'You don't believe he can make a bet?'

She'd seen Camron make challenges with Hamilton because the twins were notoriously competitive, but never something like this. Jests that went too far in damaging pride or property were Hamilton's talent. No one could stay angry at him for long; he was too good-natured for it. Despite his tricks, people still flocked around him.

But kind loyal Camron wouldn't conceive of making a bet that would potentially harm anyone, let alone make a game of the sacredness of marriage.

'Camron came up with this?' she repeated.

His eye twitched. 'Yes.'

She'd call him a liar but for the fact she couldn't remember either twin lying. Camron always told the truth, blunt though he could be, and Hamilton liked confessing to his sins. But Hamilton wasn't looking directly at her and he seemed more restless than usual. So it was possible he could be—

'He was drunk,' Hamilton offered.

She lowered her arms. 'I'm listening.'

He scraped his foot against the dirt and looked over her shoulder. 'It was the night of the festivities. He'd missed Anna while on the road.'

She understood that. Anna was a few years older than all of them and had lost her heart to a former friend of Seoc's, a man from the Maclean clan. The man, Alan, had fooled everyone into thinking he was honourable and loved Anna, but instead he'd betrayed her with another woman, another clan.

All through that, there was Camron, who, for reasons he never explained to anyone, became infatuated with Anna when he was a child. His attentions towards her never changed, even when they teased him for it. Even when she fell in love with another man.

Camron missing Anna while he was away from the clan was a certainty. Him getting drunk and making a heartless....

'Murdag made an ale challenge,' she said.

His eyes snapped back to hers. 'You know of it?'

She'd been there, not that anyone would notice. 'It was much talked about the next day. So *she* made the bet on marriage.'

He huffed. 'Why won't you believe me that Camron made it?'

Because it was inconceivable that Camron, after all these years, would betray and trick Anna like that. If she ever found out Camron had made a game of his pursuit, she'd be heartbroken all over again. If Camron had truly made the bet and he was drunk, he should have been stopped. Hamilton should have stopped him.

But even if she gave the benefit of the doubt to Hamilton, which she didn't want to do, there was the other half of the bet that was overwhelmingly confusing.

'The ale and his feeling explained Camron pursuing Anna and traveling with her to Colquhoun land,' she said. 'It doesn't explain you pursuing Murdag.'

'Murdag.' His brow drew down and he kicked the dirt again. A patch of red flushed across his cheeks and then disappeared.

Was he shy about Murdag? Had she misinterpreted his interest, or, worse, had she interpreted it correctly? Could Hamilton slinging his arm around Murdag mean what she feared—that he liked her? Why did that press so hard on her chest?

And why was he reserved talking about Murdag?

Camron was the more taciturn twin. Hamilton would boast, or at least drop heavy hints of his intent.

'Am I wrong about Murdag?' she said.

'You can't possibly be surprised about my pursuit.' He looked back up. 'You…you hinted about my being disappointed with Murdag avoiding me.'

She had done no such thing. 'When was this brilliant conversation?'

He jabbed his arms towards the village. 'At the barn, on the way down to the river. You saw her reject me. You observed my flirting and her completely shrugging me off. Don't tell me you didn't. You said it feels bad when they ignore you. You saw it all.'

Oh. So she wasn't wrong, and this man she— No, she wasn't going to think about it, not when that weight against her chest compressed.

The whole matter was too complicated and made no sense. Hamilton stood before her and told her of a serious bet, one that played with people's lives, she assumed because he wanted marriage. But she had no idea what her role in this was. If Anna or Murdag knew of this, it would be devastating for Anna and possibly murderous for Murdag.

'But that doesn't explain why you're telling me about any of this. Is there a point of you telling me—?'

'They did it again!'

Beileag swung about to see her younger sister, Oigrhrig, racing towards her with her younger brothers, Roddy and Raibert, walking quickly behind her.

'You should go, Hamilton,' she said. 'This may take time.'

The corner of his mouth quirked up. 'You might need support.'

'I won't want your kind of help,' she said quickly.

Too quickly and acerbically and Beileag felt remorse for her tone. She didn't intend to sound mean. Hamilton's quick grin faded, but his feet remained rooted.

Her shoulders sagged. As angry as she was at Hamilton, she'd control it for her family. It was horrific enough that the bet was made, but maybe when she got a chance, she could talk him out of it.

For now, she softened her eyes at him, just as Oigrhirg grabbed her hand and Roddy and Raibert skidded to her other side. They didn't grab her hand as they used to when they were younger, but they didn't stop in time and slammed into her.

Off balance, she began to fall. Two large hands seized her waist and effortlessly moved her aside.

'Sorry!' Roddy piped up.

Oigrhirg, still gripping her hand, stumbled. 'Clumsy dirt clods.'

'None of that.' Beileag looked over her shoulder as Hamilton released her. His gaze roved slowly over her features and form, and then again before he dipped his head and whispered. 'Any harm?'

She shook her head and he gave a ghost of a smile. 'See, I am good for support.'

Rolling her eyes, she turned back to her siblings, but it took her a breath or two because of the sudden heat caused by his hands on her waist, because of Hamilton's deep rumbling voice.

'Look a bit sharper than that, lads,' Hamilton said. 'Or you might not have a sister.'

Beileag almost turned around to clarify what Hamilton meant when Raibert shifted.

'Yes, Sir,' Raibert said.

'Now tell me what happened,' Beileag said. She could feel Hamilton's presence behind her. She thought she'd feel annoyed or inspected, or worse, critiqued, but instead…she felt as if there was some sort of private moment happening between them. Which was foolish given her siblings were right in front of her and Hamilton was simply standing there like a friend she'd known forever.

Like…someone who was supporting her.

When would the imprint of his hand disappear? She swore the warmth of his touch should have dissipated by now. Instead, it was alarmingly imprinted, as if his fingers had gently nestled themselves between her ribs and belonged there now. And had he taken a step closer to her because she felt the heat of him against her back?

Oigrhirg let go of her hand and stomped her foot. 'What didn't happen!'

'It wasn't us!' Roddy stomped his foot.

She loved her siblings to the ends of the earth, but her brothers were chaos and mischief and her sister was a boulder who never budged. If she simply laughed or played or reacted in any other way, life would be so much easier for her.

But her sister was rigid, everything was right or wrong, and her brothers were hell bent to prove to her they were wrong or at least that there were other ways of looking at the world. And unlike Hamilton and Camron, it didn't take any imagination at all to know they were lying. They did it all the time.

'Well enough, it wasn't you,' she told Roddy.

'Or me,' Raibert added.

She nodded her understanding. 'Neither of you caused any grief, but let's have Oigrhirg explain how she believes you have, then you can explain what you didn't.'

'There was a frog in my bed,' Oigrhirg said.

Beileag almost groaned. The boys had put frogs in her bed before and they thought to deny it? 'Let me see your hands.'

Raibert and Roddy held out their hands. They were dirty, but not muddy, and under their fingernails was moderately clean.

She turned to her sister. At sixteen, it was clear her sister would have all the beauty and none of the height. In other words, everything her mother always wanted for her daughters.

Except Oigrhirg also had most of her mother's rigidness and none of their father's absent-minded warmth.

'Where's the frog now?'

'I didn't touch it!'

'So it's still in your bed.' She turned to Roddy. 'Did you see it?'

'They put it there,' Oigrhirg whined.

'No, we didn't!' Roddy exclaimed.

Hamilton gave a snort which could have been agreement or humour, but when she glanced behind her his expression was strangely blank.

Turning back to her sister, she asked, 'Was the frog wet?'

Oigrhirg looked up, no doubt looking at Hamilton for approval.

'Answer me, please,' Beileag said.

'There were puddles.' Oigrhirg shrugged a shoulder.

'Yet the boys' clothes are dry. They don't have a speck of mud on them and Roddy's fingernails are clean,' Beileag pointed out. 'Do you ever remember them performing any jest against you when there wasn't some evidence?'

Oigrhirg started to look up to the sky again. No, not the sky, not beyond. To *Hamilton* as if he'd have an answer to a frog in a bed. He'd better not have answers to frogs in beds!

'Eyes on me,' she warned.

Oigrhirg slid her gaze back to hers. Good.

'Do you ever remember them performing the same jest twice?'

'They haven't?' Hamilton interrupted. 'Well done.'

'You're not helping,' Beileag hissed.

Raibert laughed and Oigrhirg covered her mouth. Was she trying not to smile?

Beileag blinked, then looked at her siblings who were so much younger than her, but the ties that connected them were strong. Oh, she loved them. Had she ever seen them so expectant, almost eager, when she was scolding them?

What was the difference now rather than any other time? Was it as simple as Hamilton's presence? He wasn't making any sounds, but he'd better not be making eye communication or gestures that—

'You were handing out punishment,' Hamilton whispered in her ear.

She shivered, clearing her throat to cover it up. Was he a mind reader? 'No, I wasn't.'

'You weren't?' he said at the same time Roddy, Raibert and Oigrhirg echoed them.

She almost didn't want to say anything more to soak in this moment, whatever it was. Some familiarity, some camaraderie…something shared between all of them. It felt altogether good.

Too good. Exhaling harshly, she turned to her sister. They were a family, but Hamilton behind her wasn't. She was still angry with him about the bet and games with her friends. And he intended to pursue Murdag!

'Oigrhrig, I think you need to look at other sources for a frog in your bed.'

'What?' Hamilton said.

She turned around, but instead of him looking truly scandalous, he seemed to be only mocking her. Troublemaker!

Oigrhrig looked to her brothers. 'They didn't do it, did they?'

Roddy and Raibert shook their head.

'But you know who did.' Beileag narrowed her eyes at them.

Raibert shook his head, but Roddy nodded.

'Innocent, but not. As usual.' She tried to sound firm, but failed. And it had nothing to do with Hamilton or with the frogs, but with Oigrhrig who seemed to be contemplating a change of heart...she was willing to listen and not just accuse. It had happened before, but it was so rare, and lately even more so.

'But you can see how Oigrhrig might think it was all you?' she said.

'Because we've done it before,' Raibert said. 'And we know who did it now.'

'So you were lying,' she said. 'To your family.'

Raibert, a flush of red across his cheeks now, nodded.

'Don't do it again, or—'

'Will you help me get revenge?' Oigrhrig asked.

Oigrhrig stood straight and her chin was out, but her eyes were wary, unsure, as if she wasn't at all certain her brothers, who teased her relentlessly, would help her.

Beileag swung her gaze around to Hamilton to see if he was giving hints, but he merely shrugged. Had Oigrhrig come up with this on her own? How did her brothers feel?

Raibert and Roddy were looking at each other. Their

expressions were partly astonished, partly devious. Then they looked at Oigrhirg and nodded.

Hamilton chuckled behind her.

Her siblings were talking to each other and willing to work together? Where this came about or why, she wasn't going to question it, she didn't care. She was happy!

Laughing, Beileag grabbed Roddy, ran with him and spun him around before she plopped him on the ground. With Raibert, who was a bigger, she grabbed his hand and ran in circles until they were both dizzy. When she let go, he fell to the ground, while she grabbed for Oigrhirg, who shrieked and made a run for it, but not before Roddy caught her skirts and the two tumbled to the ground.

Stopping immediately, Beileag braced herself for when Oigrhirg began to lose her patience again, but she only pounded her skirts, groaned and laughed.

That rare laughter was a balm to her soul and to the boys' as well who all joined in. Then Oigrhirg clasped Roddy's hand, Raibert at her side, and they ran back towards the village.

When had she last seen them play like that? It was a rare day indeed to see such a sight and Beileag kept her eyes on them until she couldn't see them any more.

Unable to dim her smile, she looked over her shoulder at Hamilton. 'I know nothing is solved and tomorrow they'll be fighting again, but for one day to have that I'll take it.'

Instead of the usual friendly but benign look he often gave her, there were too many emotions in his gaze.

'Hamilton?' she whispered.

He was never cruel, but she knew where she fit in the friend scheme of things. It was always his brother first, and since it was Camron, that made Anna next. Then Murdag, who was far more outgoing, and Seoc, with his mead, was mixed all in there. She was always just there because Murdag and Anna didn't let her go.

Except several times today, Hamilton had looked at her and kept looking. And if possible, this gaze was different than all the others. For the look in his deep brown eyes was both calculating and perplexed. And it didn't make her confused……but rather warm.

'You spun him around,' Hamilton said.

She'd also scolded them, given them warnings and sent them on their way, knowing she'd likely be addressing some other calamity her brothers did to their sister tomorrow.

She gave a curt nod.

'I've never seen you do that before,' he said.

She did it all the time. She might have parents who were absolutely worthless when it came to love or affection, but her siblings were much younger than her and she could pour all the love she had into them.

'You've been gone for the last six months,' she said. 'And mostly unavailable for the last couple of years.'

'It's more than that.' He looked away, breathed out. 'Something's not making sense… Probably foolish.'

Beileag wasn't certain what they were talking about. She should go, she hadn't had a chance to be in the woods yet today and, if she didn't go soon, she wouldn't have time at all while there was still daylight.

Yet a thousand expressions were covering Hamilton's features and she was incapable of walking away. He was drawn up, struggling with something, and she wanted to help. Which was simply foolish on her part since she was still cross with him.

And all her joy with her siblings was gone.

'What you think is foolish,' she said. 'I'll take it with a grain of salt.'

His eyes snapped back to her. 'No, you don't; that's not what I meant. I wasn't insulting you. It's simply...' he huffed '...you don't like games.'

Now she was certain she didn't know what they were talking about—he might not have meant to be insulting, but that's what she felt.

'I don't like games at other people's expense,' she said. 'Such as a bet which is cruel. And even if I'm inclined to believe you, which I'm not, that Camron made the bet instead of you, you should have stopped him. Especially if you think you actually like Murdag. Especially when you know your brother loves Anna. Good day, Hamilton.'

'Wait!'

Chapter Five

Surprised Beileag waited, Hamilton ran his hand through his hair and took a step back from his life-long friend.

He couldn't explain why he was about to embarrass himself—after all, he had all summer to woo Murdag. Maybe it was his notorious lack of patience. He wasn't like his twin, whose fortitude was well known throughout the land. Camron's obsession with Anna had turned to love, but still Camron had waited years for her. Hamilton wasn't the waiting kind and Murdag, as far as he knew, didn't have the heartache that Anna did. There was no reason to wait when it came to gaining her affections.

More pressing was the weight of being a twin brother. As far as he was concerned, if Camron was out winning the love of his life, Hamilton should be, too. That was as it should be. Being a twin was the best, but there was a certain responsibility that came with it as well. It wouldn't do if there were noticeable differences between them after all. People might think they were different people. Throughout the years, Hamilton had ensured that their lives stayed alike, but he'd never felt so desperate for this to be more true than since Dunbar's battle.

He knew there were more battles ahead, he needed to have his family with him in every way. He couldn't think of a future without that. And with the upcoming battles, the call to go to Stirling, he wanted something to return to. So if Anna was Camron's love, Murdag, Anna's sister, was a must for him.

Thus far, no matter how he approached her, Murdag ignored him. He was man enough to know he was outmanoeuvred. Perhaps if Anna was here, he'd be talking—

No, he wouldn't talk to Anna, not because she wasn't around, or she was Camron's interest or part of the bet. He wouldn't talk to her because Anna might not approve of him as a suitor for her sister. After her betrayal, Anna didn't approve of any man and rightly so. It made winning Anna's heart difficult for his brother, but that was his challenge.

For him, he was certain if Murdag would notice him as a man versus a friend, she would realise instantly how suited they were. Thus far, she wasn't noticing him. He feared if he did any of his usual antics, or activities that called attention to him, it would only remind her of the tricks they'd played as children.

And unfortunately, his more mature and knowing smiles were completely wasted when she was looking at a horse's udders.

He needed inside information, someone who knew Murdag, but would stay discreet. Someone who observed, but was quiet, unnoticeable. Beileag was ideal as long as she thought highly enough of him and was willing to help.

Hadn't Beileag always liked him? The fact he didn't know didn't bode well.

What also didn't bode well were their interactions

today. He'd been around Beileag all his life. She was kind, quiet and what he'd never noticed before was how expressive her gaze was. How her cheeks had flushed when she'd made the comment about Murdag ignoring him and tried to flee.

How she'd felt when she stumbled into him when he'd stopped her, and how, for a moment, his body curled around her as if wanting to protect her and not let go.

Then she stood there with that almost beguiling look in her eye, asking if she'd hurt him. He'd felt…something. But it couldn't be. It was most likely his imagination. Most definitely some desperation because Murdag was ignoring him and he needed Beileag for her advice.

She'd help him, wouldn't she?

'I need your help,' he said.

Beileag tensed. 'This wouldn't be about the bet, would it?'

Why was he asking this? She'd already said she didn't approve of the bet; him asking her to help him couldn't, wouldn't go well. Except, he had to try. The bet wasn't a game for him. He wouldn't give up at his first obstacle of Beileag not liking the challenge.

Or Murdag ignoring him, and of him touching Murdag and not feeling anything at all. Or about that moment, when Beileag played with her siblings and he'd felt an odd constriction in his chest watching them together.

No, the latter wasn't an obstacle. Seeing Beileag so free with her sister and brothers was only a reminder of how important family was. Him wanting a family, and every connection it meant, was why he wanted to press forward on this.

'It is about the bet,' he said.

'Then it's best if I'm avoiding this conversation.

You're fortunate I'm not going to take your telling me this as anything serious because if I told Anna she'd be devastated and Murdag would probably kill you… or concoct her own jest at your expense in front of the entire clan.'

This was going worse than he'd expected. 'You're not going to tell them.'

'No, I won't—first, because I don't think anything will come of it and, second, because it would hurt my friends too much. Because a bet like that is manipulative.'

Much, much worse than expected. 'You don't like me.'

She blinked. 'What?'

'You don't want to talk to me,' he said. 'And since I have just returned, I can only think it's because you don't like me.'

She unclenched her hands. 'I didn't say that.'

It was good fortune Murdag and Seoc had left. This conversation was more embarrassing than he thought it could be.

He knew he wasn't perfect and most families preferred thoughtful Camron to his bold ways. But he didn't think he was hated. After all, wasn't boldness needed in some situations? Didn't people like to laugh when tricks were played?

Apparently, Beileag didn't appreciate what were his only charms and, if Beileag didn't like it, perhaps Murdag didn't either. Maybe he was never meant to participate in the bet. Maybe this was only an opportunity for Camron to win Anna.

'Can you at least tell me why you don't like me, or if I've done something unsavoury? I think your information would prove very helpful to me in other ways.'

Beileag took a step back, looked around as if trying

to find an answer or run away. He suddenly felt it was very important that she stayed.

'Is it as bad as that?' he said.

'I should have gone,' she said.

At the same time he said, 'It's because I wanted to woo Murdag.'

She opened her mouth, closed it. Stared. Some emotion he couldn't name fluttered across her eyes and then disappeared. It wasn't laughter or confusion, but something dim.

He stared back, waited a bit. A laugh left him. 'Can you say something?'

'Oh,' she said.

'It is that bad,' he said. 'My wanting your friend?'

'As a wife,' she said very slowly and without any question.

Was her concern that he wouldn't be honourable? 'Very much so.'

'Oh, you *are* serious,' she said again. But this time her tone was much higher pitched, as though he'd poked her with a sharp stick.

'Are you well?' he said.

'No. I meant yes,' she said.

He suddenly felt as if he should wish her a good day and leave. It didn't serve the purpose for attempting to ask her for help, but he also felt as though she didn't want to help him at all because she didn't want to be around him.

Is that what she had meant when she said she should have gone? He didn't want to stand around for any pity. Nodding his head, he took strides away from her. 'I am sorry to have delayed your morning, Beileag, I understand you won't help me with the bet. I'll be—'

'You're not bad.'

'Well.' He stopped, turned around. Her expression was just as shuttered as before. What did she truly want to tell him? If Beileag wasn't honest with him, then who could he trust? She'd always seemed honest to him. Why couldn't he remember enough about her? She was always there with them when they played games or had chores.

'You like her,' she whispered.

'Who?' he said.

'Murdag.'

Yes, Murdag. Not Beileag whom he was asking for help to woo Murdag.

'She's perfect,' he blurted.

Beileag winced. 'So…woo her.'

He intended to, which was the problem. Sidestepping to ease some of the restlessness, he gazed around them. He could hear the voices of the villagers, but they weren't nearby, and Seoc had completely disappeared. Did no one like the babbling river here during the day? He rather liked it.

'It's quiet here,' he said.

She clasped her hands again, squeezed her fingers which outlined the linen wrapped there. 'It can be.'

He swung his gaze back to her. She had to be insulting him somehow. He knew he would be. This conversation was more than embarrassing. It was utter humiliation. Where was his confidence, his absolute knowledge on what to do? He'd never faltered or second-guessed himself before.

And yet, here he was.

'It can be,' she said. 'Hamilton, if you…' she swallowed '…like Murdag, she might appreciate if you were talking to her instead of me.'

'I may be having a bit of trouble with it.'

'Talking to her?'

'Wooing her.'

She pulled in her lips, then rushed her words. 'Then don't pursue her.'

'Are you jesting?'

He felt as though this was a jest. None of it made sense, especially Beileag's answers to him. She seemed flummoxed by his request. She also seemed angry, disappointed and something else he couldn't quite wrap his head around. But if pressed, he wanted to say...resigned. But none of the emotions, except her confusion made sense to him.

This was Beileag! Simple, kind, always there, always helpful when around, Beileag. But as she stood clenching her hands, he had to wonder if he knew her at all.

Were her fingers always wrapped up in those little linens? It seemed like an odd decoration for hands. None of the other females were doing it.

Her brow raised. 'How do I know you're not jesting?'

Good point. 'How many times have I jested with you?'

Another flinch and twist to her features as if she was silently schooling herself. 'You've never jested with me.'

There! That should build some trust with them. Except Beileag was standing too still and didn't act as though what he had said was a compliment, so he added, 'How about the last time I asked for your help?'

'You've never asked for my help either,' she said.

Again, he was left with the feeling he was insulting her somehow, but how could that be? He respected her too much to play tricks on her. She always seemed half frightened and timid, and if he remembered rightly, she'd disappear when the antics got too much. It was clear she didn't like to play like the rest of them.

'I'm having trouble taking this conversation with any weight, Hamilton.' She held up her hand to stop him from answering. 'And it's not because I don't like you or we're not friends. It's simply you're always jesting, and Murdag's my friend. I don't want you jesting with her.'

'Camron made the bet,' he said. 'I agreed to it because I think he needs the bet.'

'To woo Anna?' she said. 'He's loved Anna for years and years. Why would he suddenly need a bet?'

'He's loved her from afar, but nothing has come of it.'

'So you think he made the bet to spur himself forward to courting her?'

'Yes.'

'Why did you pause?' she said. 'Before you answered yes, you paused. Is there something you're not telling me?'

'No,' he said. He needed to be truthful with her. As much as he could be. He couldn't tell her that he had made the bet, not until after Camron had won Anna's heart. Once that happened, once Beileag helped him with Murdag, then this whole matter would just be something they talked about in their old age.

'Don't you want your friends happy?'

'Of course I do.'

'Do you not think Camron is right for Anna?'

She shook her head. 'There's never been any doubt, the entire clan has never had any doubt, of Camron's love for Anna. But that's not the issue with them.'

'And for Murdag? Don't you want her happy?'

Beileag's eyes narrowed. Could she tell he was twisting her words so she would be swayed his way? He needed her to be there for him. She would solve the conundrum of gaining a wife before the end of summer, he knew it. She was always observing. She knew Murdag. Beileag was the key.

Didn't she want weddings and happiness? He frowned when he realised he didn't know if Beileag wanted a husband or a family of her own.

But he knew he wanted his brother to stop longing and for Anna to gain her trust again. His brother could build a family.

And instead of Murdag always being obsessed with horses, he could be there to show her other interests in the world.

'So you'll help me?' he pressed.

She huffed. 'Why can't Camron just court Anna? He's home now and she's unattached. Why does he need some game—?'

'It's not a game,' he said. 'He's serious about this.'

'And you're serious about Murdag who has been ignoring you.'

Afraid to say any more words—he was better at actions than talking—he nodded.

'So you think I'll help by telling you all their secrets? Because I won't,' she said. 'And it'll be absolutely suspicious if I am suddenly asking them questions about their likes and dislikes.'

It would. 'You don't have to do that, you could tell me what they're up to for that day and we could be conveniently—'

'You want me to spy on them?'

He winced. 'No.'

'Lie?' she added.

Never that.

'Now you're quiet?' Her hands fell to her sides. 'I won't help you.'

He had to ask, had to know. The unsettling unease

was cloaking him and he forced himself to keep his eyes on the woman before him. He refused to look over his shoulder. 'Why?'

'Because it's lying and deceitful and people will be hurt. Good day, Hamilton.'

Chapter Six

'Anyone feeling we should let the fire die?' Seoc threw on a log.

'Feels good.' Hamilton grabbed another log and handed it to his friend. When Seoc threw that one on the fire and poked around to distribute the logs, Hamilton sat back on the ancient bench he currently shared with his brother. He wasn't ready to return home or to any proper shelter even though everyone else had said their goodnights and the heavy mist resting on their hair and clothes look like tiny stars.

Which he supposed would be beautiful if he were a child, but he knew the damp would only soak into the wool fibre until his bones were cold. Hence, another log for the fire because he had no intention of leaving. A quick glance towards his brooding brother confirmed he wasn't ready to retire either.

There was too much to think about.

Camron and Anna had returned from Colquhoun land a week ago, but his brother wasn't any closer to finding his happiness than he was. If anything, Camron was sleeping less and his renowned patience had disappeared. He was worried for Anna and Camron now, all the more so since his brother refused to confide what occurred during the trip. Only that they were forced to stay in a cave, that she was the love of his life and stubborn as hell.

'What feels good is not drinking your mead.' Camron stretched out his feet.

Hamilton knew Camron loved Seoc's mead, but he'd been refusing it since he returned. Perhaps it reminded him of the night he'd made the bet. Did he feel as though he'd made a mistake?

A niggle of conscience made him shift on his seat. Should he tell his brother that he'd made the bet? Hamilton rolled his shoulders. And then what, have everyone yell at him and drop everything?

No, it wasn't wrong. Camron and Anna were meant for each other and Camron needed the push of the game. He might seem more miserable now, but it wouldn't last.

It was just Beileag and her parting words planting seeds of doubt. She was wrong; he was right. And his brother needed to be reminded so he could stay the course.

'It was your idea to drink the mead,' Hamilton reminded him.

Seoc chuckled, winced, then rubbed his chest. Hamilton watched Camron slide his eyes to their friend's chest. Seoc's scar was hard to ignore, as were the memories from the Battle of Dunbar when they lost their laird, Sir Patrick, last March.

The world, and their clan duties, had changed much since that March. Every clan member was uneasy. Scouts slept less and guarded more. When was the last time they'd simply laughed?

'So, Camron, when are you going to tell us what happened on your travels with Anna?' Seoc sat back on his own bench.

'Not much to tell.'

Hamilton hated seeing the look of loss in his brother's eyes. Maybe if he told them more, they could find a solution. Clapping and warming his hands before the fire, Hamilton said, 'I've been trying for days to get him to confess.'

'And he's stayed silent?' Seoc said.

Hamilton nodded. 'A certainty something happened.'

'Ah, maybe he had to fight for her hand while she was with those Colquhouns,' Seoc said. 'You know how they are.'

'Persuasive red-haired devils. So was that it—did someone there notice Anna's beauty?' Hamilton turned to his brother, only to see his expression had turned more miserable, more dark.

Chuckling to cover up his worry, Hamilton pointed his thumb at him. 'See, this is how he's been. Especially as Anna's been avoiding him since they returned.'

Running his hands through his damp hair, Camron exhaled roughly. 'You going to ask me whether she's worth it? Aren't you going to say I told you so? It's not as though I wasted years thinking of only her. There were other matters keeping us occupied.'

Was it any better to think of those things? 'Dunbar, Seoc,' he said. 'Losing our Peter. Endless scouting and nights sleeping in the rain.'

'Those odd goings on with our Colquhoun cousins,' Camron added.

Hamilton rolled his eyes. 'The wedding games were good though....'

Camron looked away. 'I didn't stay faithful to Anna.'

Ah. Hell. His brother was more miserable than he could guess. He glanced at Seoc, who looked alarmed. When had his steadfast twin ever been this low?

'You weren't meant to. She had that Maclean,' he said. 'And none of the other women were her, we knew that.'

'Hamilton,' Seoc warned.

'Careful,' Camron said.

No, he wouldn't heed warnings. The bet was there as an excuse for his brother to move on from this. He would make him see reason. 'How could I doubt how you felt about her when you saw her happy with Maclean and you stepped back?'

'When we *thought* she was happy,' Camron bit out.

'Face the truth, Brother, that man did make her happy.'

Seoc cursed. 'Leave it, Hamilton.'

No, he wouldn't. He wasn't perfect—right now he was lying to everyone about the bet he'd made to force his brother into this situation. But he wouldn't give up this early.

'I wanted her to be happy,' Camron growled. 'Damn him.'

'I know.' Hamilton leaned forward and rested his elbows on his knees. 'And that's when I knew whatever it was you had felt for her was true. I could never do such a selfless act. I can't remember the last time I did anything that didn't serve me.'

Camron glanced at him and Hamilton didn't take his gaze away. Maybe he was a selfish bastard about it, but he wanted his brother happy. He wanted to find happiness, too.

'Stop looking at me like that.' He straightened. 'I can have these thoughts. And stop thinking of what was. There were other women for you, Camron, because you thought, as we all did, that Anna would marry Alan. You were trying to forget her.'

'How did you get so wise?'

Beileag thought him a fool. Why, after a week, did that thought still rankle? And why did his thoughts keep going back to her? The way she'd looked at him when he said a bet was made... He hadn't felt so doubtful since he was a child.

But that last gaze, the one right before she'd curled her fist and walked away, he couldn't forget. It...haunted him. What had she wanted to say to him as she'd glared at him? He hadn't had a chance to actually ask her for help either, he'd only said that he needed it. Frustration burned, a hard blow to his pride.

She'd been mostly avoiding him since Anna's return and, when he attempted to talk, she shook her head or walked away or...glared again with those eyes of hers, and that frown. So he hadn't had a chance to ask her if she'd help him with Murdag.

And this week proved he needed help with Murdag. He'd followed her around like a lost puppy which was equally parts humbling and puzzling. He'd never had trouble with women before. But if Murdag did talk to him, their conversations never went beyond the weather or some other non-personal topic. There were a few times, he swore, she had avoided him altogether. When that happened, he hadn't followed her. He had some pride...and his brother needed him. Unlike anyone else. Hamilton shrugged that thought off.

'I'm good with games and distractions.'

'Maybe now there will be no distractions. And Anna hasn't been completely avoiding me since we returned.' Camron pulled his feet in. 'I have been occupied teaching her brother to swim.'

Ah, so his brother wasn't above using others to make his pursuit. Maybe him asking Beileag wasn't as egregious as he thought.

'Thinking to gain her heart by befriending her brother?' Hamilton said.

'We know you love the boy, just as much as you love his sister,' Seoc said.

Camron shrugged. 'My feelings for her are the same.'

'Oh, but her feelings for you are different?' Hamilton said even as he willed himself to be quiet in these matters. What was the matter with him to goad his brother so? And yet he was incapable of stopping. His own love pursuits were failing. Maybe if he prodded his brother, something would come for him.

He looked pointedly at Seoc. 'I bet he hasn't kissed her yet. There's too much tension in him.'

'Agreed,' Seoc said.

Camron rubbed his face. 'Don't you have any of that mead?'

Seoc raised a brow. 'Haven't you learnt your lesson? Maybe you should try my new spiced ale. I've done—'

His brother was going from miserable to melancholy. 'You poisoned us with the last ale you spiced.'

'I've perfected my recipe,' Seoc grumbled.

'Like you perfected that grass water concoction?' Hamilton quipped. Since they were children Seoc had been making drinks and forcing them to drink them. The grass ale was the worst. The fact Hamilton had drunk it when dared…and was sick afterwards was something he wouldn't let anyone forget.

Camron chuckled and Hamilton perked up.

'You didn't have to drink that, just like you didn't have to drink my mead,' Seoc said.

Hamilton groaned. 'It's been less than a fortnight and my head still hurts. Why didn't anyone stop us?'

'I couldn't get you to stop drinking the grass water either,' Seoc guffawed.

'That's because there was a bet made,' Camron said.

Hamilton rubbed his stomach in memory. 'Only made us stronger.'

'You two could always stop making bets.' Seoc stood, stomped out his large feet and then sat again. They were all restless and tired.

'Then where would you get your amusement at our expense?' Hamilton said.

Camron laughed again and Hamilton was feeling much better until his brother said, 'How's Murdag, Hamilton?'

Avoiding him, completely. Hamilton looked away. 'Better than ever.'

'Murdag?' Seoc coughed, then rubbed his chest again. 'Don't you mean Beileag?'

'Last I knew my brother liked a certain woman with a thin chemise who stood on a boulder.'

'How did I miss Murdag wearing a thin chemise?' Seoc said.

'You were probably behaving honourably and not looking as she stood on the boulder in front of the fire.'

'You all made me pour the ale that night; I missed it,' Seoc said. 'Just as well if you have your eye on her, Hamilton.'

Hamilton nodded. He appreciated Seoc's comment since he could feel Camron's curious gaze on him. Murdag had been beautiful that night. Brave, funny, challenging. In fact, he was surprised it hadn't been him on that boulder, ordering everyone to drink. How well suited and alike were they! And being Anna's sister, too—it was meant to be.

Hamilton glared at his brother. 'What?'

Camron shrugged.

'You have a strange way of wooing Murdag by hanging around her friend so often,' Seoc said.

He wasn't spending as much time with Beileag as he needed to in order to make any headway with a bet. While he tried to keep his pride with Murdag, he had no concerns with Beileag so perhaps he had been in her company a bit more than Murdag's. And if he was honest with himself, he couldn't stop being near her. He didn't know why. He wanted to blame it all on his desperation to make Murdag see reason when it came to him so he absolutely needed Beileag to listen to him, to give him help. He'd even tried to apologise.

At first, she'd listened, at least in part, but he never could get any important words out since she was often around her siblings, or Anna.

But mostly she stayed quiet and then so did he as he watched her.

As the week went on, however, and he grew more bold, she ignored him more than Murdag, but the expression in her mesmerising eyes changed. It went from disdain to contemplation and earlier today, when their eyes locked, he swore he saw worry.

Her distress made his restlessness seethe under his skin. Why would it affect him if she was worried about something else? Weren't they always worried about something else?

And all the worse because she wouldn't talk to him so he didn't know if she was troubled about Anna and Camron—the tension between them was so apparent the whole village was holding its breath—or if her concern was still on the bet or something else.

Unfortunately, when he took the few steps to whisper to her that they could talk, she let out the smallest of gasps and scurried away. But he pursued her because he wanted to know why she disapproved of the bet, when it was clear Anna and Camron deserved to be together.

He was also…curious. Because now that he was paying attention to Beileag, she did things that were unusual. Such as ignore her mother and father, take care of her siblings' every need, get lost in the woods where he couldn't find her.

And he had tried to find her. At first, he'd thought to walk by her side, but she'd changed direction and acted as if she hadn't meant to head towards the woods. The next time, he remained at a distance, but he must have got distracted, because somehow, she disappeared. Afterwards, he'd tried to track her, but couldn't find any trace of her at all.

Was she going to the woods to avoid him, or had she always gone into the woods? That question frustrated. Murdag might be avoiding him, but at least she talked of the weather or horses; Beileag said nothing and disappeared on him. Yet who else could help him?

He could no more ask Seoc or Anna for help than his brother. Murdag's father was an open friendly sort, but until he had some hint that Murdag would return his affections, he didn't want to face her father. Again, he had some pride.

'I agree with Seoc. If you like Murdag,' Camron said, 'I'd stop hanging around her friend.'

If his brother was teaching Anna's little brother, Lachie, to swim so he could get close to Anna, Hamilton intended to pursue Beileag to get advice on Murdag. 'Doesn't matter. I'm going to win.'

'Win what?' Seoc leaned forward.

'Brother,' Camron warned.

Hamilton shrugged. 'Ach, come on, he's got to know

some time. He'll find out when it comes to the happy moment anyway.'

'What did you do now, Hamilton?' Seoc yawned.

'It wasn't me,' Hamilton said. 'Odd, I know, but this was, and has always been, Camron's idea.'

'Now you have to tell me,' Seoc insisted. 'Is this another challenge or a jest on someone and why would your twin, Lord of the Calm and Reasonable Manor, suggest something that even has you filling with mirth?'

'Not a chance,' Camron said to his brother.

'Not a chance for what?' Seoc said. 'Equal frowns on your faces and it's as though I've been hit on the head. I'm seeing double and double of you doesn't do it for me. Will you two tell me what's going on?'

Hamilton looked to his brother. If he was going to punch him or storm off, there'd be some indication. Instead, there was nothing, not even a challenge in his brother's eyes. So he said, 'We made a wager to marry before we're sent out again.'

Seoc looked baffled as he eyed them both.

Camron huffed. 'The less bright one with sentences is attempting to marry Murdag and I'm to try to marry Anna.'

When Seoc looked as though he was aghast, Hamilton raised his hands. 'It was Camron's wager, thus I'll win this one.'

'When have you ever won a wager from me?' Camron bit out.

'We'd be here all day if I regaled all my winnings, Brother.'

'Are you sure this is not a jest?' Seoc said, pointing at one and then the other of them. 'Because I've had to bear enough of both your jests and your bets all my life.'

Camron raised a brow. 'Bear the brunt of our jests?

'I must have been hit on my head. Or...have you put something in my drink?'

Seoc seemed not pleased, but maybe he needed a bit more information. 'Your head's fine, our friend. This may be the most awe-inspiring wager yet!'

Seoc stood and glared at Camron. 'This is true? You offered to travel with her...to be alone with her...so you could try to win a bet?'

When Camron nodded, Seoc cursed at them both and stormed off.

Did Seoc, who had been traveling with them all these years, think the bet a bad idea? 'That wasn't the response I expected.'

'What else did you expect? It's a foolish thing to bet on.'

Hamilton wanted to argue, but Beileag and Seoc had cursed at him for the bet and his brother looked so forlorn, something was breaking inside him. Was he, too, to give up so easily? Certainly, he'd lied about who made the bet, but it was for a good cause. He just needed to marry Anna's sister Murdag and all would be perfect, but right now he was having doubts. Maybe he was wrong, maybe this wasn't how to court a bride.

Which made him doubt again, because he was the one who forged ahead and repaired the consequences later. He was always out front, with his friends behind supporting and laughing with him. Now, two of them had called him a fool.

He couldn't be that wrong when everything in him said it was right. Camron needed Anna and she him. They only needed a bit of push. And if his twin was to wed, well, so should he.

'Is it true you've become close with Beileag?' Camron said.

Hamilton looked down at his feet and nodded. One lie was enough, in this he would tell his brother the truth. 'I could see I wasn't wooing Murdag properly and asked her to help.'

'She knows of the bet?'

'Don't worry, Brother, she thinks I made it.' Though he'd told her it was Camron who did. She might have questioned his veracity, but she didn't know for certain. Now he was in too deep to say otherwise. 'It matters not because she's refused to help me.'

Hamilton expected Camron to retort how he'd win then, or give him a slap on the back and tell him he'd have better fortune next time. Anything. Instead, his brother looked broodingly out in the dark while the fire dimmed and the damp soaked into his bones.

Maybe he was a fool, but he was a stubborn one. They deserved happiness and he'd feed the fire until the sun rose.

Chapter Seven

Beileag took a deep breath and blurted out what she should have told Hamilton on the day he asked, 'I think I want to help you.'

Hamilton, still chewing presumably on the chunk of bread and cheese in his hand, choked.

When he fully turned towards her, his eyes watering, his face red, he coughed some more, then turned a terrible shade. Beileag grabbed the goblet of ale at his side and shoved it towards him.

Tossing the food in his hand back on the little table outside his home, he attempted to take a drink, but it was a gasping, spluttering swallow and Beileag searched around the various houses, but there was no one in sight to help him.

How could there be no one? Hamilton usually had scores of attention and companionship. If nothing else, there should be villagers doing chores or children gleefully corralling geese.

When he was still wheezing in breaths, she gathered her courage and pounded his back until his breaths cleared, but he was still an odd shade. What if he died? She pounded harder. What if this was it and she'd killed him because she saw what he—?

Hamilton grabbed her wrist and brought her hand to his front, splayed her fingers against his chest and held her hand there. Oh.

His colouring was returning to normal. His hair curled at his forehead as usual. His angular jaw still held that confident air, the hazel-brown eyes as clear and assessing as they'd always been.

And close. And she knew they were assessing because while she'd been studying him, he'd been studying her. Why?

'You're not dead,' she said to cover up the fact she was noticing the smoothness of his jaw and how he must have shaved earlier.

He smirked. 'It was a close one though.'

He'd gone a terrible shade of blue, but he was all warm now, not only in his colouring, but the heat from his body was transferring slowly to her hand and up her arm, making her a bit flush, and the pounding of his heart was a steady thumping against her palm.

Against her palm!

She jerked her hand away from under his. From where he was holding it against his chest! Embarrassed, flustered, when her latest finger bandage fell into his lap, she reached for it.

Only to have his hand wrap around her wrist again. But she didn't want to talk of her bandages, or the blood, or her cut or lack of cuts, so she splayed her fingers to get it away from him.

And he jerked her hand higher. Frustrated now, she glared at him. Only to see his cheeks red, an incredulous glare in his eyes.

Oh. My. Word.

The linens fell in his lap. She was reaching towards his lap. The linens were small, her fingers long and...

What was she thinking!

She gasped.

'That's what I was going to say, but I didn't want to sound like a woman who was about to have her reputation ruined.'

Overwhelmingly embarrassed, she gaped.

Hamilton gave a low chuckle. 'Is it safe to release your hand now?'

He was holding her hand or wrist! Both truly, for his hands were much larger than hers. So why was she always missing the moments when he was holding her?

Not *her*, specifically, but parts of her. Why did that sound worse!

'I truly wish I knew what was going on in that mind of yours.'

'No, you don't.'

Clutching her hand now in both of his, as if their hands were locked in prayer, he said, 'Shouldn't say that to a man when he sees a flush like yours.'

Flush was a kind word, red as a sunburn from her neck to her hairline until it felt her hair was on fire was a more accurate representation. 'No, thank you.'

With a gentle squeeze, he released his hold and she snatched her hands back. She took a step away. Another, then clutched her hands before her.

Hamilton tilted his head. 'You are all right?'

She gave a curt nod.

'You know I'm only teasing,' he said. 'We're still friends?'

She wanted to nod again, but there was a pleading look in his eyes, as if he truly wanted to be assured they were friends. So she breathed deep and said, 'Of course.'

He must have meant it for the tension around his eyes eased and Beileag suddenly breathed easier.

But then his brows drew down and his head dropped. He rubbed a few fingers together before his head snapped to her hands. 'You're bleeding.'

She unclenched her hands and saw her recent cut reopened. Shaking her head at herself, she opened her satchel at her waist and drew out two linens.

She handed him one while she took another to wrap around the injury. 'Sorry, it happens so often I don't feel it.'

'What happens?'

Beileag briefly closed her eyes. What was wrong with her? Trying to laugh it off, she shook her head, 'Oh, nothing of import. Simply the normal chores and me being clumsy.'

He indicated with his chin. 'And it happens with enough frequency that you carry torn linens in a satchel around your waist?'

She gave a smile. 'I've got siblings, haven't I? Never know when I'll need them.'

He eyed the bag, then her. When he looked as though he'd ask more questions, she blurted, 'Didn't mean to scare you earlier.'

He wiped his hands and tossed the rag alongside his bread roll. 'Yes, about that. How did you get so stealthy?'

Was she? 'I approached you from the front. Just from my house to yours.'

He looked around like he'd never seen his village before, his expression more troubling. What had happened to Hamilton on this last scouting mission?

'Where is everyone?' she said.

He straightened and seemed to pull himself back together. 'My mother woke with a crick in her neck and she could barely move, and Da's knees pained him, so they're out walking to, as they say, "become young" again.'

Here was another difference between her and Hamilton: while her parents didn't hate each other, they didn't exactly go on walks together or show any sort of affection towards the other either.

'Do you think they'll come back smiling?'

Hamilton let out a rough laugh and rubbed the back of his neck. 'Can't be easy suddenly having two large men invade their home again.'

Like many of the scouts, most of the men never had their own home, rather returning either to their childhood homes or joining the other men in the large hut made only for them. A place with beds, but bare comforts. It suited many families, but it wasn't easy. Now that they'd all returned, no doubt they'd be talking of continuing to build some houses.

'Can't be easy being in a room full of snoring men either,' she said.

'Camron and I have been taking turns, but perhaps my parents like their private time, eh?'

She wouldn't know. To this day, she had no idea how her parents had conceived four children.

He slapped his knees and stood. 'We'll be out of their way soon, I suppose.'

There were rumours of what was happening outside of the clans, of England's demands, but until the clan made a decision, it was kept within the council. Still, hearing rumours and knowing the truth were two different things and a knot formed near her heart, now she knew something was amiss.

'Soon?'

His expression turned rueful. 'By summer's end.'

No time at all. The knot inside her tightened. 'So that's why....'

'You'll help us?' he said.

He kept saying that and she guessed what it had to do with, but with absolutely no experience with relationships, she had no idea how that was to be. She simply knew that this week, since Camron and Anna had returned, something had changed.

All these years, Camron had watched Anna from a distance, as if she was too precious and then too fragile to approach. But it was clear his patience had ended and Anna was hurt, running scared, but when she thought no one was looking she'd look at Camron and her eyes were sad and angry.

She wasn't uninterested in Camron anymore, but she was troubled. Beileag would do anything to help her.

'I have questions.' When Hamilton nodded, she continued. 'Since they returned from the Colquhoun clan, I've watched them and I think I understand why Camron made the bet. He made it…but it wasn't in jest.'

Some conflict flitted across his eyes, but Hamilton's answer was unwavering. 'No, very much in earnest and truly because he loves her.'

'So it was simply something said between brothers, not as a game?'

'Never a game, only…' Hamilton said. 'It's difficult to explain.'

'You're twins, you're brothers, you—'

'Want the same thing,' he said.

She expected it: she did. They'd already talked around it and she'd had a week to come to grips with Hamilton's intent.

Why it was difficult she couldn't say, she simply… hurt. It must be because her friends were gaining relationships and she never would.

Unless…unless she somehow learnt how to have a relationship or someone taught her.

Merely the thought of that flamed embarrassment through her. She couldn't get anyone to look at her—how was she to get someone to teach her how to have a courtship leading to a possible marriage?

A week of watching Camron and Anna since their return and Beileag knew her friend suffered with her own inner demons. It was a week to watch Camron struggle with his renowned patience. Between the two of them, it was like watching a storm gather and she knew it would come to a head soon.

How it would be between them, whether it would be a happily ever after or simply end, she didn't know. But she did know that as much as they had bonded, they still had difficulty...so maybe there wasn't an easy way to find love or marriage.

Maybe there was hope for her. She only needed to ask how to start.

'I truly wish there were times I knew what you were thinking,' Hamilton said.

'Nothing of import.' When he kept that steady gaze on her, she shrugged. 'I have more questions if that will be fine with you.'

'Of course.' He rubbed his hands along his upper thighs.

Which brought her gaze down to his lap and her thoughts to the feel of his heartbeat and her fumbling hands.

Practically choking on that heated awkwardness, Beileag stepped back, running her hands down her dress which tugged her finger wrappings around. Before he could discover that she wore more wrappings than she had wounds, she tightened them back around and glanced up at Hamilton.

His eyes were on her hands and she tensed, but when

he turned his chin to meet her eyes, he remained bless-
edly quiet about it, which was good because she didn't
tell anyone why she wore the linens, but it also made
her suspicious.

It wasn't like outgoing Hamilton not to continue to
ask questions. After all, hadn't he asked them before?
Was she that forgettable?

She was a fool! Did she want him to ask or didn't
she?

She didn't. Never. It was her secret and he didn't
want her for that. He wanted her…for Murdag. But how,
she didn't know yet.

'So why Murdag?' she said.

'She's beautiful,' he said.

She was. Her features weren't as striking as her sister Anna's. Whereas Anna's hair was black as night and
eyes a blue to be almost unreal, Murdag had a softer
shade of black, a softer blue. Which was ironic because
Murdag had the bolder personality…at least when it
came to adventures and horses.

'She is,' Beileag agreed. 'Inside and out.'

'I am in earnest.'

His voice and expression appeared truthful. All
week, he'd tried to talk to her while she'd avoided him.
While she'd watched her friends in pain.

'They are my friends,' she said.

'They're mine, too, but I want something more.'

So did she, but that didn't seem possible. She couldn't
imagine asking for help or someone all of sudden asking her if she wanted help finding a family. However,
she didn't need to be cruel in the meantime. She could
help Hamilton, and Murdag, if her friend wanted it.
She'd wait to offer help with Anna and Camron until
Anna talked to her about the trip they'd taken. It was

clear to every villager something boiled between them.
It was almost dangerous to ask questions of either of
them at present.

'How can I help you?' she said.

Hamilton let out a breath and straightened. 'What
does she like?'

'Horses,' she blurted.

'But besides horses.'

Adventure, freedom, jests and challenges. Pastimes
Hamilton liked, but then he'd know this, wouldn't he?
He'd known Murdag as long as she had. So he must
be after something else. Something that relationships
needed. Maybe if he revealed a bit more of what he
wanted, it would help her with finding a husband.

'I don't understand,' she said.

Hamilton looked around. She did, too. There were
more people milling about between the huts, but not
enough to interrupt their conversation.

'It's as though everyone was coming back from something,' she said.

His brows drew down and he looked bemused. 'They
are. You're not...observant, are you?'

That hurt. She observed all the time. She didn't know
if it was because of her craft or developed for her craft,
but she watched so she could get better at it. She might
not be a good listener, though, Since she was always in
her head thinking of her current project, or...just dream-
ing. Still, he didn't know that.

He looked sheepish. 'Look, I didn't mean to offend.
I don't know why I keep doing that.'

'If I wasn't so observant,' she said, 'I wouldn't know
she doesn't like you following her around.'

His apology, if it was one, disappeared, as well as
the amused curious look that lit his eyes.

Instead, a bit of colour flushed his cheeks. Good. She wasn't the only one who became embarrassed.

Hamilton took a step back, rubbed the back of his neck. 'I got that.'

I thought you weren't to be cruel?

She sighed. These were her friends! 'Maybe if you helped her.'

'I offered; she turned me away.'

'Even with the horses?'

He winced. 'No, it was in the kitchens when she was getting bread.'

She couldn't imagine Hamilton in the kitchens. Not because he wasn't capable of learning, only because he didn't have the patience to wait until bread rose, let alone the oven time to bake it. 'Do you even know how a kitchen works?'

He shrugged one shoulder. 'I know how to eat. And I'm good with my hands.'

She glanced at his hands resting at his side, then slid her gaze away. Had she ever talked to him like this before or for so long? He'd always been the twin she was most fascinated by, but these concentrated moments, these wonderings and noticing his hands, were unnerving.

She was beyond a young girl's infatuation period of her life and this man was interested in her friend! What a person she had turned out to be! Now she was disloyal to Hamilton and Murdag.

If Murdag wanted him, that is. She had avoided Hamilton quite a bit over the last week, but Beileag wanted love and couldn't, not for one moment, believe deep down her friends wouldn't want it, too. She also knew something else her friend needed.

'That's…good. You'll need those hands,' she said. 'She has a horse with wolf's teeth that are falling out.'

'Surely James could help.'

James was the farrier, blacksmith, healer, anything related to marshalcy. 'James received a message that his mother was bedridden and left several days ago.'

'But still there must be someone else who is more knowledgeable than me.'

'Are you scared to reach your hand in a horse's mouth? You understand that if the tooth can't be removed, he can't wear a bit,' she said. 'And as for someone more knowledgeable, that would be Murdag, except she may need help.'

He looked to his feet again and nodded.

He was so reluctant, Beileag didn't know if it was because he didn't like horses or he didn't want Murdag. Surely, this bit of advice and information would be treasured if he meant to pursue her? It would be hours of long work with a distressed horse to take care of the tooth. And it would cause Murdag hours of worry and strain. She always said she hurt along with her animals.

It didn't appear that Hamilton wanted to spend hours with Murdag. And whatever crazy tightness in her chest that lodged there since her fumbling hands eased right into disappointment. If someone courted and wooed her, she'd want them to spend days with her.

'You do want her?' she said.

His head snapped up. 'She's perfect for me.'

Again, with the determined voice and sure expression. Again, with her doubts which probably stemmed from her own insecurities. Murdag was perfect for anyone.

Beileag clasped her cold hands. 'Well then, you'll need to be by her side when she worries. And that means when wolf teeth cause problems. A few hours like that and I'm certain she'll look at you differently. Good day, Hamilton.'

'Where do you go?' he blurted.

Beileag pulled up short and turned around.

'When you walk to the woods, where do you hide?'

Chapter Eight

'The woods?' she said.

Let her go, you fool, she is not your concern.

Hamilton tried to make his feet and thoughts move away from Beileag, but couldn't. He was curious. There should be no harm in asking and then afterwards he would see what lively Murdag was up to that day.

'You go almost every day. I followed you and though I've been tracking game since before I could walk properly, I couldn't find you.'

She licked her lips. 'Oh. I'm simply walking in the woods. It's pleasant in there. Siblings and all that.'

'And then you're gone for hours?' he pressed. 'Stop prevaricating, Beileag, and take me where you go.'

This time she didn't flush. Her hands did not flutter, nor did she clench them in front of her. Instead, she kept those golden eyes on him and he didn't blink.

He refused to. If he was being judged or valued, he'd give all he had to, so that when she refused him, as she was certain to do, he wouldn't miss the reason. The moment stretched between them. He almost wanted to step back to laugh, to make a joke, but it was all so serious.

No, even that word didn't encompass what was happening. There was an intimate weight to it all and it felt *binding*. As if her determination on his request was of the utmost urgency. If he blinked or joked, this moment would sever and he wouldn't be any closer to the truth.

A truth he knew nothing about though he thought he should. This was Beileag, who was always there in the background while they raced around in fields and drank grass tinctures for fun.

But something seemed off with that truth. Because this woman before him, the one with golden hair and golden eyes, who stood quietly poised, could not be the same Beileag or he'd never known her at all. She had a secret and it was important enough to hide it…at least from him.

'Do Camron or Seoc know where you go?' he said.

She blinked, a hint of amusement in her voice. 'Not in the slightest.'

Something both eased and tightened in his chest. Eased because his brother didn't know and thus they were on equal ground, but tightened because perhaps she told no one. Perhaps no one ever even guessed.

'Anna or Murdag?'

'Always,' she said, complete amusement now lacing her words and features. Lighting everything between them, even that weighty bond. Now he truly wanted to know. It was more than the chase of the hunt. It was vital he knew the secret. As though he wouldn't breathe right until she told him.

'You won't let this go, will you?' she said.

When he shook his head, she bit her bottom lip. 'What will you do if I tell you?'

'I don't want you to tell me, I want you to show me,' he said. 'I want to *see*.'

She gasped.

He had pushed too hard. Taking a step back, he rubbed the back of his neck and apologised.

'No, don't,' she blurted.

He lowered his hand.

'I'll show you,' she said on a soft laugh. 'It's quick enough and you can be on your way to Murdag. It's not that important.'

He felt as though it was. The strangest of days were happening since he'd returned with his brother and friends. Seeing Murdag with the firelight behind her on that rock was like seeing another aspect of a familiar friend, but Beileag…was altogether different.

When he returned and festivities made spirits high because of their safe return, the bonfire had lit all of Murdag's outstanding charms and personality. Since that night, he'd tried to pursue the woman he'd seen, but he'd been met with the Murdag he'd always known, if a bit more surly than usual.

He couldn't remember Beileag from that bonfire night and he couldn't remember much of Beileag from before either, and it was driving his curiosity beyond decent bounds. It was clear she was reluctant to have this conversation, yet he pushed.

'Why'd you keep it hidden?' he said.

'Because it was foolish.'

Suddenly he wanted to right the wrong done to her that made her golden eyes dim and made her believe anything she did was foolish.

Everyone in the clan had felt the brunt of Beileag's mother's acerbic tongue. Was it Sian who made her feel that way, or something else? He didn't know. It wasn't something he pondered, or at least not for long, before.

All he did know was this woman was raising her siblings and giving them advice, love and a firm hand.

He couldn't imagine her doing something not meaningful. Even when she tossed her brother about, it meant something.

How could he not know these things about her until now? He knew it with a certainty even without her sharing her secret, or the fact she thought she was foolish, that whatever she was about to share with him wasn't idle or frivolous.

'Never,' he said. He didn't even know what more he could say or what must be said for her to reveal—

'Come with me.' She pivoted and strode forward. Her walk brooked no delays or hesitancy. As if she'd made up her mind and that was that.

So, he followed her. All the steps they took through the trees were familiar because he had followed her before. So intent was he to follow her exactly that when she stopped, he almost ran into her. Instead of them both falling forward, he simply clamped an arm around her waist and moved her along with him until he could stop.

'Some warning next time,' he said.

She looked over her shoulder at him. 'I forget how you charge forward.'

'Yes, my brother and I tend to do that,' he said. 'Walking, that is.'

He was rewarded by a curve to her lips. '*You* do it differently.'

Did she mean that he walked oddly? Or that she noticed him as someone different than his brother even though they were identical? Never! But he'd never explained that to anyone, other than his brother. A jest was in order.

'Walking?' he said. 'Oh, yes, you've noticed that I do this!'

His arm had never left her waist, so it was effortless

to suddenly walk sideways and forward, and any other wild way he chose to do—with her. His sudden sway tossed them both and she dug her heels in the dirt and her hands gripped his arm to remove it.

'Oh, I don't think so!' he said. 'If I walked differently, so do you!'

He lunged left and she gave a startled laugh, her body completely going lax, her hands simply holding on. Laughing with her, he spun them until he almost stumbled, almost fell over. So he lunged right one more time and jerked to a stop.

Chuckling through his words, he said, 'Yes, you're right, I do walk differently.'

She gave off a few more peals of glee. As her head rested on his shoulder, her body grew slack against his. Their bodies slowed down from the exertion and their breaths eased. Together they shared a moment of bliss before Hamilton realised everything else about the way he held her.

His front to her back because some time during the fray both of his arms had slid around her waist and now there was a natural curve as he cradled her against him. Everything had happened so naturally as to not have been noticed. He noticed now. Especially the softness of her hair tangled against his neck, the addictive smell reminding him of entering a new forest on an almost silent morning. The slender length of her limbs, the swell of her hips. The connection of their breaths.

Everything he noticed, mostly when she realised how they stood, too, and tensed, then pulled abruptly away and gave him a quick smile that didn't reach her eyes.

He imagined some similar discomfiture was in his expression as well. That, as well as confusion. A handful of times with her and they'd touched more than they had their entire lives. Why was that?

She fluffed her skirts. 'We won't get far if you, we, keep walking like that.'

Ah. She was to show him her secret. 'Do we have far to go?'

'Perhaps.'

'You do know if you show me how to get there, I'll always be able to find it.'

She placed her hand on her hip. 'As many times as you've boasted about your tracking abilities, I would expect nothing less. But I don't believe I have anything to worry about.'

He noted her jaunty stance and wanted to mimic it, but he could still smell damp leaves and crushed pine, still feel the warmth of her curves, and he wasn't certain what was happening between them. 'And why is that?'

'You followed me before and I lost you.'

'About that…' He stopped as he gaped at her. 'You *knew* I was behind you.'

She raised her brow. 'I wouldn't brag about your tracking so much.'

'It's the mud,' he said, shaking his head. 'It makes that sound, so I stayed too far behind to see you.'

'But it also doesn't hide my footprints, so I think we're even.'

All true. Maybe she was observant after all, at least about some things. But it didn't explain how she knew nothing of the council meeting that everyone except a few, including him, purposefully avoided. He knew what was told and none of it good. He didn't need to hear how perilous it all was and how close the English were to defeating them all. It was the last summer any of them would know peace, if ever again.

Right now, he needed to know he had something to fight for and return to when the next battle was done. Thus, he'd do all he could so Camron could have Anna and he'd have Murdag. Otherwise he feared the restlessness, the sleepless nights, would never end for him. That he'd always have nightmares about the wolf in Ettrick Forrest and the gaping wound in Seoc's chest. He just wanted family and all the grounding, joyous ties that it brought.

Until that happy moment for him and his brother, a distraction with a friend wasn't a terrible thing. Plus, he was curious again. How had this woman evaded him all week? 'How did you hide your footprints?'

She lifted her skirts and gave him a smirk. 'Watch.'

Watch and follow he did. There was nothing but surety in the way she made her way through the trees, but her steps were close to trunks, half hidden where the heavy foliage was heaviest. Most people walked straight through the middle where it was clear.

But that wasn't all she did to evade him tracking her. For she swirled this way and that, facing one tree, while her back was to another. It was as if she danced with them. He stood there, mesmerised by her feet traipsing up and down boulders and rocks. Until she was almost out of his sight and he scrambled to catch up.

'Keep up, oh, great tracker.' She laughed.

Half-cursing, half-admiring, Hamilton scrambled over the boulders with her. He knew these woods and always steered away from the rockier ways. After all, why travel the harder path?

Beileag appeared to like the more difficult areas. On and on they went while she continued her unusual dance and he lumbered behind. It wasn't far, but it was a fair distance from their village and home. Enough that should she call out, no one would hear her unless someone was also in the woods.

He was about to point out that unsafe fact when she stopped in a copse of circled trees, with enough sunlight to reveal…nothing. Some foliage, mud, rocks and them.

'Are we here?'

She opened her arms out and grinned. 'This is it.'

There were many footprints of different depth and all hers. This was certainly the area she came to. But this was her secret?

'This is…interesting,' he said. 'But your walk was even more so.'

She smiled. 'I created that walk when I was a child and will hardly stop now since it proved you couldn't follow.'

The image of her dancing with trees as a young girl was easy. As a woman, it was altogether different and not so innocent. But it was something else he wanted to talk to her about: the reason she did that dance to avoid being tracked.

'So this place was always a secret.' When she nodded, he said, 'Why tell it to someone now?'

'We need to help Anna and Camron, don't we?' she said.

'And Murdag and myself,' he said instantly. On reflex. He wasn't thinking at all about his brother or the bet now. Not when the memory of Beileag's hips swaying as she danced with trees and beckoned him to follow was all too fresh in his thoughts.

'I can only offer suggestions when it comes to them,' she said. 'I won't force or do any of your…tricks.'

'Wouldn't think of it.' If she knew how serious this was for him, how much he was desperate to have his and his brother's happiness secured before they left again, she'd have no doubts. But he didn't talk to anyone of what happened at Dunbar's battle. Many nights he, Camron and Seoc stayed up and none of them talked of it. It was better that way.

And this bet, which should have meant nothing at all, was a catalyst for his brother at least. With Beileag's help, he could have a happy future as well. He still couldn't believe he was here with her, in some secret spot. It was a welcome distraction from that plaguing restlessness.

She raised her chin, her expression wary, but defiant. 'I might need some help, too.'

'Help?' He looked around, but still there was nothing in the clearing, but she'd stopped. Somewhere nearby her secret was here and hidden and he needed to know why. 'With this?'

She shook her head. 'I'm showing you this secret as a favour.'

Doing his laundry was a favour, this was more, but he didn't want to push for an answer when he wasn't altogether certain he wanted one. Something was happening between them and, though it felt natural and easy, he was wary. It was like a current and it wasn't the direction he intended.

He couldn't be attracted to Beileag…not that she wasn't comely…very comely, if he was being brutally honest with himself. She'd make a fine wife for someone else. He needed to stick to the plan.

Camron wanted Anna, and Murdag was Anna's sister. Murdag did jests and played. Murdag was for him.

Being a twin and connected with his brother was important more so now after they had fled to the forest. He needed the connection with his brother. To have families together, ones so entwined no war could tear them apart. They'd be brothers married to sisters. Beileag didn't fit into the bet he'd made.

He knew he wasn't being entirely logical, but that wolf had warned him and he couldn't stop looking over his shoulder. Surely, more ties to hearth and home... to happiness would end the unease he constantly felt?

And this favour she requested...it seemed like a trap. There was nothing here and nothing she was telling him either.

All she was doing was looking at him expectantly as though he'd know the answers. He was afraid he didn't even know the questions.

She raised her hands out to him. Was he to take them?

'You've been wondering what these are,' she said. 'They're bandages.'

'You've been bleeding.'

'I've been cutting myself,' she said. 'With nothing dangerous, merely clumsiness! Oh, my word, you should see your expression.'

His expression was probably thunderous. What was this woman doing in this forest to mar her hands? 'You wear bandages constantly on different fingers, too. I couldn't think of what you'd be doing to hurt your hands that wasn't dangerous.'

She exhaled slowly, turned and hopped over a log. 'No, stay there.'

Did she have eyes in the back of her head? He stepped back to his original position and watched how she carefully lifted a peeled log covered in dead leaves. If he craned his head, he could see a pit from where she lifted a chest, then another. After, she moved to another part and again lifted a carefully concealed covering to lift out yet another chest surrounded by different pieces of wood that had obviously been carved on.

She'd found someone's carvings? 'Treasure found?'

'Hardly,' she answered, tossing the different pieces

of carved wood alongside the chests. 'Everything's still a bit wet from when that storm blew through and you'll think most of them dull, I would guess.'

It was her tone that alerted him to the creator of the crude carvings. And looking about at the ones now littering the ground around the chests, they were very rough. Maybe she was simply getting started.

'You've taken up whittling?'

'Whittling? I started that way. It's more carving now.' She tossed her hair back over her shoulder and stood to face him.

'There's a difference between the two?' he said.

A slight blush to her cheeks as she brought an almost shy gaze to him. 'Quite a bit. Tools and time. I've been doing it for years.'

'Woodwork like your father?' he said.

'I'm not building things like him,' she said. 'Only carving on sticks and such.'

Unexpected Beileag. That's what he'd call her when he thought of this woman. And he more than understood her not sharing her secret with anyone.

He picked up one of the more substantial sticks, and turned it around to see her rough cuts of different depth and length. She'd clearly been hacking at this thing using different tools. When he couldn't determine was what it was supposed to *be*. But he wouldn't tell her that. She got enough criticism at home.

It was no secret her mother disapproved of Beileag in every way. Not so common the entire village knew, but those closest to her did. How many times had he stood outside her home, waiting for her to come out, and heard her mother chastising her?

If she'd been at this for years and this was good as

she could do, and she was brave enough to share this secret, then he could be a better friend.

After all, who was he to criticise, when he could do nothing of the sort? Further, he thought himself a good tracker, but even with his talent she'd eluded him.

Nobody possessed perfection.

He looked up. 'This is interesting and I'm grateful you brought me here.'

Something like confused amusement flashed through her golden eyes, before it dimmed. As if she was surprised by his comment and then...disappointed.

Which was not the response he was trying to draw out! He didn't want to hurt her! He wanted to...a tumbling of confusing emotions battled through him from snatching her hand and pulling her towards him, to stealing the stick, running through the village and declaring this stick to be the most beautiful of all sticks.

None of which made any sense, nor probably would be welcomed.

Still, he wanted to do or say something to ease her disappointment. And of course, he shouldn't insult someone who was willing to help him woo her friend either.

Holding up the stick, he said, 'This is very interesting, and beautiful! I'm hoping you'd let me keep it?'

Chapter Nine

Hamilton looked earnest, not jesting, or smirking, or as though he was about to play a game on her.

He truly stood before her with her practice log, the one she used when she got new tools to see the sharpness and depth they wielded. The log he held was hacked in so many places it resembled nothing. An animal gnawing with its teeth could have made better patterns.

So she wasn't certain what to think of his request to keep it for himself. Part of her thought him rather sweet for being kind to her. As though the log was treasured and he was encouraging her to continue her craft. Another part of her, heavy with her mother's voice in her head, thought he actually believed she was that terrible at her craft.

For one panicked moment, she was tempted to leave it at this. He saw her favoured tree clearing with just enough sunshine streaming through to give her light and a solid enough wall of trees and boulders to protect her from the clan. Hamilton even knew she carved some pieces of wood.

In essence, she'd shared her secret. With him looking all wide-eyed at her, he wouldn't think anything of it if they simply turned back. In truth, that's what they should do.

After all, keeping him here with her instead of letting him pursue Murdag was selfish. And did she truly have the courage to ask him to help her to pursue a husband? No, she didn't.

'I have others,' she blurted.

Hamilton blinked; she gaped until she found her wits again.

'I'm still working on that project,' she clarified. Pointing to the chests behind her, she continued, 'Would you care to see more completed items?'

She didn't know why she decided to show him her little bits of wood, or why she felt suddenly shy, but she was and she did. She was also excited; she wasn't ready for him to leave, not like this. For better or worse, she was committed.

'I would,' he said.

She waved at the log where she usually sat. 'I'm afraid this is all I have to sit on.'

He gave a little smile as he spun around and sat. 'I've been sitting on these quite a bit myself lately.'

She supposed he did out on the road. He certainly looked comfortable enough as he placed his elbows on his knees.

Holding out her hand, she said, 'I'll take that from you.'

Hamilton clasped the rough log in both his hands. 'I think I'll keep this for now.'

Beileag laughed.

'What's so funny?' he said.

'No, not funny, only....' She tried to understand what she felt with him holding that hacked log like a child with a sweet. 'It's just different, that's all.'

What was this emotion she felt?

A certain nervous giddiness, but also a bit of happiness, too. Hamilton was here, wanting to see her craft, and seemed content to do so. Murdag and Anna hadn't been here for years. They knew where to find her, certainly, and they were always welcome, but they also knew how little precious time she had to herself to work, so they gave her the privacy needed.

So, too, talking and showing Murdag and Anna about this place was comfortable. After all, they confessed everything to each other and always had.

Hamilton, though a friend, wasn't the same.

Beileag knelt in the dirt, turned the chest around so Hamilton couldn't see the contents and stared at her tools.

'What have you there?' He craned his neck to see over the chest.

'Simply some things that have been nicking my hands.' She handed him the tool on top.

'An axe?' He set down the log at his feet and took the instrument.

'This is a hand adze. It smooths and carves. My father has the foot adze.'

'What's the difference?'

'A foot adze has a larger handle and is held by both hands. Though, in truth, I often hold this in two hands as well,' she said. 'My father has all the larger tools for carpentry.'

'Like what?'

She shrugged. 'Like the gimlet, braces and twybill. But he needs them for actual carpentry work such as making houses and large furniture.'

He went quiet, then said very slowly, 'You look almost wistful, Beileag, for these larger tools.'

Was that a gleam in his eye? Was he flirting with her about larger tools? She wasn't Murdag, so there wouldn't be any need to. And what did she know of flirting when it had never been directed at her? Still, she wouldn't mind having access to those tools if only to play around with them to see what they could do other than making planks of wood.

'I don't need them for what I'm doing,' she said instead.

'That is a shame.'

At his tone, she again snapped her eyes to his, but he looked back at the adze before she could determine if she was hearing things. Because that *had* sounded suggestive. Just because no one had flirted with her didn't mean she hadn't seen it before. She couldn't even count how many times Hamilton had pursued a girl or woman practically in front of her.

Not that he was rude; she simply suspected she'd never been noticeable to him before and she wasn't now either.

She wanted to shake herself! He wanted Murdag, her friend. And he was here…for reasons she really couldn't fully explain. Because it was only somewhat reasonable to ask him for a favour, but showing him all this, showing him herself, made no sense.

'However,' Hamilton continued, now holding both ends of the adze and twirling the heavy instrument between his fingers, 'what you do have is a very dangerous weapon, Beileag.'

Dangerous to her, but not to him apparently. 'I noticed.'

'And you're simply out here chopping away at things by yourself.'

Now that tone she didn't need to guess about. 'Yes, by myself, for years, and I don't need help.'

Hamilton stopped twirling the adze. 'Now, lass, I didn't mean—'

'Maybe we should go.' This was all lost. She truly should have thought this through.

'Let me explain,' Hamilton said. 'Please.'

She knew she was sensitive on these things, but how else was she to take it? 'What did you mean, then?'

He handed her the tool and she placed it back carefully in the shallow chest. All the while he stared at her and she stared right back.

Days of this when he had always been gallivanting, carefree mischief-making Hamilton. But she felt as though he was trying to understand her. Why?

Hamilton exhaled roughly and looked away before he turned back to her. 'I seem to be stumbling my way with you. Was it always like this?'

That sounded honest. So she tried that, too. 'I don't think we've ever done this.'

He tilted his head. 'True enough—you've been holding a secret. Now listen. All I meant...or at least what I was getting at...was not that you can't handle the tools. I can see from this piece here that you can chop away with the best of them.'

When he pointed at the hacked practice piece at his feet she wanted to laugh or cry. He *did* think that was the best she could do!

'But,' Hamilton continued, 'I was only bemoaning the issue you haven't shared this with anyone, when it's clear you love it.'

'I've shown you nothing but my tools.'

Hamilton grinned, then closed his eyes. When he opened them, almost all the gleaming amusement that flashed there was gone. 'It's the way you talk of them. I may mention my knives, sword or arrows, lass, but I can't talk about a tymbill like you do.'

'It's twybill,' she said.

'Exactly.'

'Do you truly want to talk about this?' She pointed to the rest of her chests. One held some of her first work, which she kept for reasons so private she wouldn't be sharing them today, but the other chest held her latest work, which she was rather proud of.

'You haven't shown me near enough.' He gazed at her face, his expression resolute. 'So absolutely.'

She dared ask the one question that seemed too laden with possibilities, but she had to. 'Why?'

'It's interesting,' he said. 'I'm finding *all* of this interesting.'

Maybe he thought if he didn't feign interest she wouldn't help him.

'I'll still help you with Murdag, and Anna and Camron, even if you're bored with my carving.'

'I'm not bored,' he said quickly. 'Though I do appreciate the help with Murdag. Camron made this bet, so his challenge with Anna is his own.'

'For now,' she said. 'I...think they need help still.'

'They do. So, are we agreed when my brother asks for it, we'll do it?'

She loved them both very much and it was clear to the chickens clucking around their pens that they loved each other as well.

'I will,' she said.

He gave a soft smile and his shoulders looked less tense, as if he agreed, but never truly believed her that she'd help.

'I did say I'd help,' she repeated.

'Yes, and almost choked me with surprise.'

'That's your own fault.' She waved around them. 'But I don't want to talk of this if you think it'll hurt my feelings. It will, mind you, but that's *not* your fault.'

He gave off a short laugh. 'I know nothing of this.'

'Most people don't.'

'I truly know nothing,' he clarified. 'And so...a little bit won't hurt me.'

She held up her hand to reveal her bandages. 'Are you certain of that?'

'I handled one of your tools, Beileag, and haven't suffered thus far.'

She narrowed her eyes on him. Mischief should have been Hamilton's first name because she just didn't know how to take him.

Still, she was the one who had brought him here and he's the one who stayed, so here they were.

Shoving the tool chest to the side, she opened the chest with the good carvings and turned it towards him. She watched as he unwrapped the linen, placed it on the ground next to the hacked piece and took out one piece after another.

His eyebrows got higher and higher, some amusement, some surprise.

Suddenly, he snatched the practice log and waved it at her. 'What's this?'

'Pine,' she said.

'Beileag,' he warned.

'It's a soft wood. When I don't want to waste a good piece of wood, I use that log when I sharpen or acquire new tools to see the accuracy of my cuts.'

'And you were going to gift this to me?' Shaking his head, he tossed it down next to the linen. 'When you had these in this chest all along?'

'I wasn't going to give it to you!' she huffed. 'You insisted!'

Laughing, he picked up the five small rabbits, and laid them in his palm.

'They're different colours.'

'I used different hardwoods, like oak, apple, elm.'

'They're even round and chubby,' he said. 'And the ears!'

'It's a stop cut,' she said. 'I'd like to make them finer with ears separated, but I'd need to use larger pieces of wood to do so.'

He placed them one at a time on the linen and reached in the chest for the next one. 'So this is what you do. They all seem to be animals except for this. How did you make a spoon?'

'With a hook knife.'

'And the polish?'

'Leather strop both sides, the smooth and suede, as well as a burnishing stone.'

Shaking his head. 'I won't settle for a practice log now as a gift, Beileag, I'm going to want one of your creatures.'

'I haven't offered you any of them.'

'We'll see...' He set down the hedgehog. 'There're so many ways you've cut. How do you start carving? Do you think of what you want and then carve, or is it the wood that's the inspiration?'

No one had asked her these questions before. Murdag wished she'd sell them to different clans for supplies or at least to free herself from her family.

But no one, not ever, had asked her how she did it. It was rather enjoyable to talk about it.

'I draw some lines first and follow along.'

He nudged the hacked log with his toe. 'You didn't draw on this first, did you?'

'No, that was all...inspiration.' She smirked.

His eyes narrowed. 'You'll tease me forever about your practice log.'

'I think that's a fine idea.'

Chuffing, he picked another animal piece out, then another. Every one he looked at and set carefully on the linen at his feet, until he got to the last, the one she treasured the most.

It was the darkest of the lot and the most polished. A wolf running, its fur made with the tiniest of marks, its ears laid back with the wind or its speed, its snout as far up and out as the back leg so it was perfectly in symmetry.

She wanted to gloat then at him when he saw her best work, but instead of Hamilton huffing out more praise as he'd done, he'd gone tense and quiet. He brought it up to a sunbeam, canted the carving and his thick neck and stared in the eyes. He gazed at it as if in some communication and traced with his fingertip every bit of her carving detail.

The more he stared at it, the more a feeling of foreboding fell until it didn't matter if the sun was shining. She didn't feel a bit of happiness at all and she didn't know why.

'Sit down a bit with me, would you, Beileag?' Hamilton said, still staring at the wolf.

She found herself simply staring at him and she wasn't looking at him as a friend, or as Hamilton, but... it was the oddest feeling. As though she was studying him as he did her as she turned a carving of her own.

When he slid to the edge, she was compelled and made her way next to him.

'You've kept this secret a long time.'

She didn't know the direction of his thoughts, for she felt they were regarding the wolf and about something else entirely. And there wasn't the easy camaraderie they'd shared a few moments before for her to tease some truth from him. So, she decided to simply answer the question.

'I've carved them for me,' she said.

'Why?'

That was a conversation she wasn't prepared to talk of, if ever. 'It's quiet in the woods, isn't it?'

They'd shared those words already together, so maybe he'd think they were enough. In truth, though, she wasn't certain he heard her.

Staring at the piece in his hand, turning it over and over, his finger sliding up to the tip of the nose and then back down to the tiny outstretched foot, he said, 'My brother doesn't know of this?'

'No, nor Seoc.' She folded her hands in her lap. 'Only Murdag and Anna.'

Hamilton tilted his head to look at her. 'And me.'

Beileag didn't know how to answer. Obviously, she should simply agree with him, but it was the tone of his words, almost militant. And his brows were drawn in so much it was as if he was troubled.

About what, she couldn't have guessed, but she tried and also racked her thoughts to come up with different words other than agreeing he was the only one of the men who knew her secret, but in the end, she couldn't.

She also needed to answer him, since he kept his gaze steady on her and the silence between them was becoming fraught with so much tension she almost wanted to shout out a warning cry of danger and hastily make her way back to the village.

'Murdag, Anna, and you are the only ones to know of this place. In truth, you're the only one who has sat here for so long and let me rattle on about the craft.'

'This is a great secret you've protected.'

His words…they were getting closer to the truth and that was somewhere she was not prepared to go. It wasn't only the secret she protected; it was herself. To distract him, she pointed to the figurine in his hand. 'You can keep that one if you want.'

'For me.' Bowing his head again, he curled his fingers around the object.

Beileag kept her quiet while Hamilton gazed at her carving and gathered whatever thoughts he had. The wolf was one of her better pieces, she'd spent weeks on it to get the fur looking as true as possible. Once that was done, it was almost impossible to polish it without ruining the tiny little lines she'd made, but she'd managed it.

Still, he hardly understood the constant correcting she'd had to undergo to complete it. And it wasn't so perfect that he'd needed to look at it with wonder, or be troubled she offered it to him. But she couldn't deny there was a little of that in his expression, too. She didn't know if she'd ever seen Hamilton like this before…so still and thoughtful.

The log didn't afford them much space, so they were almost touching, and there was a welcome warmth to him she never had in the many days she'd spent in the forest.

But because his elbows were on his knees and he was holding the figurine between his legs, he was for all intents and purposes looking up at her.

His hair had come loose at some point during their

walk and it was falling over his shoulders and shadowing the left side of his face.

The sunlight highlighted the tips of his lashes and cast shadows along his angular cheekbones.

He truly was handsome. She understood on some level that the twins were identical, but Hamilton still managed to be the one who was more handsome and gifted with charm.

And now he sat beside her and she shared her craft with him. She could almost imagine her future husband doing just this. A man who held and teased her. Who sat by her side on damp fallen tree. But this wasn't the time for imagining or wishing.

Her friend was troubled and she didn't know how to help him. There was a vulnerability she'd never sensed with him, either, and for a moment she felt the need to bundle him in the heavy linen at his feet to protect him from his own thoughts from…what? They were simply looking at her carvings.

This wasn't about battles or rumours of ones to come. Except Hamilton didn't have his easy grin about him as he gazed at her carving. His expression had turned sombre and that weary, wary look was there, the one she thought she'd imagined before. Had something changed him since his last scouting mission?

'This is one of the most beautiful things I've ever seen in my life,' Hamilton said, his voice far rougher than it was before.

No one had given such a compliment before.

'It's a wolf running, isn't it? Feral, and what is this expression…a snarl?' Hamilton nodded to himself. 'He is chasing prey.'

She let out a breath. 'No, it's—'

'Following his pack for the hunt,' he said almost grimly.

Wolves mated for life and she always imagined this wolf running back to his partner and cubs. 'He's running back to his family.'

'Running to family.' He said the words slowly as though he was testing them for truth and didn't find it. 'Have you ever seen a wolf?'

'We have dogs and Anna's father talks a lot.'

He gave a soft smile that didn't reach his eyes. 'So you did this from looking at the dogs running and ol' Padrig's tellings?'

She held her hands carefully in her lap. 'When we were children, he was always warning us about the time he came across one.'

He stared at it more and she knew, or thought she did, what he was getting at.

'You've seen one,' she stated as soft as she could. The moment seemed to call for it.

'The night before Ettrick's Forest,' he said after a long pause.

She knew what that meant. Dunbar's battle, where their laird was killed and they'd fled from the English. It was a terrible time for the Graham clan. None of the men who returned were quite the same.

She thought Seoc, with his scar, was the most changed. Now she wondered about different wounds. Perhaps the changes she could see in Hamilton weren't only because of the time away. Were the lines beginning at the corners of his eyes all from laughter, or from worry?

'Do you want to talk about it? What happened last spring, to you and your brother?' She swallowed. 'I'm a good listener.'

'I never want to tell anyone,' he said.

Yet he didn't let go of that wolf. 'But you want to keep it?'

Chapter Ten

'I intend to keep it, Beileag.'

Hamilton both resented and revered the wolf carving. The workmanship in it was remarkable, the depth of polish and cuts bringing out the natural lines of the wood and creating more movement in the perpetually running animal.

He'd felt like that since they'd run towards Ettrick Forest, as if he was perpetually running. He might be lying about the bet, but he wanted something out of it, too. He wanted him and his brother to have a home, a family to return to. He wanted to tighten their connection somehow. He knew he'd always loved being a twin more than his brother, but since he'd returned, he needed his twin. All because of that wolf, the one that watched them, warned them of the battle to come. If he'd only listened.

He was glad he was sitting because the moment he saw this wolf at the bottom of the small chest, he knew he wouldn't be the same.

Still, he picked it up. A wolf! He hadn't been the only one to see it in the forest the night before Dunbar's battle. But to see it again, almost to its very likeness, was jarring. He felt as though someone made some jest with him.

Many jests, in fact. There was something about the last few days and his interactions with Beileag. As though he was falling asleep and startling awake and seeing the world a little differently. Or at least, the world was trying to show him something different.

But what? Nothing he should want. He was a twin and he wanted that connection always in this tumultuous world. He didn't want…dancing with trees, or wolves at the bottom of chests. Still, he had come here instead of going to the stables. He'd discovered this wolf and he would keep it; letting it out of his hand seemed almost impossible. He'd always forged ahead with whatever life threw his way. Why not now?

And the creator of the wooden creature sat next to him and said nothing. He…rather liked that, truly. Which was unusual, as he'd never thought much of quiet until recently.

Until it didn't seem he could find it anymore. Not with the clans' meeting and what was soon expected of them in Stirling. More fights, more losses.

With all the upheaval, he craved quiet now. Strange that he found it looking at these wooden carvings at this side of the forest. He'd like to sit here for a moment more if not hours, again an unusual experience…but there it was in all its truth.

But then he'd be selfish in doing so. After all, he was invited to this log with its hidden treasures. It wasn't his place to stay, though he wanted to.

He turned to his host. 'I am most humbled at your craft and thankful you brought me here.'

She smiled softly.

'What is it?'

'So formal?' she said. 'When all you do is sit on a damp log so I could show you my sticks.'

'Sticks! I'll have you know that is a spoon!' He purposefully picked up the hedgehog and pretended to use it as a utensil. 'I'll never eat soup without it again.'

This time she laughed.

Maybe it was the way they sat so close that he could see how the sun played against her colouring and how her eyes lit up at his simple jest.

And it was a simple jest. Surely she wouldn't look that delightful, delighted, an expression that made his heart warm, simply because he called her art 'not sticks'.

'You should be complimented on these all the time,' he said, rushing and fumbling out the words. She should know this and immediately. Hadn't he complimented her on her workmanship? He thought he had, but then, he was so astounded by her knowledge and what he had lifted from the chest, maybe he hadn't done her sticks justice after all.

This time he wasn't confused by the emotions flitting across her features—surprise, pleasure—until all of it dimmed.

She clenched her hands. 'Murdag thinks I should sell them and keep the coin to fund my adventures.'

That would be something Murdag would want. Coin. Adventures. It wouldn't hurt with what he wanted as well. All that adventure with Murdag.

He coughed to release the words and conflicting feelings lodging his throat.

'You don't like adventures?' he said.

'I never needed them. I want…' Her eyes watered a bit before they looked out over her collection. 'It doesn't matter what I want.'

It did and she'd asked him for a favour. And if this woman wanted him to do something, he would. After all, she'd already offered to help with his brother, as well as Murdag, and she'd brought him here to this quiet, special, place.

But the wolf, which he fully intended to never let go, he wasn't certain how he'd repay that. Whatever he did wouldn't be enough.

And no doubt what she'd ask would be something simple and he'd be on his way, in her debt forever, though she wouldn't know it.

No one could know what a wolf meant to him. He'd told her more than others. He'd told his brother none of it.

Which, for him, was another first. He never wanted to lose that familiar, family connection with his sibling. Ensured everything he did kept them as equal as possible, but this day had already tipped him over.

Camron had never been here, never seen the workmanship Beileag could do, never been gifted with one of them. Never sat beside her on a damp log while she quietly waited for him to answer her.

'It does matter,' he said.

'What?'

'It does matter what you want,' he repeated. 'And you brought me here for a reason. A favour, you said, and I'm willing to pay, whatever the price.'

Beileag paled before that gentle pink skimmed across her cheeks.

The sunlight never faltered in this little clearing and the smattering of freckles across her nose evidence, no doubt, caused by many more days spent just like this.

Hidden by trees and boulders, sitting here on this log carving for hours to perfect her creations. He wanted to know more. He wanted—

'No price to pay.' She gave a tight smile. 'This was nice to show you. We should go.'

'No, we shouldn't.'

This was the quiet, shy Beileag he was used to. Most of the time it'd be Murdag or Anna who would coax her along while he was already leagues ahead. Her favour wouldn't be much—a little patience on his part now was a kindness, wasn't it?

He straightened and turned to face her more fully. 'Come now, you brought me here and I want this wolf.'

'I want a husband,' she blurted.

Hamilton knew he stared, but in all fairness to him, what this woman had said was unexpected. He couldn't possibly have heard her correctly.

'That's…good.'

She swallowed hard and looked him dead in the eye. 'Will you help me?'

'With what?' he said.

'I'm to help you with Murdag—will you help me find a husband?'

'You want a husband,' he said. He couldn't help but repeat himself. He simply didn't know what else to say. Which wasn't completely honourable, he knew. He had asked her to help him find ways to connect with Murdag. It was only fair he help her connect with whomever it was she wanted to.

He was only surprised. That's all. Surprise was why his blood froze a bit and his heart constricted. It was strong surprise that made his mouth a bit dry and his thoughts rebel from any reason.

She twisted one of her bandages. 'Why is that so hard to believe?'

'It's not…' he started to say. 'It's not difficult to believe. I simply didn't know.'

'Was I supposed to let you know?' she said. 'You're

not questioning Murdag wanting a family, why do you question me? Is it because I'm too tall?'

'What?' Hamilton bit out.

'Nothing.'

It didn't feel like nothing. In fact, he had a lot going on inside his head.

Who was it that she liked? She was wonderfully tall, as she pointed out, and Seoc would be a good match for her.

Except he couldn't remember at any point Seoc mentioning Beileag in any kind of romantic way. And she hadn't mentioned Seoc by name. Given they had been friends for life, wouldn't that have been easier?

It must be someone else, someone he wasn't so familiar with. Was there anyone new in the last year?

There was that one man, with reddish hair, who swore he wasn't a Colquhoun, though Hamilton had his doubts. Seemed like a decent sort, but…something seemed off about him.

And he couldn't think of any Graham man who would be good enough for her. Now he knew her secret, and the skill she had, plus there was the issue of her mother—that was something to treat with either delicacy or with a strong backbone if someone was to court her—he couldn't think of any man worthy of her.

But if there was someone she wanted, he'd be here for her as she was for him.

'So who is it?' he said.

'Who is what?'

'This husband you want.'

'What do you mean?'

Was she shy about this now? It was hard enough talking of this without having to be absolutely explicit. They were friends, but before this last week he could hardly say he'd talked to her at any length. If at all.

And certainly not about husbands and what Beileag wanted. He rolled his shoulders, and stretched his head from side to side.

Ah. It was the restlessness again making him uncomfortable. That made sense. Except…it didn't feel as though he wanted to suddenly run off and train or check the traps. It was something else getting under his skin.

'Come now, Beileag, I confessed my inability to woo the woman I—' Hamilton stopped, thought about his words. It wouldn't do to get ahead of himself. 'Surely you could share the name of this man who has caught your eye?'

If possible, her cheeks flushed more and she twirled one of her bandages.

'There isn't anyone in particular,' she said.

'My strengths aren't relationships, maybe you could just tell me about that particular.'

She tore off that bandage and put it in her pocket. 'There isn't anyone at all.'

'But you said—'

'I want a husband,' she said. 'I don't know who it's going to be.'

'So just any man would do?' Wanting to tease and poke, Hamilton almost bumped her with his shoulder, but Beileag seemed to be falling into herself.

She fidgeted with another bandage and pocketed that one as well, and another, until her hands were free. No blood, no cuts.

'Beileag, why do you wear—?'

'Maybe you could point me in the direction of someone who could be a good match for me. You've travelled to other clans—maybe there's someone there?'

Back to husbands again. Hamilton stared at her

hands. Old scars were there, but nothing new. Another unexpected aspect to this woman.

'Oh,' she said. 'I see. It truly is as hopeless as I've been told.'

'What?' Anger swept through him. He knew exactly to whom she was referring and her mother could not be more wrong. 'Just because I haven't come across a man doesn't mean there isn't one out there. I haven't met the world.'

'You must know more than ten men, though, whom I've never met.'

He had met hundreds.

'I was right,' she said.

He was fumbling again. Where were his easy ways? He tore his gaze away from the woman and spun the wolf around. 'No, it's me and my inability to understand all this.'

'You've had…women before,' she whispered.

Hamilton rolled his shoulders. Her stumbling over the words made it no easier to talk of. What was he doing here with this maiden, talking of his…stolen kisses and more?

And how would she know? He'd accused her of being unobservant! He didn't want to think of any of this, let alone with her. Bawdy conversation full of pleasure? No, that wasn't what she wanted.

Should he open up to her more? Expose himself more? Sensitivity, vulnerability wasn't him. He was the best at covering all that up.

Because there was no reason to tell her that even with the women he'd shared beds with, he knew it would be different when it meant something more than pleasure.

He spun the wolf again, and again, all the while

watching the eyes. She'd carved them uncannily life-like; they looked right back at him.

'It's balanced,' he said. Unlike his own life. He'd never minded being the one to throw a bit of confusion and chaos in the mix when he always had his reasonable brother to help sort it out. But now…now he wished he'd learnt a bit of reasonableness along the way himself; it might have helped with this conversation.

'Are we talking of the wolf?' she said after a while.

It was safer to do so, but he wasn't a coward. 'Why haven't you talked to Murdag or Anna of this husband you want?'

'You know why I haven't spoken to Anna.'

He did. Anna wasn't exactly wanting a husband. And Murdag?

She didn't seem interested in finding a husband either. Funny that, that he and his brother had chosen women who didn't want them. But he'd wear her out eventually. He could already imagine family gatherings and them sharing meals.

This strange time in the woods would simply be a memory between friends.

'Since I'm so terrible at this wooing, maybe there's someone here for you. Our clan is large and not only limited to this village.'

She nodded.

That truth made him brighten a bit. 'Maybe it all comes down to what you do with your other…relation-ships.'

'Other relationships.'

'The men who have wooed you.' He'd been away for most of the last few years—any number of men could have pursued Beileag. Who did she share her kisses with?

He stretched his legs and crossed his legs. He most

definitely was getting restless again. And he did not like that he didn't know who Beileag had kissed.

What a terrible friend he was turning to be!

'Other. Men?' she said, a tight tone to her voice he never heard before. As though she was mad or going to cry.

Maybe she didn't want to talk of the men before him. Or not before *him*…just men she had.

How many had tried to win this woman's hand? Probably more than he could count.

She was beautiful, accomplished. He'd seen how she was with her siblings and she had more patience than anyone, especially with the cruelty of her mother.

'Perhaps it's a matter of how much time you spend with everyone. I can imagine perfecting your craft takes you away.'

Her brow drew in, as she looked around the clearing. 'You think it's me being here that has prevented me from finding a husband?'

'Absolutely,' he said. There wasn't anything else it could be but her secluding herself behind the boulders and trees. 'Next time you're with a man and he's smiling and flirting, keep doing more of that. You can make beautiful things later.'

Ready to go, he stood. He felt good because he'd helped her and now he could help Murdag with her wolf teeth and all would be well.

Until Beileag's hands fluttered and she cried out, 'I've never been with a man.'

Again, she shocked him, but he pulled himself together, coughed to clear his throat. 'Of course, I wasn't simply—'

She made a sound of disgust and frustration. 'But I've never kissed, no one's tried, no one's *seen* me!'

Throwing the wolf on the linen with the rest of them, Hamilton grabbed those hands and pulled her up.

She was up and against him before he realised what he was doing. All he knew was that he wanted to comfort her and not let go. Why was it always like this with her?

When she gasped, he cupped her jaw, tilted her head so she'd look at him. She couldn't possibly be implying that no man had noticed her.

'No one's kissed you?' he said. 'No one's tried?'

'I wouldn't even know if they did. And maybe that's why no one wants me because I don't know what I'm doing, or I'm just that unlikeable.'

She thought…she thought it was her fault? That she hadn't tried and therefore was unwanted? What was wrong with the men here? Unlikeable? Not beautiful?

Her mother's words, no doubt. Beileag was stunning, all golden haired and long limbed!

When the sun hit her hair just so, she was almost difficult to look at. And when she talked of her craft and tools, she had this glow to her secretive smile. She'd kept the chest turned away as if there was something of great interest. Her eyes had gleamed over the edge at him as she handed him the crude-looking adze.

Which hadn't been balanced and the handle so well worn it was almost too thin in places for the heavy iron. Which also didn't look that sharp.

But still she talked of its importance and her eyes looked longingly when she mentioned her father's craft.

He'd been…enchanted, he couldn't help but tease her in return, but then she'd lost that warm expression and he now knew why.

She didn't know he'd been flirting with her. She wasn't uninterested in men or flirtation; she just didn't know how. And if someone had wanted to flirt or kiss her before, maybe she didn't know then either. Maybe... maybe she just needed to know what it was all about.

That was easy to remedy, and, as a friend, he could show her.

'I'll kiss you,' he said.

'What?' she gasped.

He dropped his hand to grab her other one when she tried to pull away. 'I'll kiss you, then you'll know how easy it is.'

'That's not what I—'

'Not what you meant when you asked for a favour. I disagree. I think it was, you just didn't know it.'

'That makes little sense.'

It did—she just didn't know that either. The more he thought of it, the more he warmed up to the idea. This was perfect truly. Perhaps it was a bit untoward, but they were friends and it didn't have to mean anything. He could simply...show her what it was like. Then she wouldn't be so unattuned with the men who were no doubt making jests about tools and falling flat.

Just kiss her, something chaste of course. And he could hold her. That wouldn't be much. He'd already accidentally been doing that for days now.

She was slender, her movements graceful—she reminded him of a young tree in a gentle wind dancing to a tune he couldn't hear and bending in ways he couldn't guess.

Fitting perhaps to what she carved—maybe there was some connection there. Another intriguing aspect to this woman...

Her hazel eyes, more golden again, growing wider as she waited for him to answer.

Was there a question? All he felt was some untoward anticipation.

'Hamilton?' she whispered.

A simple kiss, a light hold. Nothing much between friends.

Her hands trembled in his and he clasped them more fully, wanting to warm them. His eyes dropped to her lips when she pulled the plump bottom one between her teeth.

She wanted words, but he kept fumbling his words. Too much thinking and mischief was reasoned out. He was best at forging ahead and working with the consequences later.

'Ham—'

Tugging her hands towards him, throwing her off balance, he tilted his head and kissed her.

Chapter Eleven

Nothing could have prepared Beileag for the solid pliant heat of Hamilton's lips pressed to her own.

One heartbeat, two, in which a riot of sensations assaulted her: Hamilton's calloused hands cupping hers, his unique scent, like crushed parsley and ale, the warmth of his breath, the tilt of his head as he aligned their noses, the way his feet bracketed hers.

The certain way he gave and took her first kiss, jerking his head away when he was done. Then rocking back on his heels which made a distance between them that his hands, still holding hers, did not. The way her lips, still tingling from the brief contact, never would. She felt branded in a way she'd never un-feel.

One moment, two, and she was changed. From the hitch to her breath to the taste of him she swore lingered on her lips.

To the racing of her heart that wouldn't stop, even when the kiss was absolutely over, and Hamilton was looking at her with a soft calm look in his hazel eyes. Something that was both smug and persuasive.

'There,' Hamilton said.

The single word scraped over Hamilton's natural

voice. It, more than his continuation of hand holding, caused the flush of heat to her skin.

Hamilton of Clan Graham had kissed her. Her first kiss, maybe her only kiss, and he'd done it here among her trees, and he was looking at her as if it were just any other day. As if he was both certain of her response and his actions.

Which should have annoyed her to no end, or to the point where she punched him and shoved him away.

But that wasn't what she felt.

She had to get through the shock first.

'There. What?' she said.

'That's what it's like. Nothing more or less.'

They couldn't possibly be talking of the same thing. Her heart wouldn't stop the hard thump in her chest and she knew her cheeks were red from the way Hamilton's gaze kept dropping to her chest, chin, up her cheeks, as he followed her reaction.

'You kissed me,' she said.

'I said I would.'

He had said that and the surprise of it all was definitely fading, but not lessening. Instead, there seemed to be some sort of warmth roiling around inside her, making her feel restless and calm at the same time.

Making her all too aware of how the breeze brushed against the back of her hands, along her cheeks. Aware of how crisp the sunlight shone through the trees.

Everything about her little hiding spot was brighter, sharper.

'Why?'

At her question, Hamilton's calm demeanour began to crack. His brows drew inwards, just a little, but enough for her to notice because they were still standing close.

And because she was looking at him. Truly looking, not just the side glances she'd been giving him that day, or during the years of friendship where they were always in groups, and Hamilton was always ahead. In truth, she was more familiar with the back of Hamilton than his front, or any expression. From the way he'd grown into shoulders and his broad torso. How his hair had been brutally short when young and now brushed the back of his neck.

Like this, she felt free to just stare directly at him and notice how the sun had turned his skin golden and the frequent laughter had left lines at the corners of his eyes. How his lashes curled up and his nose had a shape that fit his face so very well, but wasn't something she could simply explain to anyone.

Just as she couldn't explain how standing here like this made her feel. Warm. Secure. Anticipatory.

He'd kissed her; he was done with whatever test he'd given. He'd even said *there,* as if he'd finished the instruction to the test and revealed the answer.

She absolutely didn't know anything except the warmth inside kept increasing to some heat and was pressing against her skin until she felt as though she'd burst if she didn't do something.

'You were talking of finding a husband,' he said, slowly, as if she didn't remember the conversation.

'I was,' she said.

'But you're overthinking it,' he said. 'You should just do it. There are men out there who absolutely want to marry you.'

'And you know this how?'

He cleared his throat. 'You're very marriageable, Beileag. Very.'

She wanted to pursue that, if for nothing else than she didn't know what that meant, but he made it sound like a compliment, as though it was something flattering. She felt almost giddy from the thought.

Wrong.

The word flashed through her, unmistakable in her mother's voice. Maybe so. Maybe he was merely being nice. He'd kissed her almost as chastely as a brother would a sister. And also, Hamilton wanted Murdag, her friend, so even standing here holding his hands wasn't appropriate.

It should simply be 'there' and done as he obviously intended.

But she didn't want that. Not at all.

Not when she was so close to a truth, or what felt like truth. Like something she'd pondered on all her life and was just now realising. Or perhaps what she felt wasn't that profound. Maybe she had a bit of mischief in her as well and was pushing the matter, but she wasn't going to let it go. Not yet.

Not when for the first time, she felt…she felt so free.

She clenched his hands. 'We're friends, true?'

'Always.' He clenched them back.

She looked down at their hands held up between them. Plenty of space between their bodies as to be appropriate and yet…she wanted more. Just a bit. If necessary, she'd confess tomorrow, or take this moment to the grave.

But she'd seen true kisses and she knew the one he'd offered wasn't one. For once, she'd wanted to know what it was like. Not the kiss, but…that moment right before the kiss.

The anticipation of it all.

Because, though she'd never been with a man like this, she knew Hamilton simply announcing he'd kiss her and then doing it wasn't what she needed.

They didn't have to do anything except up to the point of their lips touching. She wanted to know what *that* felt like.

'Friends,' she clarified.

'Absolutely,' he agreed.

'So, when I say I may not understand exactly what you mean by all this, would you tell me more?'

With a slight smirk, he dipped his head and looked under his lashes at her. 'When a man kisses you, or acts as if he's going to kiss you, it isn't time to be hiding behind a boulder. That's what I mean.'

'And you showed me what it's like so I'd know what to look for…and not be hiding in my trees.'

He flashed a big Hamilton grin. 'Exactly.'

'Except you told me that you'd kiss me.'

He nodded.

'No man has said they were to kiss me. Are there other ways I should be looking for?'

'Other indications?' he said.

'That a man may want to kiss me.'

Hamilton lost his grin, then it seemed he lost his words. Still she looked at him and he at her, their hands holding the entire time. Except this time, she swore she felt his hand jerk a bit as if she'd surprised him.

'There are.' He cleared his throat. 'Many, in fact.'

She wouldn't take it too far. She wouldn't. She just wanted a bit more time like this. Near a man as open and free with his laughter and life. More of this and then she could at least say she had at one time almost kissed a man.

There wouldn't be any wrong with it; there shouldn't be at least. The fluttering in her stomach and slight burst of sweat at her lower back belied that fact. But it was nervousness, that's all.

Or mischief.

Or curiosity.

Or madness.

She didn't dare poke at reasoning anymore, or she just might lose her courage to do anything at all. And when would she get the opportunity like this again? Never.

And Hamilton was Hamilton. He should be used to women throwing themselves at him. Who was she, or this moment, compared to him, compared to all he'd done? Nothing at all. Insignificant.

Which should make it easier to press on with asking him, if only she could somehow calm her body into not feeling so…expectant.

'What are they?' She swallowed. 'What is it like… before a kiss?'

His lashes fluttered and for a moment he broke eye contact, but he didn't step away and his hands stayed around hers. Although, in truth, she swore she felt a tremble there, but she didn't know if it was he or she who had done it.

'As a friend, eh?' he said.

'Always,' she repeated.

'There's a look,' he said. 'The first thing I…a man does…is notice a woman.'

Something as simple as this? Maybe Hamilton was correct and she did hide too much.

'What would that look like?'

Another smirk to his lips. 'A bit like this.'

'Like what?' she said. 'You're staring at me.'

'True,' he said. 'How about now?'

She took in every handsome feature he had and even some she'd probably never noticed before, like the way the tips of his ears poked out from the wave of his curls.

But it didn't feel as though he was wanting to kiss her. Maybe she was broken.

Hamilton huffed and released her hands. 'This may be more difficult because we're friends.'

They were friends and he didn't have those anticipating a kiss feelings for her.

Fool that she was, wanting something that she truly couldn't have. She brushed her hands down her skirt. 'We can return now. It was nice what you did. I'll pay more attention when men announce they want to kiss me.'

Hamilton huffed. 'Now there's a challenge to any man's pride if there ever was one. Are you making a bet with me, Beileag?'

She wasn't trying to.

'Let me try this.' Hamilton put his hand on his hips and looked down at the ground. She watched him breathe and toe the dirt a few times. There was nothing about his demeanour to warn her when he looked back at her.

He did the same as he'd always done, looked up through his lashes, his head tilted to the side. But this time, he barely blinked, or maybe that was her, and his eyes didn't simply stare into hers, but skimmed over her features, the tangled strands of her hair, her non-existent hips and down to her boots and back up again, but twice as slow and meandering.

By the time his hazel-brown eyes met hers, they seemed darker. And darker yet as they locked on to hers.

With that look the roiling warmth was a sharp stab of heat right down her centre and she needed to part her lips.

'Oh,' she said.

Then words escaped her completely when Hamilton's mouth curved at the corner as if he was pleased with her response. On a rough exhale, Hamilton ran his hand through his hair and eased up on the way he stood. 'That's the look you should be looking for.'

If that was the look she was looking for to see if a man was interested in her, she was ill fated.

Because no man could look at her the way Hamilton just now pretended to. She knew that with utter certainty because no man was Hamilton.

So how could they affect her as he always did and how could any other man's lashes be so ridiculously long as to both hide and reveal the mysteriousness of his thoughts?

She had an answer from him, but it wasn't the answer she wanted, or at least not all of it.

'No,' she said. 'That won't do.'

Hamilton blinked. 'What won't do?'

She couldn't explain. Taking the only step between them, she placed her hand on his cheek. She wasn't certain what she was searching for, only aware that she searched. She'd wanted the anticipation of a kiss and the look he'd given her was part of that.

It wasn't enough.

Hamilton started at her touch, but held still. Given whatever freedom he allowed her, she traced his features with her fingertips. He wasn't some new broken branch for her to twist and look at under bright sunlight.

He was Hamilton, her friend, a man, but that curious thrill of finding a sturdy branch for a new project was what she was feeling. She couldn't explain it as anything else.

For years she'd acknowledged, always to herself, that he was the more handsome of the twins. It was his smile; one he hid from her now as she traced along his jaw and ran a curl between her fingers. It was as thick and soft as she ever thought it would be.

'Beileag,' Hamilton roughly whispered, a crackle of emotion in the two syllables.

She should stop. She didn't even know why she was caressing his cheek and mapping the texture there. But he'd kissed her and he'd looked at her, and she just... wasn't the same. Just a little longer and she'd step back, clench her hands in front of her and watch everyone else play and live their lives.

She'd go back to carving some wood creature all alone behind some boulders where no one would look for her. Just a moment more, no more than that.

'I need something else,' she said. Which made no sense, she knew, because Hamilton's expression changed from calm satisfaction to a little less precise, to something that was turning a bit intense, a bit...determined.

'All right,' he said, his voice low and rumbling. If anything, he held even more still, watched her even more carefully.

Did he wonder what she'd do? She did, too. No kiss and he wasn't touching her. It was all seemingly acceptable.

It didn't feel as though it was perfectly within her rights to do this. Not with the roughness of his stubble under her palm or the softness of his bottom lip when she accidently brushed there with her thumb.

His breath felt more heated to her than when he gave her a kiss. He was also breathing differently.

What would he do if she touched the shell of his ear?

'When men are interested in women, do their eyes go dark?' she said.

Hamilton's eyes became hooded.

'And do their breaths hitch?'

'No,' he said on a hard breath.

Had eyes ever darkened to the point they were as black as the sky at night? Or lips gone so soft it was all she could do not to touch them with her fingertips?

Had his cheeks always been so drawn tight or flushed?

At what point did the pretend kiss, the almost kiss, turn to this…wanting? Because that's what this was. A want. This was what she was craving earlier, to feel this for once.

He leaned his forehead against hers, their matching heights aligning their bodies in absolute union.

The tension between them tightened to a painful level as Hamilton rolled his forehead before sliding his cheek down hers and then back up.

It was as though he wanted to kiss her, but couldn't.

'Beileag,' he murmured against her skin. It was both a warning and a call.

'Please,' she said. Not knowing what she was asking for. For him to step back, for her to? Yes, all of that. They needed to end this…whatever this was…and she would end this.

Hamilton kissed her.

Chapter Twelve

There was nothing left of any intentions. Hamilton's every thought, every feeling, was about Beileag of Clan Graham and her seduction of him.

Because that's what had happened. He'd been seduced and all the more so because he knew she hadn't done it with any intent. It was just her.

Unexpected Beileag! How could he know she was like this? That she felt like this?

Every brush and flutter of her fingers against his jaw, temple, his chin, he felt elsewhere. The tightening low in his groin, heat at the tips of his ears. The ragged breath he managed to do between each light caress. One after the other, no rhythm. No possibility to guess where her fingertips would brush or why.

He'd closed his eyes to ease the sensation, but it only made it worse. He became all too aware of his body's reactions, the roaring of blood rushing through him, the slight stuttering pant of the woman before him, the brushing of their clothing, the shifting of her feet against the dirt.

His own widened stance, preparing him for whatever else she might want to assuage her curiosity with.

Until the air surrounding them thickened with tension, tightening everything inside him until he was half-suffocated with want, until he didn't think he could breathe without her lips against his own.

Until he broke.

But it wasn't because he was weak, or a coward, or because this was merely lust. All of this was a surprise, but then didn't he seek surprises? Seek *her*?

He wasn't simply seduced by a kiss, by a touch. It was Beileag. The woman who'd beckoned him for weeks. Beileag, her secrets, that wolf, her awareness that he felt restless and out of place in his own home.

How to tell her this? Explain it when he was just barely grasping the situation as it was.

Fool! Grateful fool. It was all her. He sought *her*. And he wouldn't have known, still ignored all the signs, if she hadn't needed something else.

Wrapping his arms around her, bringing her body more solidly against his, having the joy of almost imperceptibly lifting his chin to align their lips—how had he not kissed a woman like her before? Easily answered! There was no other like her. Tapered waist, long limbs, slender, tall.

He'd been fighting his notice of Beileag since he'd returned, but he couldn't now. He didn't want to.

It was she all along whom he'd sought, his missing part of him; he could feel it, know it.

Her soft mouth yielding against his. His body shuddering, craving. Sudden, all of this sudden. But that was his true self. Everything that was right was easy, natural. Not forced.

It was just like this.

When her hands went around his neck and she brushed

her fingertips against that sliver of sensitive skin, he deepened the kiss.

Lips to tongue, the sweetness of it all, she responded with a moan that seized lust within him. This was Beileag. Beileag! Quiet, shy, unassuming. A woman with secrets. So many secrets. This place, her craft, those little bits of linen she'd pulled off her fingers.

The sounds she made when she was properly kissed. Maddening little whimpers, half in some surrendering sound he'd hear for the rest of his life, half in delight that just made him repeat the little nips, the soft caresses.

He'd thought himself so clever, so in control when he'd offered an innocent touch of their lips, a light hold on her waist. A brief moment and then his friend would not be shy around other men. Would know that it wasn't much and look for signs of their interest.

But then…then…

She'd looked at him as if he was some rough-hewn log needing to be made into one of her creatures, and his entire body fell under that gaze. He'd held still at first from surprise and then because he couldn't, didn't want to, do anything else.

With effort he kept his hands against her sides until she nipped his bottom lip, then soothed it with a tentative lick of her tongue, and then everything in him surged towards her until he was digging his fingers around her back, needing to hang on to something.

His touch, his lips just this side of frenzied, but she was there with him.

And she felt…*right* in his arms. Finely wrought to his breadth and bulk. Soft in places that he craved.

He mapped out the planes of her form, cupping her bottom, bringing her against him.

Intending to just relieve some of the building pressure, but her hips began to rub and any reasoning fled him. He was only this man against this woman, hard heat against her arousal.

A kiss, something of friendship, to find this? Absolute want and need. That's all he was, fast, sure, certain.

He broke off to taste her sun-warmed skin. When her head fell back so he could gain access to the cords of her throat, he felt his own knees go weak at her trust and he lowered them both to their knees.

All the time they remained hip to hip, her hands now exploring down his arms as his own encircled her waist to bring her up, so that he could lay her down.

His thigh between hers, her hip against his.

Down to the ground, lying above her, careful of his weight against hers, but her knees up making a cradle for his hips.

Their lips again seeking kisses, seeking taste and touch and more of the needful bliss.

A simple kiss, revealing to him all he wanted. All he craved. Here all the time, but he'd been too blind to realise it.

He'd thought he wanted Murdag with her horses and humour, but when he'd touched her, it hadn't escalated to anything.

And over the last few weeks at home, he'd spent more time trying to gain Beileag's attention.

Blind he was to the reason why! But now he knew. Now he absolutely had no doubt as to why Seoc gave him such a look as though he knew all this time it was Beileag he'd wanted.

And he did want her. Strung tight as he'd ever been with whatever shared madness this was.

He needed to share words with her, let her know in some stumbling way that he wanted only her.

But he failed at the most tempered of times and his body wouldn't release him. Not now she was in his arms and her breaths were hard pants. He needed relief, but more, he needed *her* release.

After that, he swore, he vowed, after that, he'd say the words. Let her know his intentions. He wouldn't let her have any doubt. He'd make it known in his touch. Pushing up her skirts, his rough hands on her legs.

She startled.

'Let me,' he crooned, he soothed. 'Let me, I know what to do. What you need.'

'Hamilton…,' she started to protest.

'Do you want me to stop, Beileag?' he said. 'I'll stop. You only—'

When she shook her head, relief and satisfaction ripped through him. He circled his fingers on the back of her calves, on the back of her knees, her eyes on him, her breath raising her chest in ways he wished she didn't have clothes on so he could see all of her. Everything his hands were doing were hidden, too.

He wanted to see her, but maybe it was too much? He was just like this at her touch!

'Do you feel all tight and aching?' he said. 'Are you wet and wanting?'

Her brows drew down, her lips still damp and swollen from their kisses. She looked as though she wanted to protest. 'Yes,' she said instead.

Hissing, he palmed his erection at the surge of desire her one word released.

Waited a moment, two until he was certain he wouldn't ruin all chances with this woman whom he wanted to know in all ways and all time.

How could he not want her forever?

Sudden revelation for him, but certain all the same.

Hadn't he always been certain what he wanted. Always been seeking?

Here was where he found it, was surprised by it. Surprised by her, but certain all the same. 'Then let me, let me,' he said. He didn't make sense; he couldn't finish his sentence enough to give any meaning.

But he tried to let her know what he felt through his expression, through his hands when he cupped under her knees as gently and firmly as he could so she wouldn't startle, so she'd relax them into his hold.

When he felt the tension in her lower limbs release, he lowered his head and slowly spread them.

Watched her skirts slip up to her waist, felt his heart beat with every slithering slide of linen up her thighs until it pooled at her waist, and his every drop of his blood pooled low.

'What are you doing?' she said.

A virgin, never kissed until today, shyly asking for him to find a husband for her. There would be no other. Keeping his eyes on her, he slowly lowered his head until it came just at the juncture where he held her thighs, then kissed.

Her scent, her heat was stronger here, twisting his want to an almost painful need, but he kept himself in check, he watched her and not where he was heading with his kisses.

He let instinct take over as he switched to her other thigh and kissed down. Switched again to the other side and slowly nibbled and licked there. All the while he kept his eyes on her.

Watched her wary look become nothing but slumberous heat, that flush to her cheeks intensifying.

He expected her to close her eyes, to arch her neck, to

sink into what he did, and then he realised his Beileag wouldn't do that. She was too curious.

'You're going to watch.'

Not a question. Beileag and her curiosity had got him here. His curiosity now, he lowered his eyes.

Beileag gasped. 'No, wait.'

His eyes snapped back to hers. From one heartbeat to another, she changed before him. Fading were her mesmerising hooded eyes, the beckoning glances. Gone was the flush and her plump lips drawn in.

She'd shifted from wanting his touch to not. She didn't have to say anything at all. He could see and feel it. He released his outstretched hands and pulled up.

Scrambling away, she pushed at her skirts.

'Beileag, what do you need?'

She pushed up on to her knees. 'We shouldn't do this. You shouldn't do this.'

He wanted to argue, to protest. To point to everything that had just occurred to prove to her they should do exactly this. All day, every day. Every moment. That it was right, they were right. Sudden, true, but right.

But her eyes were wide and every emotion in them was something he never wanted to see: shame, anger, disbelief.

He stood and held out his hand. 'We'll never do anything you don't want to.'

She eyed his hand warily and stood without it. 'We're not doing anything at all. Ever.'

He dropped his hand. Was she ashamed at what they did? At what they shared? Just the thought settled a boulder against his chest. Had he done this to her? Not made it as joyous as he thought it was?

At her wary expression, he feared he had. What *had*

he done? She was curious and he'd pushed her as fast and hard as if she were experienced.

He staggered back. 'I am sorry.'

She blanched.

He should have talked more, asked questions of what she wanted. His body cooled to almost ice at the horror of what he'd put her through, he could use words now.

'We won't do that again. I didn't mean for it to go so far. I—'

'No more words,' she bit out.

The words were so bitter, so cold he stepped back even more. Everything in him wanted to pull this woman in his arms and comfort her. Apologise to the end of their days about how much he desired her. What had he been thinking?

A kiss! That was well and glorious enough! To then nip at the cords in her neck, that chin? To clench her skirts in his fists and to see those long legs of hers was greed.

He'd been so sure, though. So certain she was there with him. He'd been delirious with discovering her. But he'd behaved as if they were already betrothed. He needed to tell her, to let her know there would be no other.

'No more words, then.' He stepped back again, wanting to show her that he meant her no harm.

She looked even more alarmed so he stepped back again. He'd leave if he had to.

'No!' she said.

Another step and he stumbled over the unopened chest, fell on his side, his legs kicking the chest over so the contents tumbled out.

Not many things, a few whittled pieces of wood, crudely done. Four people. Two large and two small.

She gaped at the small figurines and cried out. Rushing over she threw them in the chest, and slammed it closed. Clasping it close, she faced him.

Every bit of softness in her expression, even all the confusion, was gone. The only thing left was an anger and something else that wrenched at his heart.

'Go, Hamilton, just go.'

'Beileag, please, we need to talk. I know this is sudden.'

'Sudden!' she said. 'Like...some happenstance, something inconsequential?'

No, like something powerful. He struggled with words. This wasn't something he could repair with some jests and the promise of copious amounts of ale.

Not when she seemed racked with confusion and he felt every bit responsible.

Not when she clenched that chest to her so tightly her knuckles were white.

When he glanced at her, if possible, her fingers tightened even more. Did she think he'd take it from her?

And if he could get the words out correctly, would she hear him?

'You're supposed to be pursuing Murdag,' she said. 'But you kissed me.'

He did, in friendship, something light, but he'd quickly wanted more.

She clenched her eyes, shook her head roughly. 'Then I kissed you as well.'

She'd responded to him. To his realisation of who she was to him. But she didn't understand and he barely understood it himself.

She opened her eyes, speared him with the agony that was in them. 'I'm just as much to blame for this as you are.'

Never that. 'There's nothing to blame.'

'For weeks now you've been pursuing Murdag, coming to me for help to woo my friend. Here I am agreeing to help, mostly to help with Camron and Anna when the time comes…if they need it…and the moment I did… you want me? Who does that?'

No one.

'I can't talk to you any more,' she said.

They weren't talking now. His fault, but he knew he couldn't simply explain the change in his feelings when she stated the facts like this.

He needed more facts. Things to show her, but he had nothing right now.

'And I don't want you coming here again.'

He looked at that chest of figurines she hadn't shown him and didn't want him to see. To the wolf that was down at his feet that he knew he hadn't the right to take, but still felt drawn to.

One kiss was all it was supposed to be. One kiss and he'd gained everything he wanted.

He knew it was right when all the restlessness was gone, but he couldn't show her that.

'I won't come here without your invitation,' he said.

'Then you'll never see it again,' Beileag said. 'We'll never be…alone again.'

Because she didn't trust them alone? That boded well.

'You want Murdag.' Beileag breathed out slowly, 'You'll have to pursue her yourself; I won't help you with her.'

That mattered not when it was Beileag he'd be pursuing.

'And Anna and Camron?'

She looked away, drummed her fingers against the chest she still clutched.

'He made the bet. He means this.'

She turned to him again. 'And you were just being nice agreeing to the bet? I've never known you to lie.'

'That's because I never have,' he forced himself to say through the sudden flash of anger and frustration. But this wasn't about him and his pride, it was about trying to prove to this woman, who somehow knew him better than he knew himself, that he wanted her. No one else. But her expression turned more stubborn and he could feel whatever connection they'd made slipping away.

He looked to the sky, searching for answers, finding nothing, looking to her and only seeing her shut down completely in front of him.

'I'm to blame for this as well, but no more. If Anna and Camron need me, I'll be there as I said I would. And I give you my word, I will tell no one of this bet your brother made. But I will do nothing else.'

He needed her, but he needed to show her and that wasn't happening now. 'Very well.'

Chapter Thirteen

'Oh, when did you get here, Beileag?' her father, Ivor, said.

'Not long ago at all,' she lied. She had waited in the woods until she could no longer hear Hamilton's steps. Then she waited until she felt like carving, or at least hacking at logs. But even after an hour, she didn't trust herself with an adze or an axe or anything sharp with fear to damage it.

So, she cleaned up the surroundings, returning it to the condition where no one would happen across her work. She found some solace in burying her chests, in setting the branches and wet leaves on top until the secret she kept was hidden from any wandering eye.

But her clearing, the dappled sunlight, and bird song didn't soothe her enough, so, with little thought except needing further comfort, Beileag wandered to her father's carpentry mill.

It was a place she'd often gone to when she was younger. This old building was used to house the tools for the clan and to create more artistic furniture pieces during the cold winter. It was crowded with large tables and many stools. Unfinished bits of wood were always about and, if a person wasn't careful, splinters were a constant risk. But it had plenty of light from large doors that opened on opposite sides and the most divine smells of oiled metal, muddied thick sloped floorboards and freshly carved oak.

At this time, and on a sunshine-filled day, she hadn't expected to see anyone inside, let alone her father. After all, his work took him around the village for repairs to houses or building new structures. But he was here, shavings in his greying hair, humming to himself, sitting on a stool next to a table and methodically carving the back of a chair.

'What brings you around?' The light and shadows exposed the deep crags in her father's broad features as his whole body swayed with the even motions of his hands.

Of course her father would want to know what she was doing here, rather than how she was or that he was pleased to see her. If she stayed quiet long enough, he might even forget that she was here. He hadn't even looked up. She didn't know what else to say to him. How could she explain why she was here, when she hardly understood herself? The only explanation was that the doors had been open so she'd entered.

In her eyes, her father had always been larger than life, somewhat apart, but here she was able to fall in the childhood familiarity of watching him. And after a few more breaths, she felt a little more ease after this morning's time with Hamilton.

'I'm here for no reason,' she said. Lying to herself and to her father. She was just full of lies today.

Very well, Hamilton had told her. *Very. Well.* What did that mean? And he'd turned and left as if all that had transpired between them meant very little. Hadn't meant…everything? More than she could expect. One moment she was asking for help finding a husband and the next they'd kissed, they'd touched.

She felt overwhelmed and exactly right, and yet, the moment she wanted to stop, he stopped. The moment she'd told him they couldn't do it again, he'd said...very well. And walked away.

Back to Murdag? She had no right to carry any ache in her chest at that thought. What had happened between them? She couldn't wrap her thoughts around it. Blame him? Blame herself. No blame?

Because that's where she was. That was the overriding feeling, the one she couldn't tame: she had more than liked what they had shared. She could almost feel him, even now.

In a day, she was an utterly different person. She'd taken Hamilton to her secret place, he'd admired her carvings, asked her questions, kissed her and she... hadn't wanted to stop. She'd always had affection for him beyond friendship, but she'd kept that private. A secret. When she mentioned having a husband, it hadn't even occurred to her that it would be him.

It was one day, it shouldn't feel like anything at all despite what they had done and he had feelings for Murdag. She certainly couldn't have feelings for him other than the neutral friendship that they'd always shared.

How could they go back to how they were? Had she even given him a chance to extricate himself? And then when he...when he'd bent her knees and her dress fell and she'd felt the coolness there and the calloused heat of his hands. His eyes gleaming like something from a fevered dream of hers....

She groaned.

Her father's eyes snapped to hers. 'Doesn't seem as if you're here for no reason.'

Over the distance between them, over the large tables laden with wood shavings and cat's tracks, through all the sparkling dust motes, Beileag answered with the only truth she had left in her, 'The doors were open.'

Her father huffed and pointed to his left. 'Right there you stole my burnishing stone.' Her father pointed to his right. 'Over there you pinched my leather strop.' On a half-chuckle, half-chuff, her father carved another long strip along the chair. 'You say the doors are open as if it's no reason, but the stool I'm sitting on is the same stool you sat on when I gave you your first lesson. You don't come here for no reason.'

Her father had never given her a lesson. She had come here countless times and the only words he'd ever shared with her were warnings to get out of the way, to not touch the blade, or that the iron was too hot.

'Are you just going to stare at me, or are you going to steal my new hook knife?' he said.

'I—' she said.

'Father! Father! Come see the size of this rock!' Roddy ran through the door opposite Beileag.

Her father turned around on his stool. 'Ho-ho! That is a mighty rock and what does my son intend to do with such a beauty?'

'I'm going to add it to my collection!'

Racing steps were heard before a thud as someone slammed into the building. Raibert, his hair standing up, dirt all over his clothes and hands muddy, bounded into the hut.

'It's mine!' Raibert charged towards Roddy. 'Give it back.'

Roddy darted around a table. 'I found it!'

'In my collection!' Raibert swiped; Roddy ducked.

'Boys! No!' she cried out. This was nothing new, but

over their heads were saws and blades hanging; under their feet were bits of rough wood which could trip them on to heavy iron bars.

'Tell him to give it back!' Raibert yelled.

'It's mine!' Roddy squealed and ran jaggedly away.

'Roddy, stop it!' Beileag called out. 'You'll hurt your-selves.'

'What is going on in here?' Sian, her mother, stormed in. 'Oh, it's you. You know I can hear all your cater-wauling clear across to the baking ovens?'

The boys went utterly still and her father quiet.

Beileag turned to her mother, facing the familiar scowling disappointment bracketing her mouth. It would do no good telling her mother it hadn't been her mak-ing any such yelling when she was pretty certain she had raised her voice at her brothers.

Her mother pursed her lips. 'Honestly, do you all have nothing better to do than interrupt your father at his work? Out with you!'

Raibert grabbed Roddy's hand and the boys ran out the opposite door behind her father, who had his head down and was carving once again.

That just left her to face her displeased parent. She didn't have any hand to hold, or work to do. She could leave from the opposite door, but it would require navi-gating around all the tables and she wasn't certain she wanted to turn her back on her mother, who'd been known to throw a few things, for so long.

'Why are you still standing around?'

'I thought I could help,' Beileag said.

Her mother sneered, 'With what? There are no shelves around here.'

'She could help with other matters,' Ivor said.

Beileag looked at her father, a tiny bit of warmth

at his words, even though he hadn't looked up, hadn't come any closer and was still carving on the chair.

A tiny glimmer he would defend her and then the horror that, if this went further, her mother would ask how she could help and her father would say something about her woodworking.

'Do you need help, Mother?' Beileag said. 'There's laundry, isn't there?'

Her mother looked to her hands. 'At least you don't have those dirty bandages around your fingers.'

All that time in the woods after Hamilton had left and she'd forgotten to put them on. 'Then it's a good day to clean the clothes.'

Her mother eyed her father, then glanced back at her. 'It is a good enough day when you make yourself useful at least.'

She took the steps towards the door. Her mother pivoted and stomped out and Beileag followed her. She didn't bother looking back to her father. What would she see if she did? Nothing but him working on that chair. He'd spoken up, but what did it mean other than it could have been worse for her?

Her mother suspected she had done carving when she was younger. She'd been a child when she started and hadn't the skill to hide what she was doing. But it wouldn't do if it went further than that. If she followed her into the woods and destroyed what Beileag had created.

She should have kept it a secret. Shouldn't have told Hamilton, for he was one more person who could accidentally reveal what she'd kept hidden for so long. No one to blame on that one except herself. She still didn't know why she'd done it. Some long-forgotten impulsiveness she didn't know she had, or that he drew out of her most likely.

As for the rest...

Why did he kiss her? Why did she greedily push for more when she'd never contrived or bullied for anything? She always kept in the background, never followed her friends on the most egregious tricks. Always did what her mother wanted and took care of her siblings above her own time and needs.

But she followed that kiss and then when it heightened... She needed to make their friendship like it was before. No confusing feelings like now, else she'd suffer when Hamilton pursued Murdag or another woman as he was wont to do. It was Hamilton, after all. He was never without companionship and, with Camron pursuing Anna, he was bound to marry soon afterwards. She needed to remove herself from this day.

She needed to treat Hamilton the way she did her cherished wolf, which had taken her months to carve and polish. The piece of wood she'd found so special, she'd wanted to create something that wasn't something docile like a hedgehog or rabbits, but breathtaking and dangerous.

And that was the creation he had cradled in his hands and looked at so thoroughly it was as though he was trying to see inside. As though he was seeing inside her and he wanted to keep it and treasure it. He'd thought it beautiful...and feral. Dangerous. He'd thought it was running towards prey, but she always imagined it was towards family.

Hamilton had said *That too*, as if family was as important as sustaining food. He saw everything and somehow knew everything about her. Saw her, but she couldn't tell him that because it wasn't her he wanted to see. It was Murdag.

She should have kept the wolf at the bottom of the chest. She should have never shown that deepest secret. It was best wrapped in linen, tied in string, kept in the bottom of a chest, under branches and soggy leaves in a clearing no one knew, all but forgotten.

Just like the other chest and the people there. The one he'd kicked over. How had he kicked it over? How could it have opened? Those little figurines were her first clumsy attempt at carving. She'd never created people again, never tried to. So they were rudimentary carvings. Wishful creations of a family that would never be hers. A husband, children...

Hamilton represented none of those things. She needed to forget the way Hamilton looked at her when she came to her senses and pulled away! He was a friend at most, wasn't he?

Because for one bright incandescent moment, she thought he'd grab her right back, as if, even when reason and thought was back in place, he couldn't help himself. As if she was everything and not just some afterthought or impulse he'd followed when she foolishly pushed for more.

Chapter Fourteen

'Come train with me, Brother.' Camron slapped Hamilton on the shoulder.

A hard slap, one that had him pulling back his fist almost immediately to reciprocate. When he saw his brother *grinning*, he held back. He was glad to see his brother like this once again. However, his brother's obvious happiness made all the darkness he felt even more acute. He really did need to hit something, or run far distances, or swim entire rivers.

Except…he'd done nothing but hike the hills surrounding the village for most of the day, anything to think and try not to think of Beileag. He had to do something. He hadn't had a chance to talk to her all the day for she was never far from her family or she was doing laundry.

The walking through the rolling hills and quiet soothed him, something he wasn't used to, but it wasn't enough. How was he going to win her heart when she knew the worst of him? How impulsive he was to push for Murdag. To tell Beileag of the bet, to tell Camron he'd made the bet and that he'd solicited Beileag's help.

Too many people knew of his intentions, so much so that he couldn't possibly say it was all a farce—it'd gone on too long, too many steps had been taken down the lying path.

For what? Heartache for him.

'Not today, Brother.'

'Not today?' Camron grinned. 'I'm too awake to go to bed.'

'That's where I'm going.' Where he intended to think all night of a way to prove to Beileag what she meant to him.

'No, you're not, you're heading out to the field to join Seoc and the others by the fire.'

That, too. So he could brood as he'd been doing, as his brother had been doing for weeks. Night after night since they'd returned from scouting. Except his brother hadn't been with them last night.

Hamilton scrutinised his twin. 'Your hair's wet.'

'I've been swimming with Anna and her brother all day.'

Hamilton had seen them. Seen how Anna stayed shyly by his brother's side, but he'd assumed it was just more wooing. But his brother was too happy for that.

'And you have dark circles under your eyes.'

Camron flashed a grin. 'I do not.'

'But despite that, you're grinning,' he added. Oh, he could say more, but it would only bring to harsh light that Beileag had informed him he would have no more of her kisses, while it was clear Anna had given no such decree to his brother.

Camron clapped him on the shoulder again. 'Come on, spar with me, I can hardly contain myself.'

Maybe a few hours of training would do him well, for he feared if he was pounded on his shoulder one more time, he'd have no control over what he'd do to his twin.

'Not here, let's head further towards the orchards

and away from mothers and their children. We'll have some audience for when I win, but not too few as to save your pride.'

Camron laughed and Hamilton felt some trouble ease in his heart. His brother was happy! How could he feel so good and terrible at the same time? So happy for his brother, and so miserable for himself. The further they walked, the better he felt about this decision. He needed the distraction of a few good hits from his brother, who would give as good as he got.

'Is this a fine enough location?' Camron roared out.

Hamilton ducked, just missing Camron's first swing.

'This'll do—how's this?' Hamilton charged and slammed into his brother. The bastard held firm.

Within moments, a few men stopped to place bets on them; as was customary, none stopped them.

'If you smile any wider, people are going to think you're me.' Hamilton spit blood off to the side.

'Impossible.' Camron kept his stance wide and his arms out.

Dammit, they were too evenly matched. Swing and duck. Slam and shuffle back.

'Are you playing with me?'

Camron, covered now in sweat and dirt, slicked backed his hair. 'We're both playing, Brother.'

He wasn't. He still needed more. The longer this went on, the more people came and went, and a dark part rose within himself. That part where he wanted to lower his guard and have his brother keep swinging. But the carefree glee on Camron's face belied the fact he didn't train in earnest, only for entertainment.

Camron ducked, but Hamilton's fist made a solid blow against his jaw. His twin stumbled, but didn't fall. He was slower, but still as carefree.

How long were they to be at this until he felt weary in his body and not just his soul? His brother was happy, and had made strides with his Anna. For himself, he feared he was further away from finding true happiness than when he'd made the bet. A bet he'd made! Shouldn't he have had some fortune with it?

And the worst or best of it all—the truth, that he had to come to, blow by blow, feint by feint—was that his brother, the man who was always by his side…might not always be.

They were different. His brother was content and he was not, and if Hamilton could not find a solution, then it would always be so. Perhaps…perhaps, they'd always been different and he'd just ignored it.

In truth, they weren't exactly identical any more. The weather, the years and different scars had changed them. But there were other differences, too. He'd always taken those differences as something inconsequential. He had solidified his world around the truth that they were born the same day from the same family. Therefore, they were the same. But it took this moment, this time, these wants and longings of his to realise…they weren't.

He wondered if some of the restlessness inside him was acknowledging the differences that had come creeping in, one experience at a time. As if he was growing out of his own skin.

Now his brother was earning the chance at a wife and children, a home. While he…still played games.

Damn him for making it on a vow for his brother, but a whim for himself. He'd been still drunk, but that was no excuse. He should have thought!

Camron leapt, struck his jaw and Hamilton swayed until his vision cleared. He was losing his balance, his knees were weakening, so were his arms. He was going to lose this fight, lose his brother, lose... Beileag.

That wolf! How did she make eyes like that from wood that saw into his very soul and made him question his clan, his family, his country and his world? Made him realise he wasn't living the life meant for him, to not be so blind. Why did she rip the blindfold from across his eyes, make him see so clearly, only for him to lose what he so dearly wanted for himself, and for them?

Beileag been right, the wolf hadn't been looking at him as some prey, it was reminding him of the importance of family. Camron finding his wasn't some game that he needed to mimic, but to discover.

On a roar, Hamilton charged.

Camron swerved to avoid him and Hamilton almost stumbled to the ground. When he righted himself, Camron was swaying.

His brother was too tired to knock him out now and he'd done enough damage to his twin's comely face that Anna was certain to be displeased with him on the morrow.

'Enough?' he called out and Camron gave a shaky nod.

By that point, they had no audience for which he was grateful. Bellowing breaths, they collapsed, leaned their backs against two bordering orchard trees and stared out across the damp field.

Long moments when he was so exhausted it was almost peaceful. He could almost pretend that he had his brother back completely and they'd never part. That he'd charm his way into Beileag's heart. That he'd—

'What was that all about?' Camron said, his voice low, gravelly, worn out from the fight.

Everything. Nothing. Too much to talk about and he was too weary to solve. 'You said you wanted to train.'

'I thought we'd have some fun.' Camron rubbed the blood off his lip. 'You hit me and it hurt.'

And he was a bastard to do it. What could he say? He knew what Camron wanted, a few jests, a few swipes and feints. But he didn't. He wanted Camron to hit his jaw, his ribs, punch some reasoning into him, or just make him hurt on the outside as much as he hurt on the inside.

For once, his sensible brother wanted fun and he didn't. Just another bit of evidence that they were different or becoming more so.

'You should have ducked,' Hamilton said. 'Or do you forget who swung first?'

'We should have stopped,' Camron said. 'Or we could do it again?'

He felt exhausted and was close to breaking down and lamenting his haste to pursue Murdag. If he had waited, he might have come to know Beileag naturally this summer time. Or…what was more likely? He might have treated her as he'd always done. Impulsive bet! And yet, it gave him the gift of really seeing Beileag. Of touching her. He knew, with utter certainty, he'd needed the bet at first to talk with Beileag. As if there wasn't enough conflict in his life, he both loathed and rejoiced that bet.

It would be a long night. And no matter how much his brother hit him, it wouldn't help.

'If I thought it would do me any good, I would. But I can't feel my arms now.' He patted his arms on one side, then the other.

'That reminds me of the bet.'

Hamilton let his arms fall flat. 'The bet?'

'You were talking of your arms the morning after I'd made the bet.'

How could Camron remember everything so clearly except the fact he had lied to him? Camron hadn't made the bet. What would he think, what would Beileag think, when they discovered he'd lied?

Camron had already suffered much pursuing that bet and now his own life would never be the same.

Why did he make that bet? It shouldn't have meant anything, something said and then forgotten, and yet if he hadn't made it up, would Camron be this far along with his Anna…would he have found Beileag? He didn't know.

All he was certain of was if he'd told his brother from the beginning that he'd made the bet, it would have been dismissed as a jest. So Camron had to believe he made the bet. He and his brother finding loving families was bigger than some confessions later.

Maybe they'd all laugh about it some day, after they found true happiness.

'It couldn't have been my arms.' He picked up a rock, rolled it in his hand. 'I think we were talking of our legs not moving because of the mead.'

Camron grew quiet, stretched his legs in front of him.

This contemplative Camron was the brother he was used to, not the bounding, grinning one, but it didn't make him feel any better to see this glimmer of his brother. He felt worse because it probably didn't bode well for him. Especially if they talked about that night or the bet.

'You want to talk?'

'You wanted to train and I agreed.' Hamilton tossed the rock. It didn't go very far past his own two feet.

'That wasn't training. What's bothering you?' Camron picked up his own and threw it. It went far past his own rock.

How had his brother any more strength than him? They were supposed to be identical. But they weren't. He needed to remind himself of this. They had similarities, but they were different.

What a realisation to come to now! Was it too late? He shared something with his brother, but they didn't share everything?

Murdag was her own woman and didn't want him and, if he was honest with himself, he'd realised he'd never wanted her. If he had, even a little bit, his response to Beileag would never have been. But the moment she'd touched him, just outside that barn, he'd become aware of her.

That cursed kiss! He could never un-feel her now.

And here he was brooding and his brother noticed everything. Laughing at himself, Hamilton tossed another rock, which went a bit further. 'Sometimes I hate it that we're twins,' he said.

'I forget that we're twins,' Camron said.

'Madness!' Hamilton stretched out his legs and crossed his ankles. 'Not only are you fortunate to look like me, but imagine all the jests we would have lost over the years.'

'Unless I'm staring at my reflection in the water all day like you, I forget you look like me.'

Hamilton picked up another pebble, but didn't throw it. It was cold, round, perfectly smooth. Nothing like the warm wooden creatures Beileag created.

Each creature he'd picked up had been different... but when he'd kicked up that other chest, a whole different side of Beileag was revealed.

Four rough-cut humans. He hadn't been close enough to see what they were, or who. All he could tell was they didn't represent her own family because as tall as her father was, her mother was rather round.

He couldn't stop thinking of who they might be. From her anguished and frantic expression, she didn't want him to know.

He wanted to, very much. He wanted all her secrets. He wanted....

He wanted his brother and Beileag. But he was losing both. Everything was so quick, sudden. Oh, certainly he was always a few steps ahead, but this...this felt untenable. As though the restlessness was taking him somewhere he didn't want to go and his connection to his family, to his childhood friends, was breaking away.

Bending his knees and resting his forearms on each one, Camron said, 'It's because of Anna.'

'What of Anna?' he said.

'She always knows it's me and not you.'

'And because you love her, it's important she can tell the difference.'

Camron nodded, but he did it slowly, his gaze never leaving his as if he was gauging how he'd react.

So his brother knew he didn't like the differences.

'Why didn't you say anything to me before?'

'When haven't I said it?'

Camron's voice was exasperated, fond and sad. He didn't want his brother ever unhappy again.

'You do know it's because of that tapping thing you do against your leg.'

Camron gaped, then laughed. 'Why didn't you ever say anything?'

'What's the point? You only ever do it when you look

at her.' Hamilton rolled another rock in his hand. 'And we all know you wouldn't stop watching her.'

'I could truly murder you right now.'

'Well, get in line. You aren't the only one,' Hamilton said morosely. He truly was bad company this evening.

'Whatever it is, just say it,' Camron said.

Never! What was he to say? Oh, I went after Murdag, but now I want Beileag. His brother would never believe he spoke in truth. Beileag certainly didn't and she knew first-hand how he'd reacted to her.

How she'd reacted to him.

Could he save this? Was it possible to save them? Could he find a solution with the bet still in play?

The moment he said anything about the bet being false, he knew nothing could be saved then. Too many lies, but if his brother found happiness, then him, maybe the lie would be worth it.

But first he needed to find a way to that happiness. All day, he'd come up with nothing.

'I wish this tree we leaned upon had ripe pears,' he tried to jest, but it fell flat and he turned his head away.

He still felt his brother's stare.

'I'm not intending to sit here until autumn, waiting for my answer,' Camron said.

If only he could stay here…at least until he found a solution to wooing Beileag. Because he sure as anything couldn't ask Murdag for her help. Best to talk of happier things.

'I saw you with Anna today. That looks as though it's going well. Any hope for me may be lost.'

Camron kept his gaze on him. Hamilton wished he'd look away if just to give a bit if reprieve. He both wanted to talk and not talk of his folly.

'Wooing Murdag not going so well?'

'Murdag? No, that's fine,' he said.

'Fine? Shouldn't there be passion?'

Hamilton snorted. 'How is my stoic brother talking of passion?'

'How about a kiss, then? Holding hands. Held eyes?'

His brother's amusement at his expense should have vexed him, but the subject was all too acute. That kiss! Her eyes! And he'd held more than her hand. When her skirts fell down her thighs…he thought he'd embarrass himself with his need.

If he hadn't taken things so far with her, he could have continued to use the bet as an excuse to be around her still, to…see what she liked while he completely ignored Murdag or any other woman. To slowly reveal himself and seduce her if she'd have him.

Instead, he'd kissed her, she'd kissed him and nothing was slow. He'd been the one seduced beyond all reason and he didn't want to ever return.

'There's that,' he said slowly, trying to calm his body down. 'And that's the problem.'

Camron hummed under his breath, before looking away and staring out at the fields.

Hamilton wanted to sigh in relief, but he felt none. He knew his brother wanted to talk, and in truth, they often had in the past. What secrets had they ever kept from each other? None. Never. Mostly because he, himself, liked to talk about every problem he'd ever had with his brother. All his life he wanted to share everything.

It wasn't lost on him that he might have been the first not to share when he made the bet and told his brother that he had instigated it, but the bet wasn't all about him. His brother was happy.

'So, it's good then.' Hamilton turned his head. 'You and Anna? You were gone all last night.'

Camron smirked. 'I was with her all today, too.'

'But I'm your brother, so I want details on last night.'

He thought he'd get a laugh from his brother, instead, his brows drew in as if he was troubled.

'What is it?' he said.

'You will tell me what's wrong,' Camron asked. 'It's you we need to talk of.'

Hamilton tried to shrug it off. He'd done nothing but think about it all day and hadn't come up with a solution. Oh, he might be spinning out far beyond what was tenable, but he wasn't going to give up. Just…he wanted a reprieve. Wasn't he to get a bit of reprieve from training, from exhaustion?

'We made a bet and it's all turned out well for you. How could it be wrong when you finally have Anna?'

'I told you; I don't remember making that bet.'

Did his brother curse the bet as well? It couldn't all be bad. If it was…he might never have a chance with Beileag especially when she discovered he'd lied. 'Does it matter if it turned out so well?'

'It is good.'

Hamilton threw the pebble. 'Then all is well, especially if she doesn't find out about the bet.'

'How would she find out? We only told Seoc.' Camron groaned. 'I forgot. You told Beileag, too.'

He'd rue the day on that. 'She won't tell Anna. She promised. But I needed—'

'To gain her help to woo Murdag? You do know it's a meaningless bet?' Camron said. 'You're not taking it as truth?'

He had to. What would Beileag think of him? It had to continue on until at least Camron had Anna and then he'd find a way to woo Beileag instead of Murdag. If Camron told of the bet, he called it off, then the truth could be discovered. He couldn't let that happen. Not yet. 'It can be true.'

Camron gaped at him. 'You think I went after Anna because I made a bet? I'll make it easy for you. You win. The bet's over.'

He couldn't look at his twin. 'But you haven't asked her to marry you yet. The game hasn't even been properly played until you ask and she agrees.'

Camron's brows rose. 'You're spending more time with Beileag than Murdag. Admit it. You only want to keep the bet going because if it's not, there's no excuse to go after what, or who, you truly want.'

He didn't want to talk of this.

Camron shoved him. 'Seoc was right, we are fools and you most of all. Do you think you need a bet to tell Beileag how you feel?'

Hamilton pulled down his tunic. He needed something, but what could he tell his brother without confessing everything they'd already done? He and Beileag had crossed so many boundaries, where did he start? With the barn and the way she felt when she'd stumbled into him? Her dancing with trees and him following her as though she was some fae? He had to avoid all of that… he had to keep lying.

'If we end it…what reason do I have to talk to her? You know how quiet she is. Trying to win the bet gives us a purpose to speak.'

'That is the reason you use? You truly don't deserve her,' Camron said. 'And after all these years, I don't need a bet between us to win Anna. I've had her in my arms. The bet has already been won by me.'

He didn't want the bet for himself either, and there were many other reasons Beileag wouldn't talk to him. Just none he wanted to discuss with his brother.

When he stayed quiet, Camron shook his head and strode out towards the fields instead of to his bed.

He wouldn't return to his home either this night. The pear trees would work well enough for comfort since he wasn't to sleep anyway.

Chapter Fifteen

'Say that again,' Murdag said.

Beileag was horrified that Murdag asked her sister to tell the tale again. It was difficult to listen the first time.

And that had nothing to do with the fact she was exhausted, the sun was just cresting the sky, that Murdag had yanked her from bed with a finger to her lips to stay quiet, or that just outside her home stood Anna, who looked broken and proud. Her back stiff, her chin lifted, her eyes reflecting pools of heartache.

No words between them as she followed Anna to her bedroom and the door was closed. No words, but shared glances while Anna took the bed, Murdag leaned against the wall and she took the only chair.

Then Anna told the tale of how she'd fallen for Camron during their trip to Colquhoun land, her trust and love in him growing while they'd spent the night under the stars and spent the day playing and swimming together. Of being so excited and not able to fall asleep, so she'd walked the pear orchards. And overheard Camron and Hamilton talking of a bet Camron had made to marry her!

Beileag trembled, sweat broke out on her palms and

she clenched her hands tighter and tighter as Anna told her story.

It was as Hamilton had told her, how he'd agreed to the bet with Camron, and Anna was reacting just as she had the first time she'd heard it, with anger and hurt pride, all justified of course—winning Anna's trust shouldn't be a game. It was almost cruel for Camron to come up with the bet.

She never would have believed he had done it either, except that Hamilton told her and now Anna recounted it.

She was still upset Hamilton had agreed to the bet and was only somewhat mollified he hadn't instigated it.

Yet she couldn't deny that Anna and Camron had true feelings for each other. It wasn't supposed to be a game, yet that's all that Anna had overheard.

And Anna, being the prize for this bet, was not only angry, her trust and heart were broken. And her sister wanted her to tell the tale again?

'Why make her repeat it?' Beileag said.

'Why make her repeat it?' Murdag echoed. 'Because I can't wrap my head around it. There's no reason for it and why have you suddenly gone all pale?'

Beileag put her hands to her cheeks. 'I'm not pale. And even if I was maybe I'm just…troubled?'

Murdag scoffed and she didn't blame her. It didn't sound convincing to her own ears. But it wasn't that she lied, it was just she wasn't telling the full worrying truth. Curse Camron for doing this. She wished she had more of Murdag's fire, then she'd speak her thoughts to both of them.

And yet…hadn't she agreed to the bet as well because she promised Hamilton she'd stay quiet about it?

What would Anna and Murdag think if they knew she knew of the bet before them?

'Maybe they meant something else,' Beileag said.

'I was there,' Anna said. 'I heard everything. There's no other way to interpret their conversation. Hamilton and Camron made a bet to marry and whoever got married first won.'

'What would they win?' Murdag asked.

'What would they win? What does it matter!' Anna cried out. 'This isn't a game! They bet on our lives and I...'

Murdag looked at her closely. 'You what?'

Beileag gasped, her hand back to her mouth. 'Oh, Anna....'

'We did more than spend the day together yesterday. The night before, we might have...kissed.'

'You kissed him? What else?'

'Does there need to be anything else?' Anna said.

'You'd tell us if there was, wouldn't you?' Murdag arched her brow.

'There's nothing to tell,' Anna said.

Beileag could understand why Murdag asked. Mostly because they shared most of their thoughts and feelings, but the other was because of Anna's overprotectiveness and Murdag wanted to make a point. This would not end well.

'Anna—' Murdag warned.

'We're not married!' Anna cried out. 'He didn't ask the question and if he asks me today, he'd better like black eyes and a broken nose for an answer.'

'He kissed you, you spent the day together, and then he left you with no words?' Murdag said evenly. Too evenly.

'I returned to my room alone last night,' she whispered. 'And today, you all saw how we were.'

Murdag crossed her arms. 'Why am I feeling as though you're still not sharing everything?'

'Murdag!' Beileag couldn't stand any more. Anna shouldn't have to share any of this. They'd been so close all their lives, had told each other most everything. She and Murdag were there when Anna's trust was broken by Alan of Clan Maclean.

Murdag was obviously angry, believing that Camron was playing a game with her sister, but talking of it all was torturing her!

'Am I supposed to share everything with you now?' Anna looked like she wanted to cry. 'How much shame do you want me to feel?'

'How are we supposed to protect you from betraying males if you don't let us in on the truth?' Murdag said.

Crying out, Beileag slapped her face in her hands to hide. This was terrible and could have all been avoided if she had confessed to Anna and Murdag before this time. Perhaps told it as Hamilton did that it wasn't a game.

But how was she to tell either of them now? She'd lose both of their friendships. She knew better. Her first instinct was that it was wrong, but she held back, was persuaded by Hamilton. He needed to know what was happening!

How could Camron have made such a bet when Anna's trust was so fragile? That liar Alan had harmed Anna in so many ways. Ever since then, she'd been overprotective to a fault of Murdag so Murdag didn't get hurt. She couldn't count how many arguments the two sisters had had since then.

And now…now she had contributed to their discord

and pain. She needed to tell them the truth. But how could she cause Anna more pain?

'I thought we were done with arguing,' Anna said. 'Aren't you cross at all? The bet included you.'

Murdag closed her eyes briefly and sighed. 'I don't want to argue with you either. I don't know why I even—'

'Because I've been saying it myself?' Anna's eyes teared.

Murdag gave a tentative smile. 'Those twins are always making senseless bets. I'm certain if you talked to Camron, it would turn out to be merely a game, or something for fun. At least it explains why Hamilton was always trying to gain my attention.'

Beileag couldn't have heard correctly. 'Still? Is he still gaining your attention?'

Murdag shrugged. 'Not truly, but it was humorous while it lasted.'

'Humorous? This isn't a game!' Slamming her hands in her lap, Beileag pulled herself in. Her friends were looking at her as though she had lost her wits and maybe she had. She hurt for Anna, understood Murdag's anger and she was lying…to them, and to herself.

Because she'd never forget what she and Hamilton had shared in the clearing. She didn't want to forget. Her heart ached even thinking for a moment that Hamilton still shared his time with Murdag.

She was a fool!

'It's not a game to Anna at least,' she added.

'No, it's not,' Anna choked.

'Sister, if I could—' Murdag said.

'I know.' Anna wiped her cheeks.

Beileag twisted the linens around her fingers. Twisted again, but she felt no ease from the familiar habit. She loved her friends and hurt along with them. She should tell them the truth. This wasn't at all what needed to be. Anna and Camron cared for each other. Hamilton said it wasn't a game. At least…at least Anna and Murdag weren't arguing, not truly, but still. She hadn't seen Anna look like this ever. Not even when Alan had almost destroyed her.

Her hearing from Camron like this was worse. No, it wasn't that Anna had merely overheard them, it was that Camron had done something like this at all.

'You didn't hear everything they said, so maybe we have it wrong,' she said. She would tell them the truth. They'd be angry with her for withholding her side of matters, but it was the correct deed to do.

Anna sniffed and shook her head stubbornly.

'I would have gone closer.' Murdag glowered. 'I would have gone right up to his face, slapped it, then had a good laugh about it as they grovelled.'

Anna's expression turned dark. 'I could still harm him.'

Beileag's blood turned to ice. Anna wasn't crying now and that broken look was gone, but what replaced it couldn't be good for anyone.

'Something needs to be done,' Anna continued.

Nothing needed to be done, except people talking or ignoring each other until tempers cooled. 'Why? Can't it just be left alone? Maybe you don't have to see him again.'

'Why aren't you giving me any other suggestions?' Anna frowned. 'You don't believe those two deserve at least some retaliation? Do you also think it's just a game?'

Those were almost the exact words she'd used with Hamilton. But he'd explained it all and, though the reasoning was faulty, Camron's heart was in a good place when he'd made the bet.

Maybe she simply needed to explain it to Murdag and Anna as he did. 'What if this is all a misunderstanding? What if this was meant to be something good? Shouldn't you talk to Camron?'

Beileag could feel Murdag's narrowed gaze on her. They were going to hate her if this didn't get resolved. Surely Anna and Camron could make it work between them and it would turn out the way Hamilton suggested?

Hamilton. Had he still been pursuing Murdag after their time together? The thought of that was like a hook knife to her own heart. And didn't that make her a liar and a fool? She was the one who'd stopped their kisses, said there could be nothing between them. Hamilton was free to pursue Murdag as he originally wanted to before she…pushed him too far.

'Why don't we turn the tables on them?' Anna suggested.

Murdag pushed off the wall. 'Oh… I like this idea.'

'What idea is this?' Beileag said.

'We'll switch the game back on them,' Anna said. 'I'll go after Hamilton while Murdag goes after Camron. It'll be sister betting against brother. We'll make our own bet.'

Hamilton wanted Murdag, while Anna seduced him? All the while she couldn't ignore the feelings she had for him. 'Oh… I don't believe…' Why couldn't she get the words out! 'What if Hamilton—?'

'We already know Hamilton doesn't want Anna or me,' Murdag interrupted. 'He's not even surprising me with that ruse any more.'

So Murdag did suspect Hamilton was flirting with her, but now he wasn't. How could she keep this straight when her own emotions were everywhere at once? Relief and frustration being a few. Shock, however, was quickly taking over. She needed to put a stop to this immediately.

'What if Anna proposes to…to *Hamilton*…and he says yes so that he wins his bet?'

'I'm not going to propose to him!' Anna said scornfully.

'Oh,' Beileag answered, completely relieved. 'Good. You'll just forgive them then?'

Anna's smile twisted. 'We'll just make Hamilton believe I prefer him with words and deeds. They don't have to like it or react. Just know how it feels to be made a fool of.'

This couldn't happen. Beileag looked to Murdag for help, but she was looking as if she relished these tricks.

Camron and Hamilton, who always made bets and challenges, weren't actually in earnest. Anna and Murdag, who never did such things, were now agreeing to do one that was surely meant to hurt Camron's pride and his true feelings.

Where was all this impulsivity coming from? Hamilton she expected it from, but then her and now Anna? Anna hadn't ever done anything like this—now everything was opposite and upside down.

Including her.

She'd always admired Hamilton, but after their time together those feelings were more intense. Which made her a twice-fool because certainly Hamilton didn't reciprocate them even if he'd…kissed her as he did.

She looked from Anna to Murdag, hoping for some clarity with them, but the sisters seemed to be in a private communication with each other, thinking over the possible situations to play their hurtful game.

And her? She just wanted everyone to be true to who they were and to others. She wanted…not these games, but someone who wanted only her. Who'd vow they wanted only her, no one else, and *meant* it. No games.

This wasn't Anna or Murdag.

'Camron hurt you.' Beileag looked from Murdag back to her. 'So you'll hurt him in return? When has that ever been your way, Anna?'

Murdag huffed. 'Maybe that's been her issue. Maybe the men of this place believe they can walk all over her.'

'You don't even know if that's what they intended to do,' Beileag said. 'You haven't talked to Camron or Hamilton yet!'

'Don't you believe I'd prefer a different interpretation?' Anna said. 'All night I've thought about this. When I could think of nothing else, I had to come to you two for help. But you're not making suggestions to make this better, either, and I'm tired of being thought of as someone without any feelings to hurt!'

Beileag strangled her hands. 'What if they did make the bet, but there was an honest reason why?'

Anna's expression turned to dark. 'I. Am. No. Game! Maybe before the… Maclean that might have seemed acceptable, but how could anyone make such a bet knowing what has happened to me? Only a heartless person would do such a thing.'

'Or one who was a fool,' Murdag added.

'Are you defending them?' Anna said.

Murdag put her hands out as if holding her away. 'No, I'm all for retaliating.'

'And you want to do this because of honest reasons. Because they hurt your sister?' Beileag said. 'Or because Hamilton bothered you?'

Murdag shrugged. 'Maybe both? My loyalties lie with my sister either way.'

'Beileag, if they want to have fun at our expense, why can't we do the same?'

Now, now was the time to tell the truth. That Hamilton had come to her for help and she'd agreed because… because Camron wanted Anna and Hamilton wanted Murdag. Hamilton, who'd kissed her.

How was she to explain all that? Especially now with the sisters glaring at her. She'd lose their friendships if she spoke now, but that didn't mean she had to stay quiet forever.

She might not have Murdag's fire and Anna's stubbornness, but she had… What did she have that was any use in this situation?

Camron had made the bet, Hamilton agreed to it. She'd gone along with it. It was a mess! Yet Anna's heart wouldn't be so broken, nor would she be so angry, if she didn't care for Camron. And Murdag wouldn't be so full of revenge if she didn't hurt on behalf of her sister.

The bet was wrong…and good. Or at least, she'd make it that way, no matter what. Because she had fire and stubbornness, too, and as soon as she saw Hamilton, she'd let him know all about it.

Chapter Sixteen

'There you are!' Beileag said.

Almost jumping out of his skin, Hamilton spilt his ale.

'Not again.' Beileag skidded to a stop in front of him.

Hamilton held his breath, waiting, but Beileag rushing in to help him wasn't going to happen again. This wasn't like before, not only because he wasn't choking to death, but there was a part of him wishing he was. When she'd pounded his back, her body brushing against his, her hands reaching...

'Why do you keep lurking around me?' He tried for something humorous to take his mind away from those dangerous thoughts.

'Lurking!'

'Skulking then,' he corrected, barely keeping the amusement out of his voice at her sudden umbrage.

'I'm not skulking either,' She pulled herself up. 'I was searching everywhere for you. Pardon me for becoming a bit—'

'Of devious mischief?' he said.

'Are you implying I'm intentionally scaring you?' Beileag huffed.

Hamilton had no idea what his intention was. This woman surprised him again and was so startlingly appealing. His only defence was humour. By teasing her, even a bit, it took his mind off how her eyes had clouded with wariness when she'd skidded in front of him. Was she thinking of touching him like he was her, but no longer wanted to?

At least now with his insult, that bit of vulnerability in her eyes was gone. Unfortunately for him, she was so beautiful his heart ached.

'I'm not implying, I am revealing you have a bit of mischief in you, Beileag.'

Her eyes narrowed. 'I have no such thing, Hamilton of Clan Graham, and if we had the time to argue I'd make you take it back.'

Ah, she did have a bit of mischief and fire. How had he missed that this quiet woman was his match? That her fire and imagination were just under the surface, burning hot? For days he was racked with the knowledge of how she'd felt in his arms and the fact he might not be able to have her there again.

'Is Camron's face as bad as yours?' she said. 'And are you cradling your arm?'

'How did you know of…?' He trailed off. He wanted to know how she knew of Camron and the training. He didn't want to talk of yesterday. She was here now. 'What are you doing here? And why do we not have time to argue?'

She looked around them, but he knew what she'd find. A few people finishing their work in the fields for the day, boys too contrary to be home and sheep being rounded up by man and dog. No one paid them any heed.

'Why are you hiding out here?' she said.

He swung his cup around. 'I'm out here in the open, drinking my ale.'

'Alone,' she pointed out. 'You never drink alone.'

The fact she knew that heartened him a bit. Maybe he wasn't completely disregarded by her. 'There's always a first time.'

He tilted the cup towards her and took a drink.

'Why?' she whispered.

Which stumped him—he hadn't thought she'd ask any questions at all and how was he to answer that?

He was someone who always forged ahead before thinking matters through and suddenly he was someone who thought and roamed hills all day yesterday and fought with his brother before sleep took him. Who'd woken up this morning, wandered about before he'd entered a garden and was given flirtatious smiles by the love of his brother's life, Anna, and then was almost punched by his brother, again. He'd wanted to talk to Murdag, but when he saw her, he was given scathing looks, so he came out here to hide. It seemed safer.

How was he supposed to tell Beileag any of that? He shrugged.

A father called out for the boys to settle down and they whipped their heads to the commotion.

'We need to talk.' Twirling a linen around her finger, she looked back to him. 'But maybe not here.'

It was an open field, no one was around and it was getting late. This was as safe a spot to talk as any, except she twirled the linen around again and he stood. 'Let's go then.'

'Just like that?'

Did she expect him to deny her anything? If so, they did need to converse and obviously somewhere more private. She kept twirling that linen, so it was a matter of some import and his curiosity was getting the better of him. 'You said we didn't have time to argue.'

Releasing her hands, she turned and immediately set

off towards the woods. This time of day was the worst for going in there. It would be dark soon and under the tree canopy, darker yet.

Hamilton followed Beileag. Of course he followed her. They might be approaching the boulders from a different location, but he knew their direction. His body tightened with every step they took as if that sole time they shared had accustomed him to crave more with her. When they finally reached the tiny clearing, his mind and thoughts and needs were only on the woman in front of him.

'She knows.' Beileag turned to face him.

She. Knows. Murdag's scathing looks today—how did she realise the depth of his feelings for Beileag? He privately kicked himself for wandering the hills, when he should have gone to her with his intentions. 'How does she know? I've told no one.'

'You told me.'

He gaped. He'd tried to tell Beileag after they kissed, after he… He shook himself. It wouldn't do for any conversation if his thoughts only went one way. And there he went again, but then Beileag had just told him she knew of his feelings.

All this time, he'd thought she'd rejected him after she hadn't given him much of an opportunity. That kiss had turned into so much, there weren't enough words. But maybe she'd only needed this time away to come to the same conclusion he had: that they were meant to be together. 'So you know then it's true. You believe me.'

'How can I have any doubt when it's such a misfortune!'

That broke him from his desire. 'Then why bring me here?'

'To talk of it, of course, and come to some agreement on what to do.'

He'd been walking the hills, trying to come to some way to court her, and all this time there was never a chance. 'We don't need to talk of it; what is done is done.'

She took a step back as if what he said was horrific. It was for him, but then he'd be leaving in another month, so maybe a few battles or losses would solve that. Maybe he'd just keep battling against King Edward's campaigns and never come back. That would work well. Then he'd never have to see Beileag marry another.

'What is done is done? What about for love then?' she said. 'That's worth a chance.'

He thought so, but he'd bungled it so thoroughly between them with him being...well...him. Anything else wasn't possible. 'When the love's not reciprocated, and never will be, then why put the other through more heartache? It will only prolong the pain.'

'But that's what I wanted to tell you. She does feel love. She wouldn't be so mad at him if she didn't. So we have to do—'

'What?' His heart stopped, started, pounded. 'You feel love?'

'Me?' She paused.

It was the pause that broke him. Hamilton rubbed the back of his neck and turned away. There was just the barest hint of light now. They could make it back to the village, but not without some difficulty.

'We're talking about Anna and Camron,' she said firmly.

Not talking of her and him and any happiness. He understood that now.

'She loves him,' she continued.

Good for his brother.

'Anna knows about the bet.'

He turned for that. 'Camron wouldn't have said anything.'

Beileag stared at him a bit before she cleared her throat, and said, 'You did.'

'What?'

'You told her,' Beileag said. 'Anna couldn't sleep last night and wasn't near her home when it was turning dark—apparently you and your brother were fighting.'

Hamilton groaned. 'After we trained—'

'Fought,' she interrupted. 'It looks as though you were fighting.'

'Aye. Maybe a bit of that, too,' he said. 'Camron wanted to train and he talked me into it. Afterwards we were exhausted and leaned against the pear trees. We talked.'

'And the bet was mentioned.'

Hamilton nodded. There shouldn't have been anyone out there at that time. They'd thrown rocks towards the fields, but it hadn't occurred to him for anyone to be in the orchards at this time of year.

'How long was she there?' he said.

'How'm I to know that?'

'Does she know about you? Camron and I talked of you, and what you know.'

Beileag gasped. 'How can this be happening? No, she doesn't, or she didn't say at least.'

'Anna could be as devious as you are.'

'Are you jesting at a time like this?'

'What would you expect me to do? When she heard she was a bet, she reacted like you did, didn't she?'

'She reacted with anger because she didn't want to be a game, which means she'd be angry at me as well. She couldn't have heard everything.' Beileag clenched and released her hands. 'Still, if you thought I was cross with you, it's nothing compared to her. Her heart is broken, Hamilton.'

What was he to do, offer advice? He barely knew what to do in the situation he was in.

'And she thinks that she wants to give back as good as she got.'

Hamilton took a step back. 'Oh, that explains the garden when she…'

'She…approached you.'

Hamilton rubbed the back of his neck. 'She did.'

Frowning, Beileag twirled two linens around her fingers.

She seemed troubled. Surely Beileag didn't think when Anna, with hips swaying, approached him that he'd reacted? Anna was more family than anything and a whole herd of women could approach him now and he knew nothing would change for him.

'Camron was there, so nothing happened,'

Her hands fluttered before she stilled them. That had him wondering. It wasn't the first time in all the years he'd seen her do it, but now he watched her and he knew her hands told him stories.

Her hands…told him about *her.*

Those linens, her scars, the ways she clenched or released them. The way she fettered her fingers across his jawline. The way and what she carved. He wanted her hands on him again.

'Beileag—'

'Her heart's broken—what are we going to do?'

'You…' he started to say. 'You still want to help me?'

'I said I would,' she said. 'It's Camron's foolish bet that got him here and he should have told her about it long before they kissed. But he lied and, as a friend, I should let him stay tortured forever for doing so. For making it a game. How could he?'

He had done that to his brother and his love. He'd done it to himself. He was a fool, but telling Beileag now would only make it worse. The bite to her tongue and flash of anger in her eyes told him how much she disapproved.

He worried over what that would do to their future relationship, if he hadn't already destroyed that by telling her he wanted Murdag all while watching her skirts slowly slide down her thighs.

'If there's any consolation, I don't think a bet will be made again.'

Beileag huffed. 'Between you two? I doubt it. But how are we to repair it?'

'My brother won't give up that easily, not after today.' His usually reserved brother had broken in the garden when Anna had approached him. He wondered if even now Anna was looking over her shoulder, wondering when his twin would pounce.

She nodded. 'It's good he'll repair it and I'll do what it takes. Anna loves him and he's a good man.'

His heart burned and shrivelled. He truly was elated for his brother, but what would it take for Beileag to see him as a good man?

'What if my twin proposes something outlandish?' he teased. 'And you don't approve and there might be mischief? Even then you would help?'

Beileag almost smiled. 'What has happened between you two? Camron making bets and causing discord and you hiding away without any people around.'

Hamilton froze.

Beileag's eyes flashed. 'I'm sorry, I didn't mean anything. Just—'

He held up his hand. What she said was too close to the truth. He and his brother had changed. They were different. Had everyone noticed this and it was just he who was blind?

It was Ettrick Forest, the pain of the lost battle and the upcoming wars to be fought. It was the wolf only he saw. The fact he found that wolf again in this very clearing. A place he liked very much because she had brought him here.

'It's fine, Beileag, truly,' he said.

'So we're good with Anna and Camron?' she said. 'And I could help?'

It was dark, almost too dark to see her if they weren't standing so close. Yet still the darkness limited his sight, and he felt as though she was asking him something. 'Did you think I wouldn't want your help?'

'No, that's not it. Why did you think I didn't do it?' she said. 'When I told you Anna knew of the bet, you didn't think I told her.'

He might not know her as well as he wanted, but he knew this. 'I trust you and you said you wouldn't.'

She smiled.

He took a step forward before he could stop himself. 'What about us?'

Her smiled dropped. Damn him for his impulsiveness. Couldn't he have just left them alone? She'd come to him, was talking now and smiled. He needed to build what was between them slowly. But he couldn't do it. She'd brought him here again; that had to mean something.

'We already talked of that,' she said very quietly.

He burned for her. It wasn't everyone who noticed he and Camron were different, but she did. 'Not to my satisfaction.'

'What would satisfy you, then?' she said.

He wanted to sweep her in his arms and kiss her until she lost that pointed look and there was nothing but hazy desire. All that day he'd stayed away from everyone, especially after running into Anna in the garden. But being here with Beileag was better, far better.

What would satisfy him? This, this right here. This grove, the quiet, the absolute privacy of the boulders and the trees around them. The way there were secrets buried there, beautiful ones, ones made of hard work and passion.

Beileag stood before him, a challenge in her eye, her hands at her sides. It was just she standing in her favourite spot as the sun faded to create this misty otherworldly place.

'Why did you bring me here?'

Her brows drew in. 'I told you why we're here. To talk about what needed to be done with Anna and Camron.'

They had done that and it was time to go, except if there was one thing he knew, it was that Beileag liked secrets. And she was keeping one from herself.

He realised that now. Talking of Camron and Anna hadn't taken long at all, and there was plenty of privacy in the field. But they'd taken the long walk here instead. There was more she wanted to know from him and he was all too glad to tell her whatever she wanted.

Thus far, she'd only asked one other important question. The one that had made her smile. She'd asked him why he trusted her. He had, he did, always. He also trusted that she'd brought him here for a purpose, but did she realise it?

'You know that's not true,' he said. 'Come, I'll tell the truth first. You asked what would satisfy me? You in my arms again, here in this clearing.'

She gasped. 'I didn't bring you here for that.'

He raised one brow.

'I thought you trusted me—now I'm a liar?'

'We had privacy enough in the field to talk of Anna and Camron, but you brought me here and I'd like to know why.'

He wished he'd asked that question earlier when there had been more light, but he hadn't realised it until now. Still, he'd take what he had, as long as she was here.

'Come now, Beileag, ask me your question or show me what would satisfy you.'

Chapter Seventeen

Was Hamilton right? Had she brought him to her clearing for reasons other than to talk of Anna and Camron? Instinctively, she wanted to argue with him, or perhaps pivot on her heels and leave him to find his own way back.

But it was precisely these rash denials giving her pause. She wasn't used to these strong emotions occurring and changing so frequently around Hamilton.

Oh, certainly she'd felt emotions in her life, but she was always able to let them go. Her family practically demanded that ability. Now, however, everything in her felt tight and out of control, no matter how much she twirled the linens around her fingers, clenched her hands, or breathed in the scent of her woods.

It wasn't only the strength, it was the suddenness of the conflicting emotions. As if they were there all along and merely waiting for her to take notice. Attraction, guardedness, anticipation, wariness. How did Hamilton fit in with all this? She'd longed for someone for so long, she didn't know how to let go of that longing. As a child, she'd tried to carve a family, some little wooden figures she could play with. That was the life she wanted, that was the family she wanted, yet she'd brought Hamilton to this clearing.

Had she brought him here for something else? They were done talking of his brother and her friend, they could leave, but she didn't feel that, whatever this was, was settled between them.

She couldn't forget what they'd shared, what they shouldn't have done. He had wanted Murdag and then kissed her, and she had responded. Yet when she'd stopped it, he had agreed. Easily. She had been lying there, reeling, and he'd withdrawn. She shouldn't feel any emotions towards him after one brief encounter, yet she felt too much.

Releasing her hands at her sides, Beileag walked around the little clearing. There wasn't much space. She'd never needed it before when she'd sat for hours with her sticks and tools, but she wanted it now.

'I wish I knew what you were thinking,' Hamilton said.

That stopped her. 'You keep asking me that question as though you care.'

'I do.' Hamilton dipped his head. 'You've only shown me a glimpse and, every time you show me some facet of yourself, I want to know more.'

The urgency in his voice was demanding, his words were almost pleading. But his expression...

Everything in his expression said he told the truth. He wanted to know what she thought.

'I might have brought you here for other purposes.' At the gleam in his eye, she continued, 'However, I don't know exactly what it is.'

He took a step closer to her. 'Then we'll explore whatever that is.'

He had made clear to her what he wanted: to hold

her again. That was certainly one of her wants, but not all. 'I am unsure.'

'You brought me here, why be wary of it?'

Exactly! Her conflicting emotions were obvious to Hamilton as well. 'Because no one has ever wanted me to talk this much.'

'You have friends.'

'And we talk.' How did she say this without making her dearest friends sound uncaring? They'd spent their whole lives together, but didn't share common interests. And because she was quieter, she tended to listen more than divulge any of her activities. There were times she wished she could share her troubles with them, but Anna... Anna had part of her broken and Murdag shrugged all troubles away with a hard horse ride. They weren't the same. Still, they were her friends.

'They don't ask because they already know me,' she said, although, her friends might have trouble understanding her now. Was that why she'd told them nothing of her time with Hamilton?

That heated light dimmed in his eyes. Somehow, she'd hurt him with her careful words. 'We should have talked more. It's why I followed you here.'

Did his wanting to talk mean he had feelings for her? Not merely ones in the heat of the moment when she'd said she wanted a husband and she'd just knotted, burled, herself all over him, but *true* feelings.

How could he when she felt like a burl? Twisted, someone deformed because she didn't fit with the rest of the tree or her clan. And she felt ugly. Unless you carved into them, burls were ugly.

'What about Murdag?' she said.

'I loathe the fact I ever gave you pause to doubt me.

Yet I don't think any of this would have started between us if I hadn't approached you because of the bet.'

Did she dare hope that what Hamilton felt wasn't some impulsive act? She was tall and not graceful. She had scars on her hand and was quiet. She wasn't bold like Murdag or beautiful like Anna. Yet he had sat with her on the log and talked to her about her craft as though he'd wanted to know.

'But you wanted Murdag. It was she who came to your mind, not me.' She was aware she sounded stubborn and vulnerable, and she twisted the lone linen around her finger.

He eyed her hands. What was he thinking? It was difficult to see him in the dark, but they'd stayed in the centre of the clearing and moonlight surrounded them. The sounds of the village were quiet now and, if she stayed still, she could hear the river.

'We're here to talk secrets, aren't we?' he said.

He asked slowly as if he was reluctant to share and she couldn't blame him. 'It's too private for me to ask. I'm sorry, I—'

'Wait.' He grabbed her wrist. 'It has to do with Camron.'

Halted by the warmth and the surety of his touch, Beileag searched Hamilton's eyes. The light was too dim to see his features clearly, so it was the depth of his voice, his calloused fingers wrapped securely around her which captured her attention. She didn't understand his words at all.

'I'm sorry. What do you—?'

'The night we all returned,' he continued, 'Murdag was there, standing next to a fire. I mentioned her to Camron.'

'So he told you he wanted a bet to marry Anna and you to marry Murdag.'

'No,' Hamilton said with some force softened by a frustrated growl. 'I mean…she was there that night, but that's not why I chose her.'

It was kind of him to not mention details; she didn't need to know the reasons. One of which was obvious: Murdag had been beautiful with the fire behind her. 'I was there that night. I understand.'

Hamilton drifted his finger over her pulse before he released her. She instantly felt the cool breeze around her limb and cupped her own hand there to keep the warmth.

'Can we sit?' he said.

It would put them under the canopy with even less light. His voice was already taking on some dangerous intimacy she'd never realised before. 'Do we need to? You wanted Murdag as you should, so you told him you wanted her.'

'Sit with me, Beileag. It is not an easy matter to tell and one I did not realise myself until recently.'

Did she dare? Hamilton was asking. Further, she had brought him here—the least she could do was listen to all he had to say. But the more time spent here with him made acute everything they shared. There were no distractions, no carvings, no wind brushing against trees to watch them sway. There was only him and she felt the connection between them tightening.

'Please,' he said.

When she nodded, he strode to the log they'd sat on before and he again made space for her. All as if he'd done it dozens of times and, even in the dark, he knew where it was. For one bright moment, she thought to mention bringing another log here for next time, but would he ever want to return?

It felt too comfortable to sit down next to him, but if he didn't return, what would this place mean for her anymore?

He made to reach for her hand again, but she pulled away, and he released a breath. 'Camron is my twin brother but I am not his.'

'What?'

'All my life, I have rejoiced in having a twin brother.'

'That was apparent every time you two switched identities,' she said.

He gave a small smile. 'But he hasn't felt the same for me.'

There was no affection between them? 'I can't see that. Camron loves you.'

Leaning forward, Hamilton rested his elbows on his knees. 'I am the worst at words. You'll need to recognise this or I fear there'll be much miscommunication in our future.'

Would they have one? The way they sat, Hamilton pressed his thigh against hers. She might not have taken his hand, but she felt him none the less. Was his touch why she'd brought him here, or for more words between them? If there was this much conflict within her, they would have poor communication. She wasn't used to all this talking! 'Or maybe I am the worst at understanding.'

'I've watched you with others. You are the best of listeners.' Hamilton stopped. 'Did I say something wrong?'

Everything. She was good at listening, but not at talking or being heard, but this wasn't about her. 'No, please go on.'

He waited a beat as if to argue before he said, 'Camron does love me, as I him. But I am the twin who appreciates our sameness. Who revels in it and thinks that is how it should always be. So with Camron fully pursuing Anna, I wanted to pursue Murdag. A brother with a brother. A sister with a sister.'

That sounded callous and uncaring. It wasn't as terrible as making the bet itself, which absolutely played a game with people's lives. However, Hamilton's reasoning for choosing Murdag didn't sound as if it had anything to do with her beauty or her boldness, or anything to do with the woman, her thoughts and feelings, at all. Hamilton's decision had only to do with her being a sister to Anna.

However good Hamilton was at mischief, he was never cruel, but she was missing something. 'You agreed to the bet and chose Murdag because you loved Camron and your life as his brother.'

'Foolish, I know,' he said.

Something eased inside her, but not as much as she wanted. She wasn't sure, but in his pursuit to stay the same with this brother, did he understand it was wrong to not take Murdag's feelings into account? The bet wasn't his, it was Camron's. Maybe he had made a quick decision on Murdag when his brother put him on the spot. Maybe he'd been thinking of only his brother.

She already knew if anyone else had told her this, she would have immediately got cross and walked away, but Hamilton was trying. 'Why? You'll always be his brother and you are identical. Many people still have difficulty telling you apart.'

Hamilton laughed low and bitter. 'Because I never wanted to be parted from Camron. I wanted to keep us

the same. I didn't want us to be different because then...
we wouldn't be twins.'

She was missing something to this; maybe this wasn't
about appearance. 'Why would you force the matter to
remain the same?'

A slight hitch to his breath and movement, as if she'd
surprised him, before he shrugged. 'It matters not why
I forced the matter. Murdag is more like a sister to me
and that is not what Anna is to Camron. There was a
difference between us from the beginning; I was blind
to that, too.'

He was avoiding her question; she was certain of it.
He still sat before her, still glanced around.

This talking was difficult. Complication was never
something she would have guessed with Hamilton and
his easy smiles. She...liked it. Liked that he was choosing to talk to her.

But she felt as though he was refusing to tell her
why he needed that connection. And now he mentioned
Murdag, but it wasn't about Murdag, but Murdag in con-
text of the differences for his brother. It was as though
he still wasn't taking into his reasoning Murdag's feelings at all. But she could be wrong.

It was just...she felt as if there was more to his rea-
sonings. As if he was leaving something out. Such as
why he wanted the connection with his brother so badly.
But she did understand part of it.

'It's not terrible to be different,' she said.

He angled his body towards her. 'You don't sound
convincing.'

She probably didn't. After all, her mother continually told her how her height compared to everyone else's
was a detriment. 'I want to believe being different is
not terrible.'

'Me, too.' Hamilton huffed. 'Because if I wasn't so blind to Camron and my differences and appreciated them, I wouldn't have mentioned Murdag and a bet, and you wouldn't have my doubts about you.'

Beileag didn't know what to say. Was it true? He looked as if he meant what he said, but was it enough? And he still didn't explain to her fragile heart why he saw her any differently than he had all the other years she'd been around.

'You wanted help with Murdag, so I asked you to find me a husband,' she said. 'Then you kissed me.'

'Because I wanted to. Because I still want to,' he said. 'I should have fully realised, no… I should have told you I realised before I'd kissed you, I wanted only you.'

'How did you know?'

'Because I wanted it too much,' he said. 'Though I thought it could be a kiss shared by friends, it wasn't simple for me, but I was blind to that difference as well.'

She'd felt that same strong connection, but she should have been a better friend. 'I returned your kiss.'

'A thousand-fold. It was my joy and undoing,' he said. 'And not enough. I feel as though I haven't seen you. Not all of you.'

Kisses. His touch. The way he looked down at her, his hair tangled across his jaw. The width of his shoulders and the way his calloused hands caressed her legs. Would she ever stop wanting more from that day, wanting him? 'You came close to seeing me.'

'That's not what I meant.' His mouth curved and he lowered his voice. 'Although that was nice.'

She wanted to tease him as well, but he hinted he wanted to see her, to know her, which was all too close to what she'd longed for all her life. It was more than her heart could handle now. She had brought him here for privacy to talk of Anna and Camron, but it was also to talk more about themselves. She could admit that to herself without too many contradicting emotions.

But they were strong emotions, these wants and desires for him.

'Why do you cover and uncover your fingers?' Hamilton pointed to her hands.

Beileag looked down to where she was twisting the linens around her fingers. 'Something I do, I suppose.'

'It's never the same finger or thumb, sometimes in the very same day,' he prompted. 'Let me be a listener.'

He'd noticed how often she wrapped her hands. Maybe she should tell him the reasons—after all, he'd shared some truth about himself and it couldn't be easy especially since his rush for Murdag could hurt so many people. He hadn't made the bet, had agreed to it for connection to his brother. He did say it was a foolish idea. Had he mended his ways to not rush into a relationship with her?

He was asking about her feelings and seemed as though he wanted to know about her. Was she so gluttonous for attention she would let her questions about Murdag and Anna go for now? The flutter in her chest answered that question. She wanted to talk about the linens; she wanted that chance to be *seen*.

Closing her eyes, she turned her head away from the man sitting next to her. It seemed best since Hamilton's listening was to gaze intensely at her and, this close, she felt the entire weight of that stare.

'My mother never approved of my going into my father's mill,' she said. 'I suppose she wanted me to do the softer things. Woodworking, of any kind, would not be something a woman would do. Unfortunately, in the beginning I wasn't very skilled at carving and I

had to wrap my many injuries. Those linens were noticeable to my mother.

'I could keep the other things hidden, me being in my
father's carpentry mill, or trying to find a secret spot to
continue my whittling, but I couldn't hide the cuts on
my hands. We had many fights. She already had difficulty with me, but my need to make little creatures was
something she thought she could fix, since the rest of
me was…unfixable. Eventually I had to make up stories of why I was wearing them.'

Hamilton grew quiet. Why did she tell him so much?
Now he would ask about her height and—

'By any chance did you tell her you were wearing
them as rings?' he said. 'You put them on when you
aren't wounded.'

'How did you—?' Giving a startled laugh, she turned
to him. 'That was one of the reasons until they became
a habit. I don't know what it would feel like without
them.'

'What were other reasons?'

She nodded. 'I was hoping she'd believe, because I
was still nicking myself, I wasn't practising the craft
often; therefore, I could find a husband.'

She truly was terrible at talking. Beileag twisted the
lone linen again before she stretched her fingers and
looked away from Hamilton's gaze. Did he think now
she wanted lessons on finding a husband because her
mother wanted her to have one? It couldn't be further
from the truth. Worse, he probably thought she meant
him for a husband. Maybe she didn't talk often because
she was terrible at communication.

'You take comfort in them,' he added softly.

She looked down at the twisted band and then to
him again. 'I do.'

For the longest of beats, they just looked at each other. The connection between them was not filled with tension, but with something light and warm. It was dark under the tree's canopy and the log was damp. But they sat so very close that she didn't feel the coolness of the evening, or unyielding bark of the log, she just felt... Hamilton.

As they sat, they were almost the same height, there was no wind, so his brown hair fell naturally around his face. She'd never seen him care about his appearance, or others' opinions. Everything he took in with a natural ease. She envied that about him. What it would be like to think as Hamilton did? To simply step in front of life and it would all work out.

Except it wasn't all easy for him. He struggled to find his footing with his brother. She felt this unbearable need to touch him again, as if to study that bit of him she hadn't seen before. She recognised that feeling was the same as when she picked up a new piece of sanded wood.

'Did you cut yourself when you made that wolf?' he said.

They had been bouncing from one conversation to another since they'd come to the clearing as if, though they'd spent a lifetime together, they had too much to talk about.

Yet still, him mentioning the wolf took her by surprise. Because the question didn't roll easily off his tongue as if it was some mere quip. He asked as if it held some import for him.

'Never. I didn't start carving the wolf until I had learnt my craft as much as I possibly could,' she said. 'But it was more than that.'

He tilted his head. 'Tell me.'

'I don't know, everything I did with it came out as I saw it. As though it was meant to be.'

After a weighted pause, he said, 'I'm glad the wolf didn't harm you, Beileag.'

It was fully dark now. Travelling back to the village would be cumbersome, but not undoable. Yet she still wasn't done here with him. Not when he looked at her with those soft eyes, as if it was significant that she hadn't harmed herself.

Did this mean his feelings were true and not simply because she was convenient before he left? She didn't know, but she hoped. 'What are you thinking, Hamilton?'

His brows drew down as if what she said pained him. 'For you, for me. For any future we have.'

Without thought her fingertips were at his jaw again and she both heard and felt his breath hitch.

'Beileag, you keep touching me like this and I don't know what it means.'

She wanted to say something flippant, as though she didn't know either, but she was beginning to feel she did when she felt the whisper of his words against her palm.

When she could feel him, he was truer to her. This close that unique bright parsley and earthy ale scent of him was more acute, as was the rough texture of his stubble and the soft heat of his skin underneath. Because she could feel him, he was *here*.

'How do you keep doing this to me?' he murmured.

She wasn't doing anything to him. It was he who was changing her. 'It's all that skulking.'

'What?'

'I like to see you jump,' she whispered. 'You always seem so assured. It's rather funny.'

Hamilton laughed under his breath and she felt his

delight on the palm of her hand as she continued exploring his jaw.

He swallowed hard. 'You're not…you don't intend to carve me one day, do you?'

'I couldn't capture you.'

His brows drew in as though her words pained him. Hamilton clasped her wrist. 'Here, let me.'

Bowing his head, he cradled her hands in his to roll off the one tiny linen she had tied around a finger. It had been twisted so much around it was barely visible. But he niggled the scrap from the base of her finger, over her knuckle and to the tip until her hand was unadorned completely.

He took the finger next to that and made the same sure caress up to the tip before he descended on another. Each time, his thumb brushed across her palm. Then another, each careful caress become slower and slower.

'These hands, Beileag,' he said, his voice like gravel scraped over oak. 'These hands have created the most beautiful creatures.'

Another press of his fingers around the base of hers, another swipe of his thumb, this time a gentle pressure as if to anchor him there. He slid his fingers up so slowly, she felt as if part of her heart was being pulled along with him.

A twirl of the tip of his finger against hers and his exhale came out roughly. She had no idea if she was breathing at all. She didn't need to, for watching Hamilton do so was more important. Great deep steady breaths expanding his chest, presses of his thigh against hers. She could almost feel his breath in his touch, the life-giving warmth, the almost imperceptible movement of his fingers flowing with each bit of air. In. Out. She parted her lips to feel the cool air enter her own body in the same rhythm as his. What was he doing to her?

'But as beautiful as those figurines are, they aren't nearly as wonderous as these hands that created them.' He dotted his caress along. 'This scar, this nick. This callous, this part right here so soft it makes me ache to touch you elsewhere.'

She felt as though he was already touching her everywhere. How did they become so close? Her hands were no longer over his lap, but almost over hers. She bowed her head to watch what he did, and his head almost touched hers.

'I adore your hands, would worship them if you'd let me,' he said with another firm clasp and a brushing caress. 'When you primly clasp them in front of you, it drives me mad; when you clench them, I want to ease your frustrations with soft tender kisses against those fingers, your palm, the inside of your wrist.'

One more finger, one more caress. That's all he had left; surely that was all he had left? Because she wasn't certain she could take anymore.

'But these little ties that start off so innocent, so protective until you wind them tight— What I want to do with those,' he rumbled. 'Ask me what I want to do.'

Already taut with anticipation and desire, she didn't dare. Not when he circled her finger, but didn't move at all. Was he going to tease her to answer his question? When she raised her gaze, his eyes were roving over her own features, cataloguing how he affected her. If there was any light, he'd see the tell-tale flush to her cheeks, the throbbing of her pulse, but he'd changed as well.

Gone was the soft brown of his eyes. They were darker, more heated, the natural waves of his hair had fallen over his cheeks, his jaw, curtained over one eye.

If he hadn't clasped both her hands, she would brush it away. No, she wanted to card her fingers to feel every strand and texture against her own hands that he'd heightened with some need she never knew of before.

How had her hands, her fingertips, become so sensitive?

'What have you done to my hands?' she whispered. They practically throbbed with an aching heat that echoed in the rest of her.

A knowing smile curved his lips. 'I suspect it is something like what you have done to my jaw, and cheek, my chest when you crashed into me by the barn, my arm when you brushed across it, my leg that you are pressed against now. The fact is, I know I'm holding your hands, but I'm incapable of letting you go. Whatever this is, it's being done now.'

She was hot all over, yielding with some need, she knew what it was called—was it the same for him? 'Want,' she whispered.

'Do you?' he said. 'Do you want this? Want me?'

His voice in the dark, the way he cradled her hands and leaned towards her. They were close, it wouldn't take much to kiss again, but he held still, waiting for her answer.

She wanted this man, and with his words, and the way he talked to her, it seemed as if he wanted her, too. Was it enough?

It felt like it was enough. 'Can I kiss you?'

Chapter Eighteen

Helpless not to, Hamilton dropped his gaze to her mouth. Did he want her to kiss him? More than anything. No, he wanted her to love him.

Because that's how he felt. This was love, for the first time in his life, and he knew it with a few touches, a few conversations. Unusual, but not for him. Was this here enough for her? Because if he did kiss her, he wouldn't want to stop. Not with wanting forever, marriage, family, children, everything from her, pounding through his veins.

Not when lust already rode him hard simply because he was here and she'd allowed him to hold her hands under the darkened canopy of her trees. Holding hands! As if what they did was anything that simple. If she let him, he would brush his fingertips and worship her body in the same way.

But she'd asked for a kiss.

'Always,' he said. 'Always you can kiss me.'

'What if… What if what happened before happens again?' Her tongue darted along her bottom lip.

What would he do with that tongue or to feel the plushness of her lips? 'Hear me on this—if that happens again I will more than welcome it.'

'It felt, we felt, so burled,' she said.

Hamilton relished that slight breathlessness in her voice. It was the only indication that whatever this was between them was becoming more. 'Burled?'

'It's when a tree has an overlapping growth—' she said. 'On top of each other. Interlocked.'

He thought he was only seduced by her touch, but her woodworking terms were as sneaky as she was and made his need all the worse.

'If you want,' Hamilton rasped. 'I would do anything to be with you. Burled, interlocked…touch me, Beileag.'

Testing him, she rested her hands on his shoulders. One, then the other, and he slowly turned his body so their knees and legs brushed. He felt every one of her fingers flexing against his muscles along his collarbone. 'Keep going.'

'This time seems harder,' she said.

Hamilton clenched his eyes and gave a little chuckle. 'That's because you know if this starts, there won't be an end.'

'I don't know where this is going.'

Anticipation flaring inside him, he said, 'Exactly where you and I want to be.'

Her gaze dropped back to his lips. 'Didn't you just kiss me before? That started everything.'

Hamilton groaned. 'We stopped last time; I don't want to stop again.'

Giving a cautious nod, she slid and curled her hands at the nape of his neck. He felt her cool fingers slide against his heated skin. 'It has to come from you. You can simply do what feels right.'

'I am.'

When she brushed her fingers along his skin again, he shivered and was rewarded with a slight curve to her lips.

'Oh, you like that, do you?' he said.

She trailed her fingertip along his tunic's collar. Every hair on his body raised and her smile widened. Her arms constricted as if she was just holding back from pulling him closer.

He wanted her to pull him close.

Unable to stop from touching her any longer, Hamilton gripped her hips. 'Just do anything. I promise you, I want it. Dance with me, Beileag.'

'Dance?'

'Like you do with the trees.'

A faint hue flushed her neck and cheeks. 'Oh, I didn't walk that way to—'

'Seduce a man. Well, you did.'

'But I'm tall,' she said.

'I know.' He groaned. Since the last time they'd touched, he'd dreamed of her long limbs wrapped around him and what it would feel like with her ankles crossed around his waist. Her height only gave him more of her to touch, to kiss, to discover.

She licked her lips. 'Will that be a concern because you can't enfold me in your arms and—?'

Never. He roamed his hands up the curve of her back and down again. 'Been thinking about this, have you?'

Another nod. Her hesitancy and the vulnerability in her eyes wouldn't do at all.

'Here, let me.' Hamilton lifted her off the log and placed her on his lap. Widening his legs, he adjusted her until her skirts layered around them, her legs straddled his hips and her elbows rested on his chest.

'Like this, you're a bit taller than me,' he said. 'But that is so I can take advantage.'

'How so?' she said.

'Like this.' He ran his lips and teeth along her neck.

Ended with a soft kiss right under her ear. Feeling her skin gooseflesh, he did it again.

Beileag gasped. 'That is taking advantage.'

'Perhaps.' He smiled against her skin. The only way this could be better was if there were no clothes between them. Another kiss, the tiniest of nips, a swipe of his tongue. Beileag arched her neck, giving him more access, and Hamilton hummed in approval. He kissed along the perfect lines of her neck to her slightly parted lips, then sucked lightly on her lower lip.

Pulling back, he asked, 'Like that?'

Eyes eager, she nodded.

He could feel the pulse at the base of his throat increase, the slight shaking of his hands. He wouldn't make it through this. 'What else do you want?'

'Something. Everything.'

He, too, wanted something: her. And everything: her. He cleared his throat, which felt as though he had swallowed gravel. 'Then that's what we'll do. Hips up.'

Slowing his breaths, he hastily untied her gown, pushing it up and over her head. Was rewarded with her large chemise crumpling to the side, baring one shoulder. Her tempting breasts rose and fell so sweetly under the thin linen.

Grinning, he fisted his tunic and ripped it off. Rewarded again when she laid her hands on his chest and he felt her calloused fingertips against his skin. All the better for she was looking at him as if she couldn't take his features in enough, as if she was thinking of creating him with those hands of hers, as if he was someone special.

'What's going on in that mind of yours?' he whispered.

'I can feel your heartbeat. Your skin feels warm, these

hairs scattered here…' She splayed her fingers and ran her hands up. 'Those are different.'

He felt different, as if he was on the cusp of a desire he'd never dreamed about, and he tightened his grip on her only piece of clothing in case she allowed him to rip it off her or didn't want to go any further.

'What else do you feel?'

Keeping her eyes lowered, she palmed over his shoulders, down his arm until her hands cupped over his hands which still gripped. 'I want to feel what other textures you have.'

Tugging her closer, he kissed her again, kissed her deeply, gripped the flare of her hip and reverently cupped one of her breasts. Felt the weight of it through the fabric, thumbed over the taut nipple and captured her gasp.

More kisses along her collarbone, her thighs relaxing around him, pressing her heated mons against his thigh. Her breasts, nipples stiffening, pressed against his chest. 'Hamilton?'

Her uttering his name made him shudder.

'I feel warm, but the air is cold,' she said. 'I want… more.'

He pulled back to take in that amber gaze of hers. When she nodded, he tucked his fingers underneath her chemise and gave a tug till it fell, held on the tip of her breasts before it dropped and pooled around her waist.

Her breasts were perfect. Small, round, heavy on the bottom and tipped a colour of rose he wished he could see in the daylight.

'What surprises you have been hiding from me,' he said.

'Surprises?' she said. Her eyes were wide, taking in his reaction. What did she see, what did she feel? She was over his lap and surely must feel what she was doing to him.

'Your beauty should never be covered,' he said.

She laughed, gulped. 'Never?'

'Never in my presence, always before others.' He'd go mad if any other saw her this way.

'But my height,' she protested.

He pressed a hard kiss against her lips, felt her breasts' tips slide across his chest and they both moaned. 'Don't remind me of your height again, Beileag, or this will be over before it starts.'

'You find me beautiful?' she said as if she had doubts.

'Stunning,' he said against her lips, feeling those soft mounds against his own hard chest, her palms pressing into his shoulders, her heated core through a scrap of her chemise and his woollen breeches.

If he could stay like this, a moment in time, he would. But his blood was heating to some unknown height and he swore he could feel her damp desire through heavy wool. What he would do to taste her there.

'You say you could not capture me, but know that I feel captured.' With the softest of caresses that his hands were ever capable of, he cupped each breast, felt the weight of them in his palm, rubbed his thumbs over the peaks.

This time, without her chemise, her reaction came on a sharp gasp.

He wanted to pleasure her, needed to. Holding her like this, feeling her like this, every bit of the restlessness in him was gone. He was home, exactly where he wanted to always be.

'More?' he asked.

Her eyes were half-mast, her lips parted. She rubbed

her hands down the length of his chest. Down the thin line of hair that disappeared under his belt. 'More.'

At her single word, his body jerked in response. On a sharper gasp, her gaze dropped between them. Even in the dark, she had to feel and see the hard bulge against his breeches.

'I'm about to break in two, Beileag. When you say more…'

She dropped her hand and cupped him there, and he gave a low growl. 'Then feel me. Capture me.'

She did. Caressing with her fingertips, exploring him from the tip down to the base of him where she straddled him, then back up to trail the back of her finger along his stomach, around his chest, then flattened her palms and down again.

This time, he knew it wasn't his imagination when she grew more damp. His eyes holding hers, he slid off his belt, thumbed loose the folds at his waist until his breeches fell open.

When her eyes roamed over him as though she couldn't get enough, when she didn't remove her hands from the hard muscles along his stomach, he yanked the scrap of her chemise still between them, ran a hand up her back, another at her hips and rocked her damp softness against him.

Pleasure. So much of it. Enough for him. Enough for her to love him? He needed her to love him. On a hard gasping pant, he rocked her again and she gave a tentative canting of her own hips.

'More,' she said. 'Something's happening.'

'Then move, Beileag, like you do with your trees in the sunlight.'

He felt her flutter against his erection, pressed her

firmly against him. Until on a breath of her own, she pressed herself against him again and again.

'My good skulking lass,' he said with every bit of reverence. Would her surprises never cease?

Bowing his head, he pressed his kisses against each breast, flicked his tongue around the sweet pebbling and bit gently before sucking that tender nipple.

Her hips canted and she gave the most delicious cry. 'Again.'

He did. He'd never get enough of the taste of her or the feel of her soft peaks throbbing against his tongue.

His kisses became rougher as he, too, wanted more and again. He tried and failed to be careful, to not scrape his stubble across her delicate skin. The man in him revelled in the marked pink he left behind. With her, like this, nothing of anything he'd shared in the past compared. Nothing.

'Understand me, I want this different,' he vowed.

Her eyes opened to his. A moment, a breath, and she arched her back, her breasts undulating with her movements, so mesmerising, he lost his peripheral vision until he realised he needed to garner another breath.

Beileag rocking her hips against him, grinding, the scent of her arousal surrounding them. 'Hamilton,' she gasped.

'Let go,' he growled. 'For me, let go.'

On a keening cry, a bite and kiss along his jaw, his neck, Beileag surrendered to her pleasure.

Locking himself against her, Hamilton gripped her hips until her breaths evened.

Everything inside him, everything he was, eased and tightened at the sight of her desire. She wanted this, wanted him. Still he asked her, 'There's more, Beileag. I want you, but you need to give me an answer.'

'Everything.' She kissed and whispered against his damp heated skin. Her hands once again caressing, discovering.

Unsated, he felt something feral rise up to meet her soft touches. His chest expanded, not with his breath, but his heart, his soul, with possessiveness. He wanted all of her, every bit, he didn't want to share her even with the ground at their feet.

Enfolding her in his arms, he slid off the log and leaned back. Her straddling his lap, which put her head just above his and her body balanced all over him, was quickly becoming his favourite.

For he had the advantage of being able to touch all of her limbs from her shoulders to her fingertips, from the juncture of her thighs, over her knees and down her legs to her toes.

And that is what he did. Everything between them must be right and that included holding out long enough for her to want all of this.

Pressing her palm against his chest, Beileag dug her knees into the damp earth and lifted. Sweat collected at his hairline as he notched himself. Lifting his eyes to hers, he looked for any doubts, any hesitation. When he saw none, he gave one quick thrust.

Hugging her to him, waiting for her trembles to subside, but there were none. It was he who shuddered. He kissed her forehead, the tip of her nose, her chin.

She smiled, gently caressed his face, ran her hands softly down his body to where they were joined and circled her hands around them.

He felt her flutter and his own response. 'What are you doing?'

'I like this texture, too,' she said, sliding her hands

She giggled. 'Very much so.'

He grinned knowingly. 'You kissed this hacked branch, my sweet. I think you like my appearance very much.'

Still laughing, she said, 'What are you doing?'

'Kissing you, starting all of this over again.'

'Truly?' she said breathlessly.

'Truly.' Next time he'd have her inside where the wind never picked up and the ground wasn't damp. Where he could strip her completely of her clothing and see every precious bit of her.

'There are hours until daylight,' he said. 'And I think you have a few more surprises to show me.'

Chapter Nineteen

Beileag cursed and swung at the man hovering over her bed.

Ducking, he grabbed her arm. 'It's me.'

Blinking, struggling to wake, Beileag glared at the man, around her bedroom, over at her sister, who was still sleeping, then back to the man who was leaning over her.

'Camron?' she whispered. 'Is it morning?'

He put his finger to his lips. 'Come outside with me.'

Her first instinct was to say no. She'd gone to bed no more than an hour, maybe two since she and Hamilton walked out of the woods. She was exhausted in a very good way.

The other reason she wanted to refuse was because Hamilton's twin being here couldn't be for a good reason. 'I'll be there in a moment.'

He nodded and quietly exited.

Dressing as warmly as she could, Beileag tiptoed out of her room, and almost ran into her father, whose arms were crossed.

There was no way Camron could have sneaked in and out of her home without passing her father, but what did she say to a parent who rarely talked to her?

'You let him in?' she said.

'Would you rather your mother?' he said quietly.

Had her father made a jest? She didn't know what to say.

'Go,' he said. 'If anyone asks, I'll explain you're with...'

'Murdag,' she supplied.

Opening the door, Beileag peered out in the cold and saw Camron pacing about. There was no light yet, but there would be soon and he wasn't making himself invisible.

'What are you doing here?' she said.

'Even in the dark you knew it was me.'

'Your hair's not the same.'

Camron snorted.

She hoped this night-time visit wasn't about his twin. 'Is this about Hamilton?'

He tilted his head, which reminded her so much of Hamilton. 'Nothing to do with my brother and all to do with Anna. Did she say something to you?'

She'd said much to her and Murdag about how she'd overheard the two brothers make a bet and would enact revenge, with Anna flirting with Hamilton and Murdag with Camron.

Thus far, she knew Hamilton had been approached by Anna, which still made her feel tense, but she didn't know if Murdag had seen to Camron.

'So, you haven't spoken to Murdag?' she said.

He leaned in. 'No, why?'

'No reason.' She took a step away.

'Beileag, I know there is something wrong because you are clenching your hands.'

She *would not* reply to that.

'I didn't know you did that,' Camron said, a hint of amusement in his voice.

'Did what?' She'd said nothing.

'Cursed—that's twice now you've had words with me.'

'I must have picked it up from your brother,' she said.

Camron almost smiled. 'So, is that where my brother's been?'

She shouldn't talk until she was awake ever again.

'Have you talked to Anna?' Camron said.

It was the soft plea in his voice that made her confess. 'She's talked to Murdag and I, but, Camron, I don't want to talk. She's not sleeping again, and unhappy with you.'

Camron looked away and blew out his breath. 'I need to rouse my brother. Can you wake Murdag, but not Anna, and meet me in the woods behind the blacksmith's?'

That was near to her clearing, but far enough away from any other ears, and it was still not quite morning. If this was an elaborate jest, it would come from Hamilton. Unfortunately, she feared it wasn't. 'This isn't some jest in the making, is it?'

'You almost sound as though you wish it was, but no. Hamilton told me you know of the bet I made. I believe Anna knows of the bet. In truth, I'm certain of it, if any of her antics with Hamilton were part of it. And I can see from your expression you know much of what I speak, but let's spare our words now and I will tell all, including my plan to remedy it when we're all present.'

What else could she do? 'I'll get Murdag, but she knows less than I and this won't go over well.'

'It never should have happened in the first place.'

'What of Seoc?'

He shook his head. 'It was his mead which caused me to believe the bet a good idea, but made me so blind drunk I can't remember making it. So, no, the less of him, the better.'

When she arched her brow, he added, 'He'll know of it when he wakes. He's out in the fields, but when I last saw him, he was snoring. I'll not disturb him.'

So both Hamilton and his brother were worried for their friend who wasn't sleeping well. These twins could make mistakes, but they were good.

'I'm terrified people will be hurt, but I think they're already hurting. I'll help you, but only because of Anna.'

'I wouldn't expect anything less,' he said. 'And don't tell Murdag anything until we all meet.'

'If she'll let me.'

'Fair, I will hurry… I don't know about Hamilton.'

'Do we need to involve your brother?' She didn't know if she could keep what they'd shared out of her expression. Not when it had been so difficult to part from him. One night, that's all they'd had and she had wanted everything.

He'd given it and more so. No husband, he'd said to her. Did that mean he wanted to wed her?

Except…was what they shared love? Facing and talking with his twin, she had doubts. She knew what Camron and Anna felt was love. They'd spent years with their feelings. She and Hamilton shared…moments.

Camron almost smiled. 'You will tell me of you and my brother?'

Shuttering her expression from this too-observant man, she said, 'What is there to tell?'

Once they parted, she went to Murdag's home. Fortunately, she didn't have to sneak into her room to wake her because her friend was already dressed to take care of the animals. It also didn't take long for them to walk to the woods where Camron said to meet. However, because they were early, it was empty, which left her and Murdag…and all her questions.

'When will they get here?' Murdag demanded.

'Camron said to bring you here and he'll get his brother.'

'And they want to talk of my sister?'

Beileag had hoped for Camron to be here already, so that she didn't have to answer any of Murdag's questions. It was bad when Anna had confronted them and she and Murdag had concocted their game to play on the twins, but since then, she'd managed to avoid lengthy conversations with them. Now, she couldn't and, given the hour and the subject, Murdag wasn't wanting to wait for answers.

For all her patience with horses, Murdag didn't have any when it came to people.

'Camron wants to talk of Anna; I don't know of Hamilton,' she said.

'She's been crying and angry since the orchard,' Murdag said. 'This is worse than when she was betrayed before. I believe he should keep apologising to her.'

'He wants to do something else.'

'How do you know what he wants? Is that the reason you brought me here, to make another game against my sister? To trick her since the old game didn't work?'

'No!' Beileag said. But as vehement as she was, there was too much truth in it and she couldn't hide her hurt or her remorse.

Murdag hugged herself. 'Sorry. I didn't mean to hurt you. She was crying for hours tonight; I don't know when she fell asleep. It's only because she was exhausted that she didn't hear you. Because she's upset, so am I.'

'Me, as well. No games, but I do believe the twins

aren't purposefully being cruel. Camron making this bet is uncharacteristic of him.'

'Not telling Anna about it was wrong.'

'I agree,' Beileag said. 'But then we don't know if he intended to…at least eventually.'

'I expect this kind of game from Hamilton.'

She did, too. 'But not so cruel.'

Murdag's eyes narrowed. 'You sound as if you're defending them.'

'No, but maybe there was a good reason for it all; maybe that's why Camron wants to speak to us now.'

'Better he speaks to Anna,' Murdag said. 'Has Hamilton said anything?'

'What?' Beileag's heart stopped. She hadn't gone to bed last night, but she thought she'd kept her time with Hamilton discreet, but between Camron and now this, maybe she hadn't. And how was she to think when she was so tired?

Murdag shrugged a shoulder. 'I wondered if he told you anything. He hasn't been speaking to me lately.'

'He hasn't?' Beileag silently cursed herself. She sounded entirely too hopeful and now Murdag was staring at her. Truly staring and everything in her seized. Everything she said was coming out wrong and far too revealing. She needed to not blurt or talk. Just listen, she was good at listening.

Murdag glanced at her clenched hands and cleared her throat. 'If there's something you're not—'

They turned to see Hamilton and Camron entering the small clearing.

'Took you long enough,' Murdag muttered.

Beileag's entire body leapt at the sight of Hamilton. His brown hair was loose and fell about his shoulders. It didn't look any tidier than when she had run her fingers through it. She wanted to do so again. Last night, she couldn't get enough of the textured waves curling around her fingers as he'd looked at her through his lashes. He'd get this quirk to his lips right before he'd said something humorous or kissed her.

Those kisses! Hours of them, as if both of them would never get enough. As he cradled her against him she felt secure, wanted…loved?

No, she couldn't do this. It was too soon to see him; she still wanted him too much. She was going to shout out something inappropriate or something that would give them away and ruin everything. It wasn't about her or him, but Camron. She should leave; Hamilton should leave. Was he looking her way?

'Why does he have to be here?' Beileag blurted.

Hamilton swung his gaze to the trees, but his brows were raised and he looked as though he was about to laugh.

'He's my brother,' Camron said very slowly, looking at her as if she'd gone a bit mad. Maybe she had.

'You think if he's not here, it's going to stop Hamilton from making any of his own mistakes?' Murdag said.

Murdag laughed perhaps to hide the bitterness tinging her words. She was the only one of them who didn't know of the bet until Anna had told her and hadn't had a chance to talk to Hamilton or Camron like she had.

What would Murdag do when she found out Beileag knew more than her? Because she might be tired, but she wasn't completely without thought. This absolutely would happen any moment here in this clearing.

Maybe if she said something now— A snapping of some sticks had them all turning.

'What?' Ducking his head from a low-hanging

branch, Seoc entered the small clearing. 'You thought you all were being subtle? I could see you from the field.'

Camron turned to her. 'Are we to see Anna here, too?'

'She shouldn't be up for a while.' Beileag glanced at Hamilton who actively kept his attention on his brother, so she looked away, too, in case Murdag became any more suspicious.

Did he love her, did she love him? They should have shared more words, but any time they were near each other...words became difficult. Such as now— she wasn't trying to converse with him and felt tongue tied, as though she was sure to give herself away by gawking at him.

She swore she could still feel his kisses. Her lips still felt plump and her chin was a little abraded. Could they see that?

Murdag paced and Seoc, who said some words to Hamilton, leaned against a tree opposite her. That left only Camron to notice, but he seemed lost in his thoughts of Anna.

There was no doubt he loved her friend. It was there for everyone to see. Beileag dreamed of a love like Camron's for Anna. No one doubted his love for her, except for Anna whose trust was broken. What would it be liked to be loved like that?

What her parents had wasn't hate, but it wasn't love either. Never did she see them giving open affection-ate touches or words, not like Hamilton's parents did. Had she just doomed her own fate to a love like that? Because here she and Hamilton were, openly avoid-ing each other.

Chancing a glance at Hamilton, she caught him looking at the dark woods, in the direction of the boulders and her clearing. As if he could sense her, he dipped his head and looked her way.

Beileag couldn't look away.

What they'd shared wasn't what Camron had for Anna. It couldn't be love like the one she'd always dreamed of, but what was it? Because…she wanted what they'd shared last night, wanted it again. The way he looked at her right now was enough, but maybe that's because she'd never felt anything like it and this little bit was better than the years and years of longing for a true family.

Or maybe it was something closer to desire and wouldn't last. She didn't trust it. Troubled by her thoughts, she still couldn't look away and watched Hamilton's eyes dim from secretly delighted to something closer to hurt. Or maybe he was troubled by his feelings for her, too.

Wrenching his eyes away from her, Hamilton asked, 'So does anyone want to talk about how Anna knows of the bet?'

Camron looked to Murdag and groaned.

What was happening here? Did she miss something? 'I didn't tell her!'

Murdag stopped her pacing and stared at her. Beileag squirmed.

Rolling her eyes, Murdag looked to Seoc. 'Am I the only one who didn't know of this marriage bet before my sister overheard it?'

Seoc shrugged. 'I may have.'

Turning back to Camron, Murdag looked half murderous. 'Apparently while you were nattering away with your brother in the pear orchards, you didn't look behind you.'

Camron looked gutted. When he looked to her, Beileag nodded.

'You're a fool,' Murdag told him.

Her friend was justifiably angry, but she still believed they didn't mean harm by the bet. And if Murdag was going to be angry at them, she might as well be frustrated at her as well.

'As am I,' Beileag said with a sigh. 'I already knew of the bet when Anna called us to her bedroom to tell us.'

Murdag glared at each of them. 'Am I the only one who hasn't betrayed her? Did none of you think to mention it to her so she'd have some defence against it!'

'Murdag...' Beileag said placatingly.

'Don't!' Murdag bit out through her teeth. 'At least now I know why you were trying to reason with her that it was all simply a miscommunication.'

'*I* asked her not to tell,' Hamilton said. 'There's only one evil person here and that's me.'

Beileag looked at Hamilton; they all did. It wasn't so much his words, but his tone. This troubled him more than he let on.

Murdag seemed to hear it, too, for the venomous light in her eyes eased, but there was no kindness when she looked her way. 'At least we know where your loyalties lie.'

Did Murdag think she wasn't a friend, that she didn't care? Anna was hurt and betrayed by the man, but Camron had loved her almost all of his life.

Beileag yearned for that kind of love, for that kind of family. If she thought, even a little bit, Anna didn't care or love Camron in return, she wouldn't have kept the bet a secret, wouldn't have agreed to help Hamilton.

But Murdag was right, Anna did deserve to know.

'I'll tell her I knew,' she said. 'But you know it's

him, Murdag. You know if there's any chance for her, it's him.'

'It didn't mean they had to play a game.' Murdag crossed her arms.

Beileag was all too aware of the brothers and Seoc listening to every word. 'And that didn't mean Anna had to retaliate the way she did in the garden. I told you it wasn't a good idea.'

Seoc laughed, Hamilton looked strangled and Camron cursed.

'How is she?' Camron said.

'My loyalty lies with my sister, as you well know,' Murdag said.

'She didn't overhear everything we said, did she?' Hamilton pointed out. 'Maybe with a good conversation this can all be resolved.'

'Anna is past a good conversation,' Murdag said. 'In truth, I don't think she should give you any moments. Because even if you talked, what does it matter? The bet was made.'

'But she clearly didn't hear Camron was against it all along,' Hamilton said.

'How against it could he be when he made it?' Murdag said.

'Are you going to stay quiet on this?' Camron turned to Seoc, who was looking far too amused.

At Murdag's one raised brow, Seoc huffed. 'I'm with Murdag on this; you're all fools. The bet shouldn't have been made and, Hamilton, you shouldn't have agreed to it. I told you all that before.'

Beileag tried to catch Hamilton's eyes, but he wasn't looking at any of them.

'Enough,' Camron said. 'It's Beltane today and I

asked you here to help me get her near the fires and the biggest crowds. We'll surround her and I'll talk.'

Beltane was a celebration about renewal and love. So many people pledged themselves to each other. And it was public, so she couldn't simply avoid Camron. Anna hadn't liked Beltane in years, but now that she was hurt again, she truly wouldn't.

'She won't want to go.' Beileag looked to Murdag for help. She wanted to help, but she wouldn't do anything without Anna's sister.

'I won't miss it,' Murdag said. 'Camron will provide entertainment with his humiliation in front of the whole clan.'

Beileag looked to Camron, but he didn't seem any different with Murdag's bitter words, but then she knew he was tortured. Seoc slapped Hamilton's shoulder and whispered in his ear. When Hamilton shook his head, Seoc frowned.

'Should we be off?' Seoc said. Shrugging, Murdag locked elbows with him and they disappeared.

'Beileag?' Hamilton said. 'Can I talk to you first? Alone?'

She needed to talk to Murdag, to form a plan for tonight, to ask her for understanding that she didn't tell her of the bet.

But she wouldn't tell her of Hamilton. It'd been weeks of keeping everything to herself, but after last night, how could she hide it anymore? No, she'd avoid Hamilton. Tonight wasn't about her and him, it was about Anna and Camron.

After Beltane they could talk. What they had shared was her first time with desire. And she'd liked it. He'd made her feel as though it meant something. But she'd seen Hamilton with other women—he understood desire, and she needed to understand it better, too. All she knew was that what they shared wasn't love. Most assuredly not as important as what Anna and Camron had. After tonight's conversation, and Camron's fervent words that was utterly clear.

What she and Hamilton shared had been special, but it wasn't Camron wishing for just a chance to patiently talk with Anna special. It wasn't Camron's years of enduring love. It had been...too effortless, too wild and needful to be with Hamilton. As much as she wanted it to be more, it wasn't love like she knew love should be.

No matter how much she thought about it, and wished otherwise, it just wasn't, and she needed time to reconcile that.

'Later, I have preparations to make.'

He looked to protest, but his gaze swung to his brother. 'Very well.'

Chapter Twenty

All throughout the Beltane preparations, Hamilton never had a chance to talk to Beileag. He didn't bother her as she and her sister wove flowers in their hair and decorated the houses. But he almost drew her aside when she scolded her brothers for attempting to steal the bannocks from the bottom of the bags. That bread would be necessary for people to find the burnt ends and claim their good fortune for the year. When she shook her head at him, he left, thinking there'd be time later.

But then before it turned dark, he needed to help with building and lighting the bonfires so their ash and smoke would bring the clan prosperity. Then he had to harness livestock, which would be driven between those fortune-bringing bonfires. Food and ale were brought out, and someone started the music and dancing. All of it so people could pledge their vows together in private. He loved Beltane, the first of May, and the welcoming of summer.

Mostly because it was a night of laughter and mischief. He usually spent weeks preparing some great hoax, but not for this one. Seoc had asked him, but it hadn't occurred to him. The war, his brother, that wolf... Beileag...had plagued his thoughts.

She plagued his thoughts even now. They'd shared a few glances while Camron and Anna had fought in front of the clan, but had had no chance at words. Not the ones he wanted.

Not until he handed the reins to his brother so he could take his Anna away from the crowd. When he turned, Murdag and Seoc had already joined the festivities. But Beileag stormed up to him.

'Did you know your brother would do that?'

'Ride off with Anna? I put him on the horse myself,' he said. He was half in merriment for the pure happiness for his twin, half in torment because Beileag looked anything but pleased.

'He told us to bring Anna to the festivities, and we did,' she said. 'He said if we encircled her and he could speak to her, he would make it better.'

'He did all that.'

'Better! He threw a sack over her head and tossed her over his shoulder like she was some harvest vegetable!'

It was the perfect deed, and Hamilton had been so jubilant. Everything up to that point had been as they'd discussed. Anna had come to Beltane. Her friends had encircled her just when everyone was reaching into the bannock sacks to pull out burnt ends.

Camron had been there as well with his sack, but it didn't have bread, only flowers. As Anna protested against everything Camron told her, she threw flower petals at him until she reached the very bottom…until his usually calm brother closed the sack around her and rode off with her.

Hamilton still wanted to laugh with joy about that, but Beileag didn't.

'You're angry,' he said.

'Of course I'm angry,' she said. 'I'm surprised Murdag's

not here yelling at you or getting her own horse and riding off to rescue her sister.'

So was he. Beileag's temper would be more what bold Murdag would do, but Murdag had simply given Camron a wave goodbye.

'She's not here because she's tasting Seoc's mead and celebrating.'

Frowning, Beileag looked over her shoulder to see Murdag, with head tipped back, laughing. When Beileag turned back to him, there was a line of worry between her brows. That wouldn't do.

His brother would sort everything with Anna and now, finally, inevitably, he had Beileag in front of him, talking to him, looking at him. She hadn't done that since last night. Merely the thought of last night shot lust through him. Made all the worse with Beileag's pouting pink lips and eyes flashing annoyance.

'Maybe she knows something you do not.' He leaned in. 'That Anna wanted to be thrown over his shoulders.'

Beileag pulled back. 'With her head stuck in a sack?'

He swiped a goblet of ale from a passing cousin, who protested, but Hamilton had already taken a large drink and his cousin was dragged away.

Hamilton wiped his mouth with the back of his hand. 'The sack surprised me, too, but perhaps a man has to improvise when he's wooing a wife.'

Would such a thing work for him? He could almost see Beileag now, rump in the air…no. With her long limbs, her legs should be wrapped around his waist, her arms around his shoulders and his lips slammed on hers.

'Do not get ideas,' she said.

'Wasn't thinking of any shoulders for you,' he answered honestly.

Her eyes narrowed. 'Do not get *any* ideas.'

Ah, she knew him well. Part of him wanted to think himself a fool for not recognising her earlier in his life; the other part was congratulating himself he had her now. Last night…he'd wanted more of that, all of that. When his brother woke him, he'd been in too good a mood despite his lack of sleep. But the conversation in the woods had sobered him of that soon enough. As the day progressed, he'd headed towards a foul mood when he couldn't talk or sneak a kiss with Beileag.

But now with her amber eyes flashing and her hands clenching at her side as if she wanted to throw a punch, he was almost giddy. Except for the frown on her beautiful face, that wouldn't do. How was he to ask her for her hand, for forever, if she was angry because of something his brother did? If that was the case, he feared Beileag would constantly be unhappy with him.

Though that thought brightened him, too. Camron was usually the reasonable, boring one. His brother never made enough mischief to cause anyone's annoyance. That fact he did it now when everything counted? He *loved* that his brother threw the love of his life in a sack. That boded well for their marriage. The fact Beileag wasn't happy didn't bode well for him.

'Are you cross with me now?' he said. 'You can't blame me for what my brother did and you liked me fine enough last night.'

Her stunning eyes became cautious and her hands clenched. Now it was his turn to frown. That truly wouldn't do.

Maybe all his words hadn't been said, but his actions had spoken. He'd laid by her side, played with her hair and been fascinated by her talk of teaching him woodworking. He couldn't wait to be in that peaceful clearing, letting the sun hit them, side by side as he nicked his hands and she laughed over his shoulder.

The mere thought of being in that clearing with her made the wolf, the Battle of Dunbar, the upcoming war in Stirling, fade. He wanted his life with Beileag.

More laughter and someone shouted at him to join them. He waved them off, but Beileag blinked and seemed to come into herself.

'I should go.'

When she pivoted away from the crowd, he followed her. 'We'll go, then.'

'We're not—'

'If I didn't know better, I'd think you were avoiding me.'

She stopped, gaped, seemed to come to herself. 'I wasn't avoiding you. I was busy, you as well!'

All true, except her expression now was pure guiltiness.

'You *have* been avoiding me today and you intend to tonight?' He grinned. 'Is it because if we do what we did last night we'll be wed?'

She looked away. 'Today's not about us, it's about Anna and Camron.'

Ah. His lass had a soft heart and wanted his brother and friend to do well. 'They are as good as wed. But they're gone now and we have us.'

'Are you implying we're like them?' At his eager nod, her brows pinched together. 'We're not a game.'

Setting his cup on a tree stump along with a dozen others, he said, 'No, we're not.'

'Your brother doesn't think so.' She strode off again, further from the crowd, but everyone was milling about when she stopped again. 'He made a bet to win her, dragged you, willingly, into it. Tonight, however, he asked for our help. I helped. I *lured* Anna to the very centre of Beltane's fires and he made it a game when he tricked her into that sack!'

Is that how she saw it? He saw it as his very reasonable brother meeting a very stubborn lass and was left with no other resort. He also saw how Anna kept arguing and engaging with Camron. If she truly didn't want him, Anna wouldn't have been so angry. No, his brother needed the privacy—both he and Anna were quieter folk. It was wise of his brother to take her away. Yet Beileag saw it as something regretful?

'That wasn't love,' Beileag said. 'You're twin brothers and I thought one of you was different. Your brother's actions weren't anything like they should have been.'

'Not love?' he said. 'That had everything to do with love. His every action announced to the entire clan he'd have her as a wife or else.'

'I'll…have to think about that.'

'You can do that,' he said easily.

'You'd know him better than I,' she added.

'More than I know myself,' he agreed.

Looking more unsettled than relieved, she walked some distance away before she rounded on him again. 'But he's been patient with her.'

'I think his patience ran out.'

She opened her mouth, closed it. 'It's not supposed to. It's— Never mind, you wouldn't understand. And I've been taught even less.'

He waited for her to explain, but when she simply pivoted and walked away, he went with her.

'Why are you still here?' she said.

'We're talking.'

She frowned. 'No, we're not.'

They were far from the bonfires. It was cooler, but

quieter. Beileag kept looking in the direction his brother had gone and seemed troubled by what had occurred with Anna. Soon though, she'd see Anna only needed to realise she already loved his brother.

Did Beileag love him? It bothered him that he couldn't guess. She'd lain with him; he'd given her his body. In between, they'd spoken of her figurines, his past pranks which had gone remorsefully wrong, but mostly, he'd held her. Everything had felt right between them. This morning being woken by his brother was unexpected, but it would work out.

Why couldn't he feel with certainty it would fall in place for he and Beileag, too? She'd seemed distracted, distressed. However, Hamilton felt an urgency for this conversation. If he waited until tomorrow, they'd be able to sneak to her spot in the trees for privacy and perhaps she wouldn't be distracted, but she'd avoided him today. Perhaps she was nervous about what was between them and, if so, then long talks were reported to help with that, or so he understood.

But it was his brother with patience, not him. He didn't know if he could wait to hold her through any conversations let alone lengthy ones.

'Can we talk of last night and about these last days together?' he said.

Her shoulders rose and fell as if she emboldened herself. It didn't appear she wanted to talk—maybe they were more alike than he thought. Maybe this could all be resolved with touches and kisses. When had they got so far apart? Easy enough to fix.

Hamilton took a step towards her and her eyes darted back in the direction of his brother and Anna. Or... maybe they could talk of something else.

'Why don't you tell me of the family you made,' he said.

She turned to him again. 'The family?'

Ah, he had her attention now. 'When we were in the clearing and you showed me that hedgehog.'

'The hedgehog had no family,' she said.

Why was it, when it counted, he was terrible at this talking? Of course, pulling pranks on people didn't require words either, but that shouldn't matter. He rolled his shoulder and looked around them. A familiar and unwanted uneasiness was overcoming him.

'In the other chest,' he said doggedly. He was imagining feeling that restlessness. There was no wolf in the woods. He was with Beileag on clan ground. His brother was as good as wed and it was Beltane, his favourite time of year. 'In the chest you didn't show me, which had nothing but linens and four stick figures. That's the one I'm talking of.'

When she stood there, staring at him with a thousand emotions and her hands hanging loosely at her side, he feared he'd made everything between them irreparable.

'Beileag? Those were a family, weren't they?' He gave a short laugh. 'They were a little crude, but probably not as terrible as I will carve when you teach me.'

She swallowed hard. 'Those were smaller hacking sticks.'

She was lying and he'd never known her to lie before. Beileag showed everything in her words, in her eyes and those remarkable hands. Except she stood there as if she had no emotions at all. As though she'd just disappeared.

He'd had some ale, had some happiness this festivity, but not now and he didn't understand why. 'They looked like a family to me. A husband, wife, two children.'

She gave a weak shrug. 'Oh, those. I forgot about those.'

He gave a little smile, tried to coax one from her. 'You kept them separate from that wolf, didn't you? And it looked as though you didn't carve people again...so they were simply something you did in the past?'

She tried to return his smile, but it didn't come anywhere close to how she looked when she rested so sweetly against him. 'Not important at all.'

He still didn't believe her, but now wasn't the time to push on it. What more could he say? She'd tell him when she wanted to.

Perhaps she was nervous because he hadn't declared himself. She couldn't still be shaken because of Anna and Camron. She'd see tomorrow that they were good.

And this couldn't be about the bet anymore. She didn't know he'd made it, but that shouldn't matter. The results were the same. Of course, he'd tell her, he wanted to tonight, so they'd have no secrets together. But all that, too, wasn't anything she knew to be distressed about.

So this had to be because this was Beltane and she was unsure where he stood. Since he was in front of her and had her attention, he'd tell her.

She was reasonable and, after last night, after all they'd shared, he should have no trepidation on asking her if she'd pledge. And she kept talking to him, like Anna did his brother. Surely that meant she had some care for him, otherwise she wouldn't keep engaging him. It was good that he told her this now.

'I'm in love with you.'

Her hands fluttered. 'What?'

'I love you,' he said with all the truth in his soul. 'I want to be the carved man, with you as my wife and two kids, more if we're blessed. I want to see you spin our children around like you do your siblings.'

Her beautiful amber eyes searched from the top of his head to his toes and all the bits in the middle. Those bits noticed, too. He'd have to make his truth telling and declarations quick and get them away. Preferably in a different direction from his brother.

'You...believe this,' she said.

She was listening to him now. Truly hearing him, but it wasn't good she sounded stunned. She had to know. They were so alike, she *had* to know.

He nodded. 'I do. But there are things you should know first before you accept my love.'

She blinked, but she stayed still and was listening to him. His heart warmed at that. His Beileag did have some feelings for him.

He regretted the timing of telling her of the bet, but not that he had to do it. It shouldn't matter who made the bet, after all, and now with such happiness between them,, they could all simply laugh about it later.

So, no, the timing wasn't perfect, but since he intended to ask for her to marry him, he wanted no secrets between them. Tonight many people would pledge vows to each other in front of others and in private. That could be Camron's fortune if Anna would have him.

He wanted it for himself, too. Not because Camron was asking Anna, but because...he couldn't wait anymore. He wanted her. Would she deny him?

No. There was no reservation inside him and he'd given her no doubts. He'd confessed his feelings; he'd shown her with all his touches and kisses.

He needed to tell her the truth. Tell her because this bet had taken on too many unexpected twists and needed to be put to rest. So they could begin anew, like Beltane.

'I made the bet.'

She blinked. 'Another one? Why would another bet need to be made?'

'It's the same one,' he said. 'The one with Camron marrying Anna and me marrying Murdag by the end of summer, before we leave for Stirling.'

'That's the one…' she licked her lips '…that's the one you agreed to in the heat of the moment, after much drinking and not thinking. The one you said was wrong now because it was made in haste and you should never have agreed to it.'

He didn't remember saying all that, at least not in that way. Certainly, some of that was true—he'd wished he'd thought about Murdag more and realised they didn't suit, and that it was Beileag all along, but the rest… Beileag seemed very emphatic about it all. She must need more. Except he could feel the unease within him again.

He hadn't told anyone of Dunbar's battle and of fleeing to Ettrick Forest. When he and Camron had dragged a barely alive Seoc back to Graham land, he'd thought that enough. Of course there'd been many council meetings since then, especially because they'd lost their laird and afterwards Balliol was ousted as Scotland's king. But that battle, that forest, were his secrets he had wanted to take to the grave. Why did she need to know all that horror? There were battles to come very soon, but how to explain any of this to her without making it all sound worse, or talking about that wolf?

Yes, he'd rushed matters with Camron because his brother had little time left to woo Anna and, yes, he'd thrown himself in that because didn't he deserve some happiness, too?

'I made the bet and I wasn't drunk. I knew what Camron wanted and thought I knew whom I wanted.'

'Is this some Beltane mischief or jest?' she said.

He shook his head. 'No jest this year.'

Beileag gasped. 'But if you made it, you lied this entire time, even when you knew Camron wished he'd never made it. And Anna, whose trust is completely broken, felt betrayed by that bet. When you told me of this bet, I warned of this. I told you people would be hurt, but you didn't listen. I didn't listen and look what happened! She screamed at him tonight, Hamilton, in front of the whole clan. I know that I said she loves him, but maybe he broke that love.'

'It's not a game,' he said again. He couldn't understand her upset on this. Camron might have pursued Anna anyway. It was just something to spur him on.

'Oh! So you meant to be cruel, to manipulate people's lives,' she said. 'You're almost worse than my parents. No, you are! Because with them, I at least know they mean the unkindness they give to their children. You lied about it. I don't know who you are anymore.'

'Camron will win his Anna and I apologised about thinking I cared for Murdag when it was you I love.'

Her hands were nothing but fists at her side. 'And yet still you do not see what is wrong. The bet takes in no consideration of Anna, or Murdag...or me! About how I would feel to be some person you needed to be wed before you're off to war. The way you're making it sound, it doesn't matter if it was Murdag or anyone else!'

That night and every time since, he had just thought of how sad his brother was. He hadn't thought of Anna because he knew that, though she didn't trust him, she wanted Camron, and he'd thought nothing of Murdag and him because... Murdag, if she was ever betrayed, would mount a horse and run a man over. Her heart and soul could weather any storm.

But Beileag was different. Everyone in the clan knew of how indifferent her father was and her mother's calloused ways. When he'd been younger, he couldn't remember how young, he'd asked his parents if he could rescue Beileag, but they'd told him she was better off than he thought.

He was a child then, so he'd let it go. Up until now, he'd forgotten he'd even said that. But now he wished he had rescued her. Because he could hear in her voice the same agony Anna had cried out at his brother.

Beileag's heart had been hurt along the way by her family and when he'd so happily found her through the bet, he didn't think how she would take it.

But she wouldn't like any falsehood that manipulated people who were already hurt.

'You don't have true feelings for Murdag or for me,' Beileag said and her voice cracked. 'You couldn't. It was just some impulsive act for reasons you won't tell me, or maybe you have none.'

'I love you.'

'Love isn't something that is forced into a slot because of some bet made.'

'I didn't make it that way.'

'Why did you do it then?'

He stepped away, look around them. 'It was a harmless bet, hardly anything that should make any difference,' he said.

'No difference?' she said, her eyes sheening. 'All my life, I want someone's only enduring thought to be—' She stopped, wiped her nose with her sleeve. 'Never mind, someone as impulsive as you will never understand.'

'What is it? I'll give you anything. Everything.'

'Not you,' she said. 'I've been manipulated enough in my lifetime; I don't need lies on top of it.'

'I don't lie!'

She smiled at him then and Hamilton's heart went cold because her tears were falling now.

'You lied about who made the bet,' she said. 'How do I know you're not lying about this? How would I ever know the difference?'

Hadn't he shown her enough? Everything he felt within him was worlds of difference from what he felt for anyone else. It was a bet. Not a jest, but still nothing to be forced as some barrier between them.

'My brother, blind drunk, didn't come up with the idea,' he said. 'If I said I made it, Camron would have dismissed it as another jest of his twin. But because he thought he'd made it when he was at his lowest, when he had no hope at all, Camron believed he must have meant it. That there was something within him telling him to not give up on Anna.

'It wasn't a real bet. It mattered to him to think he made it, that's all.'

She paused just long enough to believe he'd said something good this time. Something that would make a difference between whether he'd have her in this life or not.

'If it mattered to Camron,' she said very slowly, 'have you told him?'

Hamilton flushed. 'No.'

Her tears began again, but her eyes accused. 'Because you know it hurt him and Anna.'

Had he truly lost her? 'Doesn't mean I lied about us.'

'Even if you mean it, it's not true. You forget, I've observed you over the years. Between one infatuation after another. While you pursued Murdag, you fell for me? That's not the kind of love I want. Not now, not ever.'

He didn't need the sunlight to see the finality of her features as she pivoted and walked back to the Beltane fires and away from him.

How could this have gone so wrong?

It was just a bet; it shouldn't have mattered who made it.

All he'd wanted was to encourage his brother to pursue Anna, so he could pursue his own wife. Then when they were all happy, he'd tell them and they'd all have a laugh.

But he hadn't taken into account how deep his restlessness was. How reckless and blind it had made him and he'd thought his friend Murdag was the woman for him.

He didn't take in how deeply Anna had been hurt, how delicate it would be for his brother to win her heart and how she'd feel if she'd known about the bet at all.

He didn't consider how Beileag, with her family, would take it. Beileag who didn't want any more lies and manipulations.

Beileag was no game. He loved her, but she wouldn't believe him now. He'd given her his body, his heart. He'd given her all the tenderness he was capable of in his life. It wasn't enough, but he loved her. What else could he give, what would be *different*?

For him to have patience. Perhaps he should have waited to tell her of the bet when they knew how Camron and Anna would be. He had to admit, Anna had looked both wrathful and in agony at Beltane. Was there a chance she wouldn't accept Camron?

Probably. But then Camron had done something different and hoisted her over his shoulder and rode away.

What could he do for Beileag to prove he could be different for her? For that's what she'd almost said to him and stopped, wasn't it? She wanted someone who thought of her, who wanted only her.

He did want her and, if he wasn't a fool, he would have seen she was the one for him.

But how to prove it now? Something with no more impulsive actions. Something which would tell her he was taking her feelings into consideration. No more lies or manipulations. Something to show her he had patience and he could be there for her. That this wasn't some passing impulsive act.

But first, he had to talk to his brother and Anna.

Chapter Twenty-One

Over the next week, Beileag did everything she could to avoid Hamilton. It appeared, too, that he tried to avoid her which was all for the best. She'd given him enough opportunities to come to the right conclusion: that people shouldn't be manipulated with bets and games. Or if he did, he needed to see it from their point of view.

Either he didn't understand why he should, or he was purposefully avoiding the reasons. He'd said it was a push for Camron to pursue Anna. But he didn't fool her. There was more there.

There was the issue of why he was so determined to keep his connection to his brother. They were brothers and identical—wasn't that enough? And just because it was good for Camron, it didn't mean it was good for Anna. The absolute agony and rage in Anna's voice and her words at Beltane spoke of the depth of her feelings of betrayal.

And that very night Hamilton had said he loved her. He didn't know love. Love didn't bully itself at a person and wasn't sudden like some surprise, or jest. It was based on years, patience and overcoming adversity. Like Anna and Camron's.

How was she ever to believe that while Hamilton

pursued Murdag, he'd fallen in love with her? Ridiculous. It was simply another game, another manipulation.

Love was everlasting and not some potent whirlwind. She wanted a man who loved her for her, not on some lust driven whim. Someone who yearned for family and children with the certainty she did.

Her immature carvings from years ago of the family, so crudely done they weren't recognisable as people, were testament to her true longing. She'd wanted all that for years! Not simply because…*because*.

She was justified in this, so why was there this restlessness since Beltane? All that day as she'd joined in the preparations of the festivities, she'd kept looking over her shoulder. Hamilton had been watching her, wanting to talk to her, no doubt, but she hadn't wanted to talk. What they had shared was too powerful, too potent. It wasn't simply the way he held her or their kisses, it was the words they'd shared before she'd touched him and he'd jokingly asked if she intended to carve his likeness.

There had been a mad moment when she *had* wanted to carve a likeness of him. It was afterwards as they lay content, his smile had been so easy, the light in his eyes pleased. They'd shared everything and she had floated in warmth and the way his arms felt around her. When he'd laughed in remembrance of some folly he had done in his youth, she had wanted him to just stop right there, draw, carve, hold that moment for as long as she could.

It wasn't love…it was too natural when they talked, too much fierce need to touch and kiss him. It all felt too sudden between them. Suddenly conversing, suddenly wanting.

Her family never taught her love, but Camron and Anna did. And she was right about them, their love did endure even after Beltane. There was nothing *sudden* between them.

No…it was love for them, but not for her. She couldn't reconcile Hamilton and his lies. So she…let him go.

But why did this unease keep getting worse? It'd been a week since Beltane and she wanted to return to her way of life, but she didn't attempt to go to her clearing and carve away the time on a new creature. It bothered her that she might not be able to return and would need a new place.

With no outlet, she was left with chores or disciplining her siblings, none of which she wanted to do, and oddly, her siblings hadn't been arguing. What did she want to do?

The mill. The doors were wide open and people marched in and out. Her father was probably there, maybe he would—

'There you are!' Skirts lifted in her meaty fists, her mother hurtled herself towards her. Beileag held her ground.

'Where have you been?' Sian huffed. 'Hardly any of the chores have been done and I can't find my knife— you know, the one with the broken tip.'

She knew her mother's knife, everyone in the household did; she also knew why the tip was broken, as her mother had, in a fit of anger, stabbed it into the table in front of her. At the time, she and her siblings had been arguing about who knew what, it was years before, but of course, she was blamed. Her mother's explanation had been that she was the eldest and knew better.

'The chores are done and the last I saw your knife was this morning, when it was in your hand.'

Her mother dropped her skirts and gaped. Beileag almost did as well; she'd never been rude to her mother in public before. In fact, when had she displayed any strong emotion to any of them? Never. She'd always wanted to present a loving family to the rest of the clan and, since her mother defeated that at every turn, she'd taken it upon herself to keep a peaceable happy family. More than that, she loved her siblings and wanted them to grow up in a loving family.

That meant not giving her opinion or talking in a way to aggravate her volatile mother. Beileag braced herself for whatever was to come, but she wouldn't avoid her this time. After everything she'd witnessed at Beltane, at what she thought she had with Hamilton, she didn't have it in her to do so.

'Sian,' Ivor said from behind them.

Beileag turned to her father, who was standing at the threshold of the mill. His expression and stance were casual. In his hands was a blackened linen that he used to slowly wipe his fingers.

'She didn't mean to disturb you,' Sian said. 'I was just going to have her complete her chores.'

He indicated a direction with his chin. 'Oigrhirg needs your help with the boys. I'll take care of this.'

Her mother pursed her lips, all the while turning different shades as if she was just barely holding herself back. Beileag had never seen her mother refrain from anything.

'She needs no help—' Sian said.

'Maybe now she does,' Ivor said.

Beileag couldn't take her eyes off her mother, who looked frustrated, resigned and worried. Especially, when her snapping eyes turned to her again. Beileag tried to get her own stance neutral, but she knew she was failing. Especially when her mother's eyes narrowed as though she would start another tirade.

Feeling the familiar hammering in her heart, Beileag desperately kept her hands to her side. The moment she clenched them, she knew her mother would pounce.

Sian gave a loud huff. 'Oh, you never let me worry about any of the children. Just let them find their own way. If that means anything to you.'

'It means something to them,' her father said. 'But some insight a time or two couldn't hurt.'

'They need fortitude first,' her mother bit out.

'They get that from you.'

Beileag swung her gaze back to her father. His affectionate tone of voice stunned her.

When she turned back around, her mother was gone.

'Give me a moment.' He turned his back to her and said some words to the people in the mill. Almost immediately, Beileag heard thuds of heavy wood and tools being set down.

'All's clear,' her father said as he walked into the mill.

Beileag looked over her shoulder—her mother was still gone. When she turned around her father had disappeared into the mill.

Everything was quiet. She hadn't been invited in, but hadn't been told to leave either. When she felt she was garnering stares from some children nearby, she marched into the mill.

There was only her father inside.

'They went out the other door,' he said.

Her father had asked clansmen to leave for her, but it wasn't the other men she was thinking of at that time.

'She went.'

Her father gave a low chuckle. 'She does that.'

Her mother had never done that, never backed away from a fight.

'You should know we talked, but she didn't want to mention your Hamilton,' he said. 'So that left me.'

Her mind was in turmoil, that was why she wasn't understanding this conversation. 'How did you know?'

'How could we not know?' Ivor said. 'Even when you were little, you always lit up when he was up to something. Haven't seen those particular expressions since...until recently. A few people commented on if we should expect some vows at Beltane. When it was just Camron and Anna celebrating afterwards, your mother surmised it was Hamilton's fault you weren't also celebrating. It was, wasn't it?'

Beileag felt behind her for a stool and slowly, carefully, sat down. This entire conversation, her father didn't look at her. Not once. Instead, he was simply striding around the mill, cleaning, and straightening things. If he wasn't actually talking to her, she would have guessed he hadn't noticed her.

Except, he did notice her. And by the accuracy of this conversation, he noticed her very much.

'I wasn't... I didn't...' She didn't know what to say. Was she to suddenly confess her feelings? Or blame Hamilton? Was he to blame? Most assuredly for the bet, which she wasn't completely certain her father knew about, but then, what did she know?

'If you care to know what we think, I believe he's a fine man, your mother not so much, but then she's harder to please.'

Her parents...talked about her. Talked about her in a way that caring, concerned parents would. She'd originally come to the mill to ease her restlessness, but this was more than expected. And absolutely, under no circumstances, did she want to discuss Hamilton.

Right now, she wanted to understand her parents.

Her father...noticed her. Knew her. And she came to another realisation. He hadn't been ignoring her all those years. With an adult's eyes and a crafter's knowledge, she could look back at how her father sanded in the mill always in an angle facing her. The same thing with a hook knife, and the adze. He completed all those tasks, all those skills, so her child's eyes could see what he was doing. Her father had been training her.

Something warm bloomed in her chest. Her father might not have treated her the way he had his other children, but he had cared for her. Yet why so differently?

'When you were using that riving knife to cut that oak into planks, did you cut yourself on purpose or because you were standing at an angle to show me how to use it?' she said.

'The riving knife....' Her father's expression cleared. Lifting his thumb to his face, he wiggled it about. 'Never heard the end of it from the rest of the men after that. Even when I confessed what I was doing...that made it worse.'

It had been a terrible cut, requiring stitches, but he still had almost lost his thumb when it became swollen. Her father's suffering turned her towards carving versus building large structures.

'I'm sorry,' she said. Not only for the pain he had suffered, but no doubt the carpenters would have given him a difficult time training his daughter in the craft. And he still risked his livelihood and his place in the community by doing so.

'And I'm grateful.' When his eyebrows raised at that, she added, 'For you letting me borrow your tools.'

'Steal,' he corrected. 'Now about your mother.'

No, she didn't want to talk about her.

As if her father knew her thoughts, he looked up and she was truly grateful she sat.

Because he kept looking as if coming to some decision, but Beileag had no idea what. He wanted to talk of her mother, she didn't. What else was there to say?

'She worries about you,' he said.

She wanted to laugh, or shout, but her father wasn't a liar. So what did that mean? Her mother was worried and it manifested itself with cruelty and blame.

'She hates—' Beileag stopped. She couldn't complete that statement. Her mother hated her and nothing her father said would change that. Still... 'She hates... my height.'

Her father snorted. ''Course she does. Your towering over every young buck here makes it more difficult to find someone to marry. She worries.'

She had no answer for any of that and her father seemed to know it.

'She won't like me telling you all this, but it's past time. Your mother shows her care wrong, but her heart is in a good place.'

He set down his knife and block of wood, giving her his full attention, which shut down any argument Beileag ever had. Her father never looked at her.

'You should have known her parents,' he said. 'Cruel, evil people that they were. Always forcing their children to be one way, when they really were another. Because of them, not one person in any clan in all of Scotland wanted her. She was terrified of what would become of her. If she didn't marry, she'd be stuck with them and wouldn't have any chance of happiness, you see.

'But *I* knew what was underneath all those thorns, and was kind of proud of myself about it, too. Now look what I have: four beautiful children, who have the gift to be exactly who they want to be with no interference from us.' He gave a quick smile which starred the deep wrinkles at the corners of his light brown eyes. 'Though I believe she has been interfering by being a bit abrupt to ensure her children leave the nest and all.'

Beileag sat there listening to her father talk, with a combination of words he'd never used before, in a tone she'd never heard before. Never.

Because it sounded as though her mother's anger at her was concern her daughter wouldn't marry and find happiness. That she didn't want her home at all, was purposefully mean to her to make sure she wasn't home…to find happiness. There was so much wrong in all of that, she'd be here for years trying to unravel it.

But she didn't want to talk of her mother, though that would have to be addressed later, after she'd wrapped her head around it all. She wanted to think about her father and his voice, and words, because it sounded as if he loved her mother. No, that wasn't love. It…

Beileag gripped the stool she was on. Locked her feet around it and held on tight. No, no, it sounded *exactly* like love. Her father had been proud to have picked her, to have *seen* the woman underneath the thorns. All the while she'd been standing there, reeling, feeling as if the world had shifted under her feet. Her world, her family, wasn't what she thought they were.

Her father loved her mother. Loved her enough to go against her parents, probably the entire clan. Then they'd made some sort of agreement to not interfere with their own children. To let them grow up exactly as to who they wanted to be. Or at least how Sian thought they wanted to be. All Beileag truly wanted was a happy home, but then…

No, it wasn't the time for her to reflect on the relationship with her mother. That would take time to come to any understanding of what her father meant. It was all the rest she wanted to think about because there was a vein there. Like something revealed when she started carving into a piece of wood. Something she wanted to follow very much.

Because her father hadn't told her all of this for nothing. He'd done it because he cared. Now she wondered how long he'd cared. Did he love her when his daughter sneaked into the carpentry mill to watch him work? When she'd stolen his tools?

That was easy to answer. Just one brief memory of her father almost losing his thumb revealed in all its clarity that he cared very much, that he knew she wanted to learn, that he was teaching her in his own skulking way.

Beileag felt as though she'd faint, as though she'd shoot off the stool and fly. Because what her father revealed, what he told her, was that it was past time she understood that her parents loved their children and each other in their own way. Loved in a way that wasn't like Camron and Anna's, that wasn't like anyone else. Did she doubt it was love? No. Because it was a challenge understanding her mother, but her father spoke affectionately about her. And when Ivor had asked his wife to give him time to talk to her, her mother had listened. They loved differently, but it was love, none the less.

'I think I made a mistake.' Her voice sounded reedy, as though she couldn't get the words out of her suddenly dry throat because she'd been sitting there…gaping.

Her father, who had returned to his project after his great speech, didn't look up at her. But then, she now understood he probably wouldn't. Unless she asked him to, because he was leaving her alone and letting her grow as she wanted.

She doubted Hamilton loved her because it was different than anything she'd observed. But she wasn't very good at observing, was she? Not like her parents, apparently. Which meant Hamilton had told her the truth, he loved her, and she'd ridiculed it. She'd hurt him, purposefully. He'd tried to talk to her, to explain, when he could have thought her not worth the effort and walked away.

But he hadn't left until he'd seen she was completely closed off and nothing would have got through to her. When she'd told him she knew better than him.

It took her mother, her father, her parents to teach her that lesson on love. That it was powerful enough to be many forms. To be different than expected. She wished for one strong moment that someone else was here to observe this. To verify it wasn't some figment of her imagination. That she had parents, a family, like she'd always wanted.

'I absolutely made a mistake,' she repeated more firmly.

Her father hummed under his breath. 'Your mother will be pleased it was your fault and not Hamilton's. That'll make it easier for her to accept him.'

It was too soon to think of her mother's conversations; just hearing her father talk of them was overwhelming. She needed to repair whatever was left between them, if Hamilton would have her.

'I'm going to leave now,' she announced, though she'd never announced such a thing before.

'No more stealing from me?' Her father's brow was arched, but now he was sanding and still not looking at her.

He wanted to talk of woodworking? 'I have everything I need.'

'Not everything.' He pointed to the door. 'Go after Hamilton. Never thought a daughter of mine would be chasing that mischief maker.'

'I like his mischief,' she teased just to see what would happen.

Her father's head snapped up at that. 'Ack, that's too much talk now, you're as bad as him, be gone with you.'

Elated and terrified, Beileag bounded out of the mill and slammed right into Murdag.

Slapping her hand on her forehead, Murdag cursed. 'Ow!'

'How did my elbow reach your forehead?' Beileag rubbed her arm.

'That's because you're tall.'

For the first time, Beileag felt no sudden shame. 'I am, aren't I?'

Murdag's gaze turned searching. 'I'm surprised you're here.'

She pointed behind her and whispered, 'I was in the mill, talking to my father.'

'Your father talks?' Murdag repeated.

That was her reaction. 'I don't know where to begin on all that I have to tell you, but I can't right now, I need to go.'

'I would say so.'

That pulled her up. 'Why do you think I need to go?'

'Beileag, Hamilton left for Stirling. I returned from a ride and he was already mounted.'

'What?' Beileag clenched her hands.

'I thought you should know.' Murdag took her elbow and pulled her away from the doorway and around the corner.

'He left for Stirling.' Beileag twisted a linen around her finger. 'He's gone.'

'About an hour ago,' Murdag said. 'I was on my way to find you.'

'He doesn't leave for weeks.' She felt as though she was repeating herself, but she was still reeling from her father's words and her own revelations. She needed Hamilton here so she could tell him, but he had left and Murdag saw him.

'You talked to him?' She twisted the linen the other way.

Murdag nodded. 'That's how I knew he was leaving for Stirling. He told Anna and Camron that he'd made the bet.'

There were too many revelations, too much information.

'What did they think?' she said.

'He said they laughed it off, but then, they're happy, aren't they?'

So he'd talked to Murdag, but not to her. He'd talked to Anna and Camron, but not her. He'd revealed everything and then left her. What did she expect? After every word they'd shared, after every touch, she'd called it all false. He was probably glad he was heading off to war to get as far away from her as possible.

'Was he happy?' she asked, though she didn't deserve to know.

Murdag grabbed her hands and pulled her closer. Beileag could barely feel the warmth in her friend's hands. Everything in her was cold. What a fool she was! She knew that burlwood was ugly on the outside, but beautiful within. That if she took her time and had patience, the beauty of Hamilton's love would be revealed.

'He's been as miserable as you.'

He was probably miserable because she'd hurt him.

Murdag sighed. 'Tell me what happened between you two. I may have worried for my sister, but you are my friend. I regret you've had to endure something and I haven't been there.'

'I wouldn't exactly use the word endure.' Beileag squeezed her friend's hands and let go. 'Let's go sit; this may take some time.'

When she was done telling her everything, except the most intimate details, Murdag snorted. 'You may be a bigger fool than the twins. A bet, Anna's trust and Hamilton pursuing me…all in a few weeks. At least I understand now why Hamilton offered to help me with the horse's tooth and then suddenly disappeared.'

'You're not angry?' Beileag said. 'I thought you'd be angry.'

'Because I was kept in the dark? Hamilton had acted odd since he returned. He was everywhere I was and then gone. Then I heard of the bet and that you knew of it because of Hamilton. It didn't take much to realise two somebodies were spending time together. I just didn't know… I didn't know you had grown that close.'

'I didn't tell you how close.'

Murdag slammed her hands over her ears. 'I do not want to hear every detail. He's like a brother to me!'

'Do you think it odd that I've never seen him like that?'

Murdag shook her head. 'You held back when we were setting up all those jests in our youth. You absolutely saw him, saw all of us in a different light. Remember when he put the bucket of water over the stable door, so that the next victim would get soaked?'

She hadn't been there for that, but she'd been there

afterwards with everyone laughing so hard, Camron holding his stomach, Seoc with tears running down his face. And Hamilton, not quite a man, his tunic clinging to his torso and outlining the broad bones of his shoulders, the muscles beginning along his stomach. She'd blushed for days after that.

'That wasn't that long ago,' she said. 'He said he loved me and left.'

'Then you decided to stay around and tell me all about it. Good thing I've already got ready a horse for you and some food. If you hurry, you could catch up.'

'I was so mean.'

'You could never be your mother,' Murdag said. 'Although I don't even know if your mother is your mother. Will you forgive her?'

'My father loving me is difficult to understand,' she said. 'I don't know what I'll do with her.'

Murdag grabbed her hands and pulled her up. 'Well, you have the trip to figure it out.'

Chapter Twenty-Two

'Move any closer and I'll gut your entrails and feed them to vermin.' Hamilton stayed in the dark shadows of the trees. For most of the day, he had been followed, ever aware of the danger of travelling alone and where he was headed. That soon he'd be skirting around English camps on his way to Stirling. Hamilton kept his head straight, but his eyes constantly searched the surrounding area.

It didn't take long for him to see and hear the person following him, nor any length of time to know they were alone. So, he wasn't too concerned; but since he'd rather be thinking about other matters, and not some thief, he was annoyed.

If the person who followed him was a friend, they would have approached differently. Called out, or at least made their presence more known. However, the person skulking around boulders and trees, who stayed well back and wore all dark, obviously thought they were being clever. He didn't want to bring this enemy any closer to the Scottish camp, so he'd made a plan to draw his stalker out.

He dug a little ditch, made a little fire, pretended he

was hunkering down for the night as the sun set. When the person stayed hidden in the trees, Hamilton came behind him. He'd rather actually have been pointing the knife at said entrails, but any closer and he knew he'd give his location away. So he kept to the element of surprise, stayed well behind the man who stared at the meagre camp he'd made. And victory was his when the heavily cloaked person jumped at his voice.

'I don't know how much innards I have after you kept me on the road so long. I've barely had anything to eat.'

Hamilton lowered his dagger and stepped away from the tree. 'Beileag?'

She turned and lowered her cowl. 'Who else did you think it was?'

Hamilton, both surprised she'd come and equally displeased she'd travelled with no protection, couldn't answer her question. The woman he loved, who didn't trust him for good reasons, stood in front of him. And though the fire was at her back, and he knew he was more revealed than she, his mind filled in all the details because he was starved for her. The way her eyes stayed steady on his, the length of her eyelashes, the number of spots across her nose. The top curve of her ear he could only see when she was underneath him and her hair was fanned back.

'What are you doing here?'

'Hoping for food,' she said. 'Barring that, perhaps an apology will do.'

The fire behind her haloed the top of her golden head. He'd missed the top of her head, but he swore he had apologised and it hadn't resolved anything between them. He would have sworn it made it worse the way she looked at him at the end as if her heart had been ripped out. His certainly had.

'I don't understand.'

'I'm hungry, Hamilton—why don't you feed me first?'

That he could do. Food and preparing it would give him something to do. Gesturing to the small fake camp, he said, 'I don't have much, it's not a long journey.'

'Let me get my horse first.'

'Of course.' Shaking his head that her travelling on a horse absolutely slipped his mind, Hamilton followed her around the bend in the road and to the trees on the other side.

'You left him all the way over here?' he said.

'I tried to stay far behind.'

He didn't want her to know he had been able to hear her for almost the full day. 'But you left him here without knowing I was stopped.'

'I took the chance,' she said. 'Wasn't the first time when I thought you were stopped and left him behind only to run back to get him. You left no more than a few hours of time before me—if I was as good a tracker as you, I would have caught up.'

He grabbed her reins and they walked back to his horse and satchels. 'I thought we'd proven I wasn't that good of a tracker.'

'Well, it's now proven I'm worse than you.' She petted her horse's neck. 'Why do you have very little food with you?'

He knew they should talk of more important matters, but he was grateful she talked at all. 'I have provisions for the camp, but there is no need when hard bread and dried meat will do.'

'So no comforts on this journey. I noticed you haven't been setting fires.'

He didn't feel as though he deserved comforts. 'I didn't want to be seen in case there are enemies.'

She put her arms around her, as if she was cold. 'But you did now.'

He brought her horse around to his and began to unsaddle him. 'I wanted to catch a thief.'

'You had not thought it could be me?' She went around the other side to help him.

She looked so surprised he hadn't known it was her, but after he left, he didn't think he'd see her again, not when his heart was so battered and not when he'd vowed to himself he'd learn patience. Because that's what should have happened before he made the bet. He should have seen what his brother would do with Anna, then he should have waited until he was certain he had feelings for Murdag, then he should have waited…for so many other things when it came to Beileag.

The restlessness and that battle rode him hard, but he should have thought!

The night was clear, the moon not full. The light was fading fast and he felt robbed he couldn't see her as clearly. He loved her hair in the sunlight. Dropping her saddle next to his own, he threw more kindling on the fire and poked it with a stick. He didn't intend to make any flame for fear of truly being seen by an enemy, but if Beileag was hungry and wanted a meal, he'd risk it for now.

'Please sit.'

She took the only bare rock available. 'Do you truly think an enemy would see this fire?'

'I made certain we were still a way from Stirling,' he said. 'In fact, when I knew I was followed, I turned us partly around.'

'You did?' She smiled.

Hamilton was glad he was hunkered over the fire for even that small bit of smile weakened his knees. Was this how Camron had felt wooing his Anna? Completely at a loss as to what to say or what to do, only longing for the answers so he could get his heart's desire.

Yanking at his satchel, he carefully untied the bundle holding the loaf of bread, tore a piece and handed it to her. Beileag took the bread, set it on her lap and uncapped her water skein. After a quick swallow, she nibbled on the hard bread.

Hamilton was riveted by those bites. 'Do I dare ask why you are here?'

'I'm here to eat.'

She tormented him, but he was pleased she was here, so he took that gentle tease. If she never wanted to give him a straight answer again, he'd take it. As long as she was near him, as long as she was talking to him and assessing him the way she was doing now, with her eyes holding that curious warmth, he'd take it. But he was still greedy for more.

She sipped her water, took small bites of the bread and her eyes never left him once.

Unwrapping the seasoned dried meat, Hamilton tossed it into the small pot with water before setting it on the fire. 'The meat will be soft in a bit.'

'Culinary skills you learnt in the kitchen?'

He snorted. 'Hardly.'

She eyed the pot. 'You're not going to eat?'

'I'm not hungry.' Hamilton wanted many things, but not food. He'd left Graham land less than two days ago. It seemed like far longer because in those hours all he'd contemplated was a lifetime before him without her. Yet, here she was, following him.

'So you truly tracked me since home?'

Another of her half-smiles. 'You stayed in the middle, clopping your way towards Stirling. If you didn't want to be followed, you should have danced with the trees.'

No, he was wrong, he couldn't take her teasing. Not if she continually tortured him with half knowing smiles. He'd never borne the patience of his brother and he knew he was utterly at fault, but merely the thought of Beileag and that dance and the trees was enough to make him beg.

'Please tell me,' Hamilton said.

'I wondered when you'd break.' She grinned.

He was already broken. 'Would you believe I left to learn patience?'

She tossed the bread on to the linen on the ground. 'Not when you left in too much of a hurry to tell me you were going.'

'I didn't think you wanted to talk to me again. I can see I was wrong about that as well. But I want you to know, I know now of what you were talking. I *was* only thinking of myself, of my brother and nothing of Anna's or Murdag's emotions when I made that bet. It was never a game, and my love for you is true. I just… should have had more patience with it. I should have waited for my brother to woo Anna in his best way and I should have wooed you in mine.'

She looked to her hands which bore no linens before she looked at him again. 'So the way you show me is by leaving to go get yourself killed before we resolve anything?'

'I didn't think we could,' he said. 'That's why I left. I could see nothing I could do or say which would make it true to you.'

'Time,' she said. 'Time would show me.'

And that was all the truth there was between them. Beileag watched Hamilton take the pot of meat and water off the fire and put it to the side. When he pointed to it, she shook her head. She wasn't hungry for it anymore.

Not when what she truly wanted, this man, came over and sat on one of the rocks near her.

'I had to leave,' Hamilton said. 'If not two days ago, then soon.'

Blinking back the tears, she nodded. 'I know and that's out of your control, and we have little time.'

'I thought I had little time.' She swore Hamilton's eyes welled before he turned away. 'Like I said, I left because I need to recognise how to wait.'

'And I thank you for your apology, but I was wanting to give one of my own. It's why I'm here.'

He dropped the stick into the fire. 'You don't owe me an apology. You never did.'

She wanted to reach out to him. To take his hand, to brush his hair out of his face. To…touch him as she always seemed to want to do. But after she'd said all those things to him, she didn't feel as though she had the right.

There was a part of her that wanted to trust Hamilton's wary, hopeful looks he gave her now, but they'd both come to too many wrong conclusions before actions or kisses…or touches distracted both of them. This time words would be said. So there was no miscommunication and whatever would happen between them would be true.

'I need to give you one because I demanded you love me…that you fall in love with me as I always dreamed of.'

He straightened his arms and legs and looked as if he'd reach out and grab her as she wanted to do with him. But he held back and she had to think, to *believe* that was good. He wasn't merely forging ahead as he was wont to do and, instead, was allowing her to do so.

'I always expected love to be obvious,' she said. 'I know, humorous, isn't it, when I'm the quiet one? But the love I saw, the ones I thought were true, were there for all to see.'

'Camron and Anna,' he said.

She nodded. 'And your parents.'

'Too noisily,' he added ruefully.

'Recently, I learnt of other kinds of love,' she said. When he raised a brow, no doubt to remind her of what they shared, she gave a low laugh. 'Not…that, but my parents.'

When he looked surprised, she laughed again. 'I know, it's truly hidden, but it's there.

'I thought my father didn't love me because he never told me, never gave me much affection, and when my mother shared her caustic ways with me, he never defended me. Then I'd watch him have affection for my siblings, or at least treat them differently. I thought he was as disappointed in me as my mother was.

'But then he told me how, all those years ago when I was a child in his mill, he was showing me how to use the tools. I didn't realise it at the time, but he was secretly angling his body so I could see.'

Hamilton chuckled under his breath. 'Didn't he almost cut off his thumb because he was holding, I can't remember what, wrong?'

'It was a riving knife and that was for me, too,' she said. 'If I'd got closer, he wouldn't have had to bend his body around.'

'Everyone laughed and made fun of him for years and you say he did that for you? That is love. But your mother—' He shook his head. 'At least I can now understand why your father hasn't gone mad or bitter as he stayed with her.'

'My father loves her, understands her. And as terrible as it is, she has tried in her way to love me, too. Her anger at me has been worry.' She shook her head. 'I neither want nor accept that kind of love. It's still too difficult to understand. All this time I'd been hurt because I thought he was avoiding me and she enjoyed making me miserable. Whereas he was avoiding me to give me the freedom neither of them had had and she was cruel to push me away and find happiness.'

Hamilton chuffed. 'Maybe some patience with them as well.'

'No, I'll do what you do and forge ahead by warning my siblings and sitting down to talk to them about what works for them may not work for anyone else. I've always dreamed of them having a better home.'

'I've seen you with your sister and brothers. They know they're loved,' he said. 'But wouldn't you telling your parents about how you want to be raised differently feed into their belief to let children alone and they'll grow up as they want to, with ideas of what they want?'

He was right. However, if there was one thing she'd learnt it was the need for words to be used, for feelings to taken into consideration. And that if love existed in all different forms, then it would still exist after she sat everyone down. 'No, still jumping ahead on this one.'

'You may have less patience than me,' he said.

'Only now understanding that? I rode after you *hours* after you left. I kissed you more when you were pulling away and—'

Hamilton's breath hitched and so did hers. She gave him a small smile. 'I'd better continue.'

'Hurry, Beileag,' he said.

His voice, the way his eyes locked with hers and then travelled from her head to her toes and back again, made her want to forget the words and simply be with him.

He loved her and she believed him now, but she needed to tell him why she believed him. Thus, when she said anything at all about her love for him, he'd know she was telling the truth.

'Maybe underneath it all, I knew my parents cared,' she continued. 'But I didn't want their kind of quiet love, I wanted that longing, loud, only-one-direction love.'

'Like Anna and Camron,' Hamilton said. 'That love tortured my brother for years. If that's the love you want, it's the one I have. When you walked away and I thought all was—'

She held up her hand. 'I thought that was the love I wanted.'

Hamilton pulled back on the rock.

'I thought true love, one that was patient and lasting...was forever,' she said. 'We all knew your brother loved Anna, even she did. But you—'

'Fell in love with you immediately,' he said. 'So you didn't trust it.'

She nodded. 'I didn't trust it. I had no example for it. You were right about those sticks in the other chest. The one I didn't show you, that I never showed anyone.'

'I'm sorry I brought those up,' Hamilton said. 'I somehow hurt you by mentioning them.'

She fluttered her fingers. 'I didn't know what to tell you. They were the first figures I tried. When those came out so poorly, I tried again, and then stopped. All my life, I felt as though I didn't have a family and that I couldn't even create a decent one. Thinking I was broken because of my height, because I wasn't worthy,

I shoved them in the bottom of that chest so I would never accidentally see them.'

'Then I mentioned how I wanted to be that family,' he said. 'You stopped carving them, but you didn't throw them away either.'

How did he know her so well? 'I yearned for a family, I guess I was desperate to keep those little hacked-up ones.'

'I do still think they'd be better than anything I can carve.'

'Different then I'd carved,' she said.

He huffed. 'Different. Maybe families can still be family, even if they're different.'

'Oh!' she said. 'How I hope so. But even if I knew of my parents' type of love, I had no comparison to trust us.'

'Because of the bet?'

'Partly. Though I know you and your brother do loads of them and they are all in fun, this one felt different. I kept feeling you weren't telling me everything.'

'Because I made it all up and then stubbornly kept lying about it when I could have clarified everything with the communication between my brother and Anna and you and me.'

'Did you know you were that stubborn?'

'No, but I knew I was that scared,' he said.

'Scared?'

'You told me I kept to the lie, forced everything to keep the connection with my brother, and you were right,' he said. 'It was because of Dunbar, because Seoc was hurt, because I knew we'd be returning to it all in Stirling. It was because I'd already come so close to loss that I wanted to tether myself in every way to family.'

'Hamilton—'

'It was because of that wolf.'

That stopped her. 'The wolf?'

'At Dunbar's battle, at Ettrick Forest, the night before we lost our laird, Seoc was almost gutted and we had to flee. That night, I saw a wolf staring at us. It was the most beautiful, dangerous thing I'd ever seen.

'My heart pounded; I thought I'd pass out, but I couldn't look away. When I thought about it afterwards, I realised it wouldn't come charging towards us, it was too far from everyone. But at the time, I was so connected to it, I felt it was right there on top of me like a threat. I thought it a portent to what happened the next day. As something terrible, that we were prey and it had been a dark warning I should have heeded.

'I've had this restlessness plaguing me. I haven't been able to sleep very well. None of us has, Camron, Seoc and I staying up all night by the fire. That wolf, that moment, that battle, is also why I wanted the connection with my brother more than ever. Why I forced, as you said, that connection and it made me blind to everything else. I was terrified.' He laughed bitterly, almost to himself as if he couldn't believe how foolish he was. 'And then suddenly at the bottom of your chest was *your* wolf.'

'My wolf?' she whispered.

'The one you carved is unerringly alike to the one I saw in Ettrick Forest the night before the battle. I was the only one who saw it and somehow have tied all the misfortune and the warnings of what's to come to us, to our clan, to that wolf.'

Beileag couldn't stay quiet any longer. 'But you wanted it,' she said. 'The one I carved, I mean. If the wolf represented the war, and losing our laird, and Seoc almost losing his life, why would you want it?'

'Because you told me it wasn't running towards prey or with the pack,' he said as if she would understand.

And she did. That day, or perhaps a few moments before, had changed her entire life. 'I told you it was running towards family.'

He closed his eyes as if in pleasure before he gazed at her again and she swore her very soul reached out to his. 'That was when I knew the truth. That the wolf wasn't a portent of any evil, but of something good. It was you. You who began to carve that wolf maybe on the same day I saw it. It was leading me to you. When I'm with you, I don't look over my shoulder, I like dancing with trees and sitting in the sunlight.

'I want that wolf, Beileag. The one you carved so carefully it didn't hurt your hands. And so beautifully it should never be hidden.'

She couldn't stop looking at him, this man whom she'd known since she was a girl and he a boy. Who had travelled and changed and she had as well. Enough to say, 'And I'll have you.'

If she thought he'd looked pleased before, his eyes now lit with utter delight and relief. That pained her. 'Did you think I wouldn't?'

He lowered his chin and looked at her through his lashes. 'A man could hope.'

'But you didn't have any. You left for Stirling almost immediately.'

'I wasn't two turns away from Graham land before I was already thinking up ways to return to you.'

'If you had, you would have seen me behind you,' Beileag said, then realised the truth of that even more. 'Time.'

'Time,' Hamilton agreed. 'Patience.'

'Patience,' she repeated. 'Because of that wolf?'

His lips curved. 'Now you're getting it.'

'I got angry with you for that bet because all I ever dreamed of was having a family of my own and you just thought you could make a game of it. Everything came so effortlessly for you. Then, even when I realised your life wasn't always easy, I still didn't understand why you would toy with others' lives.'

'I know that now,' he said. 'I understand, as well, that it wasn't just the bet, but the fact I didn't tell you I made it and you felt as though Anna was being twisted around like your mother does to you. I want to believe... no, I do believe I would have realised that if I had given myself the chance, the time, because it took me but a moment to truly understand.'

'But I was already storming off.' She laughed low. 'And if you told me then that you suddenly saw the truth, I wouldn't have believed you. We both need to work on our patience.'

He laughed low. 'Quite possibly. Or maybe we're only meant to recognise we don't have it.'

She was beginning to believe that to be true. Not only to recognise faults, but good things as well. 'Can love be as simple as that? Can there be so many kinds that we don't always recognise it?'

'Would it help to know I don't fully understand it either?'

'No,' she said.

Hamilton laughed. 'I know whatever this is, is sudden. It is for me, too.'

'You invented sudden.'

'Thus, because I often do this sudden, you thought what we shared wasn't significant.'

She nodded.

'But that's how I knew it was right,' he said. 'I've

known you all my lifetime Beileag, and all I needed was a little nudge to see you.'

He did see her; she knew that now.

He cursed. 'I didn't stay around and wait, as my brother had done.'

'No, you acted brashly, forging on ahead as usual,' she said. 'But I wouldn't want you any other way. You stayed true to that and then I knew you cared for me. Well, that, and talking to my father, mother, Murdag and everyone else who thought me a fool.'

'You, too?' He smiled ruefully. 'Apparently, I can't recognise I need patience when I left suddenly to find patience!'

Oh, she was so glad she had caught up to him. 'I wouldn't want you to change.'

'Good, because I should have known I wouldn't be like my brother and wait around longing and brooding over a woman. That some day I would run into her, throw her off balance and have to right both of us again so we keep standing. I should have known she'd keep surprising me with her secrets and her lurking ways.' His teasing grin dimmed. 'I regret how the bet was discovered, but I can't regret it or how it turned out.'

She couldn't either.

'So, yes, this is sudden. Because that's what I do, follow you around and fall in love before you even trusted or liked me.'

'I liked you; I…more than like you,' she said. Oh, she loved him and he knew it, and now that all the words were shared, all the reasons, she could tell him, too. But something in her, something gleeful, made her hold back.

'More than?' He arched his brow. 'How much more? Because as far as I'm concerned, we belong together.'

She could see how much this bit of patience was costing him and she liked it. She truly liked the word belong. She'd felt so out of step her whole life, but not anymore. Now she had a man who loved her, who listened to her talk of woodworking, and they could spend hours in quiet companionship. She just needed to torment him a bit first.

'I always admired you a bit more than any other man,' she said.

His eyes narrowed. 'More than my brother?'

That surprised her. 'You want to talk of Camron now?'

'I want more than my brother,' he said stubbornly. 'I want…time. Beileag, you know my brother and I will still be called to Stirling.'

She nodded.

'When I return, I want to return to you, our family, and that uncomfortable log in the woods so you can abuse my hands.'

A family of her own, one she could show her love to, with a husband who matched her in ways she was just beginning to understand. 'I'll even put linens on them to match mine.'

'We could have some of that now. I believe I may have been hasty in leaving Clan Graham.'

She'd almost lost any chance with him because even if he survived whatever would happen in Stirling, what would be next? The English King had his campaign and Scotland was already changing.

'Do you want to talk now of what happened last spring?'

He gave a slow nod. 'On the way home, I will tell you, Beileag.'

His voice was sombre, but soft, and that told her he

thought of that time a bit differently now. But she didn't want all their time travelling to be about past pain.

'I suppose since we're returning and will have days and days ahead because we're certain to get lost, I can give you *different* than your brother.'

He hesitated and she just bit back her laugh. Not only because the way she said it, and the way he was obviously taking it, had nothing to do with each other. But also, the idea of his brother and he being different was still new. Maybe in time, she'd tell him he'd always been her favourite twin, that she'd more than admired him long before she'd realised what those feelings were, but not now. Now she felt a little mischievous.

'What kind of different?' he said, lowering his voice and looking at her through his lashes. 'Anything to do with dancing?'

'Perhaps.' She smiled. 'And that alone makes you different from your brother.'

'I do not want to be thinking of you dancing and my brother in the same conversation, lass,' he growled.

She laughed. 'No worries, there's lots of other differences you'll have that your brother won't.'

His eyes narrowed. 'Such as?'

'I'll be teaching you how to hack at pieces of wood now. That's something different from your brother,' she said, keeping all the teasing in her voice. She couldn't help it. The more Hamilton glowered, and his eyes promised retribution, the more she wanted to torture him.

She pursed her lips. 'And I have brothers and a stubborn sister, which means so do you.'

'Why does that mean I do, too?' he said, his voice low and coaxing.

'Because you have me,' she said. 'But I already said that, didn't I?'

'*How* do I have you?' His chest expanded and his grin flashed wide. 'You've got mischief in you, Beileag, and I love it, but if you think I'm going to—'

'I love you,' she blurted.

Without warning he snatched her hand, tugged her down and across his lap so that she was again straddling his lap and looking straight into those brown eyes of his she loved so dearly. But she especially loved them now when they were promising her every bit of teasing, love and mischief she'd ever want in her lifetime.

'Good,' he said.

After all they'd been through. All the miscommunication and doubt. All the struggle to realise that this was true, that was all he said?

'Why?'

His brows drew down, but his mouth quirked as if he held some secret.

'I'm not impulsive, or truly mischievous,' she added.

His eyes glinted. 'You are when I kiss you. When I touch you. You respond and then take me far beyond my expectations with all your burling and dancing.'

She laid her hand against his mouth. 'Why do you have to keep reminding me?'

He kissed her palm and laid her hand against his chest. 'I like my wife to be greedy. I like it when she surprises me.'

She gazed at their clasped hands against his chest, wiggled her fingers until he released his grasp and she laid both her hands on his chest. Felt the hard beat of his heart and the slow rise of his chest. Felt him, the man she had fallen in love with even though it wasn't how she expected to. 'Except, eventually, won't there be…enough things we've done, there won't be any surprises?'

He grasped her hips and pulled her closer, laid his forehead against hers and skimmed her lips with his. 'I know you'll come up with something.'

And before she could argue his choice of words, because she knew exactly what he meant, Hamilton kissed her. He kissed her and when she responded and felt that greedy impulse where she simply wanted more, she feared, she knew, he was probably right.

When it came to him, she'd always come up with something. *Everything.* Except…

'But can we eat first? I truly am starving,' she said.

Epilogue

September 1299—Clan Graham

'You understand, if you keep spinning her around like that, she'll be sick on you,' Beileag said.

Stumbling, Hamilton clutched his daughter, Teàrlag, closer to his chest and pivoted around. 'How, after these years, can you still sneak up on me?'

But he'd take his bonny wife like this despite her sneaky ways, hands clenched in front of her, her hair radiant from the sunlight and her eyes flashing false umbrage. She was getting good at showing the fire she'd kept hidden for too long. He liked to congratulate himself on bringing that out of her.

The fact she'd called it exasperation was beside the point. Because when Beileag was exasperated she gave this vexed smile that dazed any man. And if possible, those amber eyes of hers were more beautiful than ever, especially when they looked at him.

He loved her. Loved her more than he could ever express, for despite their time together, he continued to fumble over his words when he tried to tell her all his feelings. At least at night, and whenever possible during the daytime, he showed her how much he loved her. Which was beginning to sound like a fine idea right about now since she was currently twirling an adorable linen around her finger. He wanted to nibble on that finger and take that linen slowly off with his *teeth*.

'I cannot possibly sneak up on you when you lead entire scouting trips and are the best tracker in the clan.'

He often wondered about this himself and came up on one theory that was as good as any other. 'Oh, but I may like your surprises, my wife.'

At the sharp tug at his temple, Hamilton extracted the wily fingers of Teàrlag, his older daughter. Older by only a moment. It was just his fortune he and Beileag had twin girls with hair like their mother and brown eyes like his.

Two beautiful girls, who were almost sixteen months of age. This was all despite his journeying to Stirling and other scouting trips and back again. For as much as he loathed parting from her, the returns to his home, his wife, were very, very sweet…and productive for Beileag's stomach was newly rounded with another mischief maker or two on the way.

Beileag arched her brow. 'You may like surprises, but I refuse. Especially when you seem to be hiding our other daughter. Where's Teasag?'

'She had her turn but a moment ago. I finally put her down so this one could get her chance.' Hamilton slowly circled around. When he faced Beileag again, Teasag was in her arms.

His wife smirked. 'Did you know this one escaped?'

'No escape, she was hiding behind your skirts again.' Hamilton waggled his brows at his daughter.

Arms out, Teasag arched her back and lurched forward. Hamilton grinned as both his wife and other daughter were suddenly closer to him.

'You did that on purpose,' Beileag accused, as she placed Teasag in his arms to settle her on one of his hips, while he adjusted Teàrlag on his other.

'If I did?' Hamilton kissed one little dear forehead, then another, before looking expectantly at his wife.

'Are you wanting something?' she said.

'Will you make me beg for your kiss now, Wife?

'You only have to ask.' Hips swinging, Beileag sauntered right between the two girls, placed her hands on his chest and kissed him. When her lips lingered and he felt that hint of languid heat, he tensed, prepared to pull back, but his wife wound her hands behind his neck and pulled him closer. When she nibbled his bottom lip, all but begging him, he tilted his head to give her more access and deepened the kiss.

Arms wrapped full around his girls, feet apart to brace himself, his body reacted to his wife's ministrations. When she pulled back, her amber eyes a bit dazed, her lids heavy laden and her lips looking ready for more of his kisses, he was well rewarded.

And full on ready for her, though there wouldn't be a chance. Not when Teàrlag's grip was ripping his hair out of his head and Teasag's hot, wet breath indicated his tunic would be well drooled upon. How she could be teething still was beyond him.

Yet he could hardly pay his daughters any attention, not when his wife looked so prettily down at what she did to him. 'To think you once believed you had no mischief, Wife, when you put my antics to shame!'

Ducking his head again to capture her lips and put her in the same state as he—

'Here you are,' Camron boomed. 'I thought you were going to help me with Ùisdean and Uilleam!'

Exhaling roughly, Hamilton circled around his wife to put her in front of him so they could face his brother. Which also had the benefit of coverage so his twin wouldn't see how Beileag tortured him so.

Camron stopped. 'Oh, Beileag, I didn't see you.'

That's because Hamilton had been attempting to embrace his wife while holding his daughters. He might no longer have restless nights and was rather fond of that wolf now, but if he could somehow enfold them all in his arms and never let them go, he would. The English King's campaigns against Scotland might not be over despite the Pope decreeing a cease and desist. But there were rumours that Edward's new wife was making him happy, so there was hope. However, Hamilton no longer worried because every time he had to go away, he came back to a pregnant wife and a growing family, and such overflowing happiness that he might just start developing some odd desire for more scouting about.

'Hello, Camron.' Beileag held up her arms and Teàrlag fell into her hands as if she knew what her mother wanted.

After Beileag set her on the ground at their feet, she did the same thing to Teasag. Then as quickly as she could, she reached into her pouch and produced two linen-padded wooden rabbits. The girls quickly took their toys and waved them around.

Both of his daughters were absolutely fearless and beautiful, and kind, and just about as perfect as his wife, whom he now could pull close to him. His daughters were unlike Camron's twin fiends who had obviously taken their toll on his patient brother. Camron's hair was standing straight up, his tunic was ripped at the sleeve, and the boys were nowhere in sight.

'I need more of those toys,' Camron said. 'Many more.'

Once Hamilton had accidentally stolen one of Beileag's little wooden creatures and then somehow even more absentmindedly left it around the village, Beileag's carving secret was out in the clan. She never had the time to be cross with him because immediately there were requests for her to make more. Now Beileag was always working on another creature. He'd never seen her look happier than when she placed a new hedgehog on to a little outreaching palm of one of his clansmen's children.

Well...there were many other times she was happy. He only hoped he could rid himself of his brother and find a person or place to take his children. Perhaps her father was at his carpentry mill, or even her mother, who had softened so considerably after their marriage that she was almost unrecognisable from the woman he had known.

Of course, there were still times her quick tongue reprimanded the younger siblings, but even that had eased. Yes, it was a sound idea. Either one of her parents would do, then he could take his wife somewhere secret for a moment or twenty.

'Your boys keep losing their toys,' Hamilton said. 'And it seems as if you lost your sons as well.'

Camron pointed behind him. 'They're climbing all over Lachie, Raibert and Roddy so I could try to find you. You were to teach them tracking today.'

Lachie was Anna's brother and they were sure to all have torn clothing. 'Can't you handle a few children on your own to teach them tracking? You're getting soft in your old age.'

'I'm the same age as you.'

Camron was born first, a fact Hamilton liked to now point out. 'It has to be your old age. Because I don't have trouble with my girls.'

'Much trouble,' Beileag whispered.

Camron glowered. 'Your girls are untroublesome because you spin them until they can't stand straight.'

'I knew it!' Beileag said.

'I do it slowly.' Hamilton bent his head and whispered in his wife's ear, 'And I learnt to spin and dance with them from you.'

Beileag blushed and he wanted to follow the flush that went down her pretty neck. He growled. His thoughts were not helping his situation and neither was his wife who was pressed against him.

Forcing his gaze back to his brother, he asked, 'Where's Anna?'

'Still looking for mint,' Camron said. 'One of Murdag's horses had some digestive problems.'

'That herb is everywhere,' Beileag said.

'Not since last night when Seoc used all the mint in the land for his new sauce,' Hamilton said.

'Is that what that was?' Camron said. 'I wasn't going to look too closely in case—'

'Do not say her name. Ow!' Hamilton caught Beileag's elbow in his rib.

'You deserved that,' Beileag said nestling back against him. 'You should be happy for your friend.'

'I am happy for him,' Hamilton said. 'I also believe it's safer not to say her name too many times.'

Camron nodded his head slowly. 'It might conjure her.'

'You two are terrible,' Beileag said. 'Barabal is perfectly lovely.'

'Perfectly terrifying,' Hamilton muttered, but he couldn't deny the Colquhoun lass who'd come to Graham land made Seoc more than happy. He also wouldn't admit he might have a soft spot for the woman who had healed his friend.

Camron's shoulders slumped. 'You're not going to help me, are you?'

'Not a chance,' Hamilton agreed.

Beileag craned her neck. 'I think I can see Anna coming this way.'

Expression hopeful, Camron turned. 'All I see is a pile of boys. I've got to go.'

'Did you truly see Anna?' Hamilton said after his brother ran the other way.

'I see elbows and knees in the air. If those boys have more torn clothing that Anna needs to mend, it may be a while before you see your brother.' Beileag turned in his arms. 'All this and I haven't got around to telling you why I interrupted your making our daughter sick.'

Hamilton patted the tops of his daughters' heads. The girls demanded a good spin as well his wife knew. 'What's happened?'

Linking her fingers behind his neck, Beileag leant back. For a moment Hamilton was entirely distracted by his wife's tall lithe form arching enticingly in front of him.

'I spied your parents shutting themselves up in their home,' she said.

When she held him like this and looked at him like that, why was she talking of his parents? 'I do not want to hear about my parents being alone at home in the middle of the day.'

Beileag smiled. 'Yes, but they wouldn't mind if we gave a little knock and left two adored bundles with them, would they?'

Oh, so *he* and Beileag could be at home alone in the middle of the day. 'It is as if you have been hearing my thoughts, Wife. But you're knocking on their door because my parents in any dishevelment is something I do not want to see.'

Her mischievous laughter shot lust straight through his blood. Grinning, Hamilton swept his daughters back in his arms and tried to capture his wife, but she skipped merrily ahead of him.

Looking over her shoulder, she taunted. 'Now what were you saying about my surprises, Husband?'

That he liked them. Very, very much.

* * * * *

If you enjoyed this story,
be sure to pick up the first
instalment in Nicole Locke's
Lovers and Highlanders miniseries

The Highlander's Bridal Bid

And why not check out the latest titles in her epic
Lovers and Legends miniseries

The Maiden and the Mercenary
The Knight's Runaway Maiden
Her Honorable Mercenary
Her Legendary Highlander